# LOVE on tour

MCKENZIE BURNS

*To anyone I've ever met while solo at a concert.*

# OTHER WORKS BY MCKENZIE BURNS

THE WORLD OF FROM THE SHADOWS
*From the Shadows*
*Through the Flames*

THE RAVINIA DUOLOGY
*Legacy of the Night*

WRITTEN IN THE STARS NOVELS
*Starstruck*

WORKS WITH APPEARANCES BY MCKENZIE BURNS
*Magic & Moons: A Fantasy Anthology*
*Chaos & Curses: A Collection of Unfortunate Tales*

*Love on Tour*

# Chapter 1



*HEATHER*

I'D ALWAYS WONDERED why, when people thought of music, the first cities that came to mind were places like New York or Nashville or Los Angeles. Sure, that's where most of the budding musicians planted themselves while they waited for their big break, making connections or writing for other artists who had already landed some sort of deal.

But for me? I'd grown up in small-town Wisconsin. If I'd wanted to enjoy live music as a teenager—and I most certainly had—I'd needed to hop in my beaten-up Toyota sedan and drive three hours south to the beautiful, bustling city of Chicago.

Mom and Dad had never minded; they'd been groupies during the prime of The Grateful Dead, so they saw my desire to travel to see my favorite acts as carrying out the family legacy. Fitting, since they'd met at one of the concerts when Dad had let Mom take a hit out his bowl—and a few more after that, from what he's told me since I've gotten older. Mom denies her involvement in any of these sorts of recreational activities, but regardless, their love of music resulted in marriage, which resulted in me.

And I was just as crazy about the high as they'd been.

Not the weed kind. I hadn't gotten that kind of high since college. I was searching for the high that came with being in a crowded room, your favorite act on stage, bodies pressed against one another in the standing-room-only venue, the feel of the bass vibrating the floor, rattling your bones from your feet up, until your heartbeat had no choice but to match its rhythm.

Music was sensual. It was freeing. And seeing as I didn't have a single musical bone in my body to satisfy the craving myself, I'd chased that feeling at concerts all the way through college and into the workforce.

"Sup, Benny," I said, lifting my press badge for the bouncer as I walked straight through the front door of the venue.

Benny knew me. I'd been coming here for years, first as an attendee then later as a member of the media. Showing off the badge was more for the eager fans already waiting in line. I'd learned early on in my career that there were crazies out there. Most concert-goers knew the unspoken rules, but the novices weren't used to everything yet. They saw me walk in and thought that was a one-way ticket to ask permission to enter themselves.

Not true. Not even close. I'd spent my time in those lines, freezing cold or sweltering in the extreme midwestern seasons. I'd paid my dues the same as any other devoted fan, and now I got to reap the rewards of knowing what took a concert from good to great.

These newbies that were there more so for the social media clout than the actual art of performing would learn eventually.

"Well, well, well, if it isn't Miss Heather Hansley."

I smiled and flourished my arms in a mock grand entrance as I strolled into the small bar that greeted guests as soon as they made it into the venue. Liam, the bartender who'd greeted me, chuckled as he continued to shine a cocktail glass.

"Same as usual?" he asked when I sat down at one of the bar stools. I was the only patron at the moment and wanted to get my drink—and moment of peace—before the concert-goers flooded through the doors. I wouldn't need to be back by the stage until closer to showtime when I'd do a quick interview with the opening act per our agreement with her PR team, then stay to watch the headliner.

"Double shot tonight," I replied.

Liam finished with his glass then got to making my regular order: a whiskey highball.

"You haven't been around in a bit," he said. "Job taking you elsewhere?"

"They've had me over at Soldier Field covering all three nights of Taylor Swift's latest tour." Liam chuckled again when I fake gagged. "I don't know who I pissed off to get that assignment."

"Well, your misery's over, and now,"—he slid my drink to me—"you're back where you belong."

I nodded once and lifted my glass in a toast to his statement. "Covering the up-and-coming acts of the world."

"The ones that *should* be getting the radio play over the washed-up pop divas," Liam added.

"Here, here." I took a sip then replaced my glass on the bar top. "You heard of these guys that are headlining tonight?"

Liam shook his head. "I looked them up before I came here, but didn't recognize any of the songs. They weren't bad, though. I think they'll be a nice refresher for you after Miss Swift."

I smiled. Liam and I got along not only because he supplied me with a steady flow of drinks while I was covering concerts at The Sound Hall, but because he was as much of a music afficionado as I was. I knew he worked at another restaurant during the day, and had nabbed this gig so he could enjoy concerts for free. He couldn't always watch them diligently, but that's where he was like me. As long as he could feel the music—and he very much could since the back wall of his bar was the shared back wall of the venue—he was happy.

"They're synth-y, right?"

Liam nodded. "With a little tech fusion in there too."

"Interesting."

"You'll like it. I promise."

"Hopefully." I separated my actual enjoyment of the music from how I reviewed shows. Sometimes even the blandest artists could pull off one hell of a concert. Listening to a song through my headphones didn't always give the full story of the artist. Most of my favorites only earned that title after I'd seen them on stage.

Still, it helped when I wasn't bored to death the whole time. I'd been to plenty of acoustic and folk shows where the singer forgot there was anyone there aside from themselves and their guitar. Sometimes, it was magical. Other times, it turned into a snoozefest. And when it happened on a random Wednesday night…

I opted for coffee over liquor at those shows.

"When do doors open?" I asked, checking my phone.

"About thirty minutes from now."

I cursed under my breath, knowing what that meant. The people standing outside wouldn't be let in right away; they'd be corralled in this very same bar until the main venue doors opened for them. But I needed to be done with the interview by the time they were. I'd promised a video component to the opener, and the stage would be better for that. Small venues meant small or nonexistent backstage areas.

The rest of my drink went down the hatch, and I passed the glass back to Liam. He looked impressed that I'd managed that, and rightfully so. I'd kept my face pretty controlled considering the burning in my throat, caused by the liquor.

"I'll try and catch you after the show," I said.

"You know where to find me."

I gave my friend a wave before I got up and made my way to the back.

Time to work.

✕ ✕ ✕

EVEN THOUGH I spent time with each of the acts I reviewed before they went on stage, I never wanted them to feel the pressure of needing to over-perform. Given how many shows I'd been to in my twenty-nine years of life, I could pick out pretty easily which ones turned it on for the sake of my review. I wasn't an amateur, after all. I did my research just like any journalist would, except my research usually included watching YouTube videos of prior performances from the acts I was going to see.

Sometimes, I was lucky. Sometimes, I wasn't. Smaller acts,

like tonight's, hadn't necessarily toured in the past, leaving me to guess if they were laying it on thick or if their energy and crowd interaction was just *that* good.

This one was proving they fell into the latter category.

I bobbed my head along to the upbeat tune they were performing, the two lead singers bounding around the stage, playing off one another and interacting with the crowd in the first few rows.

The music-lover in me felt a pang of jealousy at that, and I needed to remind myself I was here for work, not pleasure—regardless of the fact that I was actually enjoying myself. I had a front-row-or-don't-go mentality usually. I'd lived that lifestyle since I'd been a teenager, hence why I'd endured so many conditions while waiting outside venues. I was still getting used to life in the back of the room, but music was music, and I was happy to enjoy it in any capacity.

I cheered along when the female lead jumped into the crowd, allowing them to lift her into the air as she belted out the bridge of a song.

It seemed I wasn't the only one who was excited, since the guy next to me threw his hands up too. Except he must have forgotten he was holding a beer.

"Ugh!" I groaned as the amber liquid rained on me.

I flicked my arms down, trying to shake it off. Some of the concert-goers around me backed away. Maybe they'd been splashed too. But I'd definitely gotten the biggest shower.

At least the culprit had the decency to look ashamed.

"Oh my god, I'm so sorry," he said, jumping into action.

I watched as he panicked, searching for somewhere to put the rest of his drink before he finally settled on holding the plastic cup between his teeth. He was quick to remove his jacket and offer it to me.

"It's a towel now for all I care," he said when his cup was in his hand again. "I wasn't thinking."

"Lost in the rhythm," I said, half-heartedly, still deciding if I wanted to take the jacket. As much as I wanted to dry myself off, he sounded genuinely sorry about what he'd done. I didn't need to make him have extra laundry for it. "I'll be fine. Thanks, though."

"You sure?" the guy asked again, and I nodded before I finally looked up at him.

Even though the lights from the stage were flashing around the room, casting shadows on everyone's face in between the spurts of color, I could without any doubt decipher that the beer-spiller was gorgeous. Like, belonged in one of those Korean boy bands that everyone was gushing over lately gorgeous.

"I, uh, yeah," I said like a true, educated woman. Hundreds of years of fighting for my rights, and that's what my foremothers got out of it. I nodded at his cup. "Still got anything in there?"

He glanced down, and when his eyes found me again, he

was smiling. His straight white teeth glowed in the otherwise darkened room. "Enough. But maybe that was my sign that I should slow down."

I smiled back. "That's half the fun of concerts, right? Having an excuse to wake up hungover on a weekday?"

His chuckle was heard even over the bass of the backtrack. "So does that mean you do this a lot?"

I reached down and held up my press badge, still dangling from the lanyard around my neck. "Kind of have to," I said. "But I like going to shows even when I'm not being paid, too."

I hadn't thought it was possible, but his smile widened. I allowed my eyes to stray back to the stage. That's where my attention should have been, not on this handsome stranger standing beside me. But I couldn't help myself. Missing one song wouldn't make or break the review that I cranked out when I got home.

"And here I thought I'd found another Stray Land fan."

I gestured to the sold-out venue around us. "I think you've found at least two hundred."

"But I didn't spill beer on any of them."

"I didn't realize that was an honor," I replied. "Is that your way of marking your territory?"

"It's more like a way to scare away the people around me so I have more elbow room."

"So… marking your territory," I repeated.

He shook his head, smiling. "I suppose you're right."

I couldn't help grinning. I liked this one.

"What's your name?" I asked.

"Ethan." He extended the hand that wasn't holding his drink. In fact, he pulled that one further away, as if he was afraid of spilling on me again. "And you?"

"Heather," I replied. I scanned the space around us in earnest for the first time since I'd fallen into my spot in the crowd. "You here with friends?" Of course, I'd been watching the stage more than the fans, but after so many years of going to concerts by myself, I'd developed a pretty keen eye for noticing the people around me. Lonesome female and all that. I hadn't been giving Ethan my full attention, but I also hadn't noticed any movements that would have indicated he was talking to anyone else.

As much was confirmed when a shy smile appeared. "Guilty of being the loser loner?"

"I'm here alone too, remember?"

"But as you pointed out, you're being paid."

"I go to shows by myself for pleasure, too."

His brows rose at that. "Really?"

"Have been since I could drive myself to the venues." I wasn't deaf to the pride that accompanied the statement.

I couldn't hear it well, but the shape of his lips let me know that Ethan let out a low whistle. "I'm standing next to a true professional."

"And you?" I asked, shooting his own question back at him.

That same shy smile reappeared. "Would you believe me if I told you this was my first time?"

A slow grin spread on my lips while I nodded slowly. "We've got a solo show virgin. Okay, okay."

When a few of the people standing around us glanced over at us, Ethan grew visibly embarrassed. Given the volume of the current song, they'd likely only picked up on the part of my statement that any mature adult would.

"What made you finally decide to pop your cherry?" I continued. Again, people looked and I couldn't help laughing when Ethan practically curled into himself in horror. For most men, I would have thought of it as a fragile ego. For Ethan, I genuinely believed it was because of my choice of words.

"I've loved this band for years, but not a lot of my friends listen to their stuff," he explained. "It's hard to get people to pay money to stand for three hours and listen to a sound they hate."

I couldn't have said it better myself. "I admire the dedication." I nodded back towards the performers on stage, allowing myself to watch a few seconds of the current song. "They're pretty good. I hadn't given them much of a listen before now."

"This is all stuff from their newest album," Ethan said.

"You've got to go home and look up the deep cuts. I'd say their second EP is my favorite, but there's a few singles they released when they were first starting out that I like too."

"Oh yeah?"

Ethan nodded. "I think the EP is when they really started to develop their sound. Up until then, it seemed like a lot of experimental stuff. Releasing songs and seeing what attracted a crowd and all that."

"So you listen to a lot of music then?"

We'd gone back to facing the stage, only half turned towards each other, but at that question, Ethan faced me in full again. "What makes you say that?"

"Not a lot of casual listeners will be able to notice things like that," I said. "When an artist finds their sound."

"Well, lots of artists evolve."

"You just keep proving my point."

I allowed myself to drag my attention away from the stage to watch Ethan shake his head, his face turned down. Was he trying to hide that million-dollar smile?

"I suppose I am," he agreed. He might have said more had the band not transitioned into another one of their upbeat synth-rock songs. His face absolutely lit up, and it wasn't because of the stage lighting that was flashing over the crowd, inviting us to join in the energy of the band members on stage.

I ducked out of the way as Ethan lifted his arms in the air

again, cheering along as the guitarist stepped up, front and center, to perform a solo, his fingers moving at super-speed in order to keep up with the pulsing backtrack. The floor shook under my feet, and I couldn't tell if it came more as the result of the jumping crowd or the bass blaring from the subwoofers.

Despite his enthusiasm, Ethan noticed my reaction and lowered his beer again—but only enough so he could retrieve his jacket from where it had been draped over his arm. I couldn't help the laugh that escaped me as he single-handedly put the hood on my head, then wrapped the rest of the coat around my shoulders, ensuring I was protected from any further damage.

"This is my favorite song," he said. "I'm not responsible for anything I do while it's playing."

I couldn't help the laugh that escaped me. It sounded practically silent over the singing crowd, booming music, and powerhouse vocals of the singer, but I knew Ethan had heard it from the way his eyes drifted down to me before they went back to the stage. He was one of the many blended voices after that.

My eyes narrowed, assessing, before I let the jacket remain on my head, my arms in the air, my body swaying in rhythm with the music.

I hardly ever let myself get lost in the music while I was on a job. Sometimes, when I covered bands I was familiar with,

I couldn't help myself, but for the most part, I was nothing but professional, analyzing every moment of the show in a way only a true concert afficionado could.

My eyes shut, and a small smile curled up the corners of my lips. Behind my closed lids, I saw the flashing lights, felt the vibrations in the floor more intensely.

This was a band I could get used to listening to. Ethan was definitely on to something.

When I opened my eyes again, he was watching me, his expression curious. I couldn't say I blamed him. I could only imagine how much of a weirdo I looked like when I truly tried to lose myself.

"What?" I asked him. "Never seen a new fan being born?"

He smiled.

"Hell yeah," was all he said before he went back to singing, allowing me to join in beside him.

× × ×

"AND THEY DO that *every* show?" I asked as Ethan and I filed out of the venue with the rest of the crowd.

He nodded. "Sick, right? It's a different song every time, so no one knows when it's coming. But all of a sudden, Allegra just jumps into the crowd and sings from there."

"She's putting *so* much trust in the fanbase." I'd heard horror stories, not only on the news but from different forums I was a part of, about fans getting a little out of control when put in close proximity with the members of their favorite bands.

"No kidding," Ethan agreed. "I don't know if I could do it, but I love that they do. I only wish we'd gotten something other than a ballad, but hey—beggars can't be choosers." He shrugged.

I smiled, about to respond, when I noticed his attention stray, eyes lighting up. When I followed his line of sight, I found the band across the bar by the merch window, greeting fans.

"You gonna go meet them?" I asked.

I wasn't sure why, but the enthusiasm that had just made him glow dimmed a little. In fact, he looked torn between wanting to go see the band and…

No, I was being dramatic. There wasn't any way he actually wanted to still talk to me. I'd been through this song and dance plenty of times before. I go to a concert. I'd end up talking with some people. They'd welcome me into their group. We'd follow each other on social media—or exchange emails before social media was a thing; stranger danger meant no phone number sharing as a teenager. We'd interact for a few days, maybe a week, two if we were really devoted. Then it all disappeared. We'd lose contact. We'd eventually unfollow.

That little bubble of post-concert euphoria bursts and the

reality that you'll likely never see any of the people you were just surrounded by again sinks in.

Ethan was going to be one of those people. I knew it.

The only difference was *he* didn't know it yet, which was why he was so conflicted about what to do.

"You should go," I encouraged, giving him a little nudge.

"Do you want to come with?"

I lifted my press badge. "I had a quick chat with them before the show when I was interviewing the opener," I said. "I also have to head home to start the review." It would need to be up online the next day, and between actually drafting and running it past editors…

My job might allow me free access to hundreds of concerts, but it wasn't a breeze by any means.

"Shit, I forgot. Work," Ethan said. He did that uncertain double-take again, his attention darting to the band before it returned to me. "Well, I'm pretty into the music scene around here. Mind if we exchange numbers in case we're ever at the same show again?"

And there it was. The hope that we would remain in contact, heightened to the point of actually trying to meet up with one another again.

I smiled, going through the routine I was used to at this point, and pulled out my phone.

"Yeah, go ahead and add yourself," I said. "I'll shoot you a text." And I would. I wasn't an ass. Besides, I'd liked talking to Ethan. I wouldn't mind a few more days of his charming yet shy commentary in my life.

I watched as he input his information into my phone, then smiled as he handed it back to me.

"I saved you the trouble of needing to text me," he said, and sure enough when I looked down, my screen was still on the brand-new text string he'd started with himself. A single bubble that said "Heather" sat at the top under the gray bar with his name. "It's the least I could do to apologize for spilling beer on you. Especially since it sounds like you'll be having a late night."

"I appreciate it," I said through a laugh. "It was nice to meet you, Ethan."

"You too, Heather." That glow was back in his eyes. "I hope I see you around."

I didn't allow myself to create too much false hope for him before he headed off to meet Stray Land, and I headed out the front door.

It was hard to ignore the unusual sad cloud that seemed to hover over me as I went.

# Chapter 2



*HEATHER*

"HOW WAS IT?" Nia, my current roommate and best friend since high school, asked. She didn't bother looking up from her bowl of… I believed that was spicy ramen I smelled. She didn't even look like she'd so much as turned her silk-bonnet-covered head to make sure it was, in fact, me that had walked in and groaned as soon as I'd shut the door.

It probably wasn't a very serial killer thing to do. Plus, serial killers didn't usually toss their keys onto the front table either.

When I didn't respond and plopped down on the couch next to her, Nia finally decided to draw her attention from the episode of *The Bachelor* she was currently watching.

"You can have some of my edamame," she said, nudging the to-go container filled with the green bean pods closer to me.

"I'm good," I said, my head tilted back, my eyes on the ceiling. "I just needed to sit on something comfy before I'm stuck in my desk chair for the next two hours."

"Good review or bad?" she asked before slurping more of her ramen into her mouth.

"Good. Very good, actually."

"No new-band, first-tour jitters that makes the lead singer vomit on the front row of the crowd?"

I chuckled, remembering the particular tour Nia was referring to. "No vomit involved in this one, thankfully."

From the corner of my eye, I caught my roommate finally turn her attention away from the TV to me. "That was my polite way of asking why you smell like a dive bar that hasn't been cleaned in the current decade."

"Ouch," I replied. "But it's nothing." I'd almost already forgotten about it. "Some guy just got excited and spilled his drink on me while he was singing. Total accident."

I groaned as I pushed myself off the couch, my feet aching in protest from not being given enough of a break. After standing for two hours, I'd walked home since Nia and I's apartment wasn't very far from this particular venue. I'd need a solid eight hours of horizontal time in bed if I ever wanted to feel the bottoms of my feet again.

That likely wouldn't happen, seeing as it was already nearing eleven at night, and I still hadn't even started my write-up yet.

And what would have been a wash-the-day-off shower, was now going to get the bonus wash-beer-out-of-your-hair time I hadn't accounted for when I'd planned my day.

"Enjoy your ramen," I said, already half the short distance to the bathroom. "I'll tell you more about the concert tomorrow."

"I'll save these sides for you if there's any left," Nia called after me. I'd just stepped into the bathroom, making sure I kept the door open a crack so I could still hear her. "I guarantee you're going to want a midnight snack so don't even tell me no."

I chuckled as I closed the door. She wasn't wrong. I always found myself going to the kitchen mid-way through my write-ups to find something to eat. I usually didn't have a chance to have dinner before the shows I covered, since my involvement started when most other concert-goers were enjoying a nice meal at a nearby restaurant. Finally smelling food made me realize how hungry I actually already was.

I wouldn't dive in until I made some progress on my review, though. And that wouldn't start until I washed Ethan's beer off me.

I EMERGED FROM the bathroom clad in my black bathrobe

and my hair in a towel, a cloud of steam following me out. What should have been a quick shower had turned into the most luxurious thirty minutes of my life, as it often did when I was on a deadline. I liked treating myself before I locked myself away in the wee hours of the night to work.

The living room was dark, hinting that Nia had finally called it a night. In other words, she'd locked herself in her room, but was probably still awake. Her overnight shifts at the hospital screwed with her sleep schedule.

When I walked past the kitchen to get to my room, I noticed a new sticky note on the door of the fridge.

**Edamame is yours! There's also some kimchi and dumplings left :)**

The Best Roommate Award officially went to Nia Thomas.

I didn't grab anything yet, knowing I needed to use some sort of reward system if I ever wanted to get going on this review. I could only indulge when it was done. Then maybe I'd catch up on my own trash TV while I enjoyed it. Nia had made a massive influence on what I now liked to watch. I hardly ever found myself turning on anything that didn't involve at least two single women getting into a catfight as they vied for a desperate man's love.

Then again, I couldn't say I blamed the women. Maybe that's why I liked the shows so much. I, too, was getting to the point in my life where if I saw so much as a glimmer of hope that a man might be worth my time, I would briefly consider doing whatever I needed to in order to make sure I got him.

Emphasis on briefly.

So far, not many had proven they were worthy of even that much of my effort. And if they had, they'd eventually fucked up.

The same could be said for a lot of people in my life.

I unwrapped the towel on my head and gave the ends of my long, dyed-red hair an extra squeeze. That's when my phone pinged with a new text notification.

My brows scrunched as I made my way over to where it sat on my bed. Who in the hell was still up and trying to get a hold of me?

An unknown number.

When I opened the text, I couldn't help my smile.

There was only one other text bubble above the silly selfie that followed: my name, sent so the receiver knew who my number belonged to. The picture confirmed the identity of who was reaching out to me, though.

The longer I looked at it, the harder it became to hold in my laugh. Ethan was grinning like a fool. It seemed like the lead guitarist of Stray Land had taken his phone and stood in the front of the group gathered behind him. The drummer had his arm around the shoulders of the fan in the center of the crew. The female lead singer held up a peace sign, one of her eyes shut and her tongue sticking out, while the male lead was smiling like someone who'd just played a nearly two-hour show: absolutely exhausted.

It was a cute picture.

Another text popped up below it: This is Ethan Morimoto btw

I snickered to myself as I texted back, How bad do you think my memory is? Lol glad you got to meet them!

A reply came in seconds later. They were great! Even got a baseball cap signed.

Another picture was delivered, showing off a black hat covered in silver-marker signatures.

How much you selling that for?

How much are you willing to pay?

10 bucks?

Ouch! I thought you LIKED the concert?!

The verdict will be out in the morning ;)

Ruthless... ;)

Ethan was catching onto my default sarcasm quickly.

I had a great time, I assured him. AND I even managed to get all the beer out of my hair! ;)

Damn I'm sorry about that😆

Don't worry about it! You helped me procrastinate lol

At least let me make it up to you

You'll give me the hat for 5 bucks? ;)

Lmao! Orrr I could buy you a drink. Another text came through while I was reading the first. I work at a restaurant. Stop by and your drinks are on the house.

A mix of confusing emotions ran through me upon reading both those texts. I ignored them—and my heartrate—as I typed out my reply. What's the name?

If anything, I'd drag Nia with me. We hadn't had a good girl's night in a while.

My phone pinged again.

It's Mellow Cat Kitchen over in Roscoe Village

Hm. It sounded jazzy. That could be a good vibe for the weekend. Staying out until two in the morning wasn't in the cards anymore, and sleep would need to be my friend after the last few weeks I'd endured for work.

Speaking of…

Maybe I'll stop by this weekend, I said, then followed up with, Gotta go write that ruthless review now ;)

Good luck! Can't wait to see how you hate on my favorite band!

I chuckled again as I locked my phone and tossed it on my bed. I hadn't even changed out of my robe yet, let alone done any of my skincare routine.

I sighed. This review was never getting written.

My attention slid back to my phone, and that emotion cocktail returned.

No. I needed to write. If not because it was quite literally my job, then because it would serve as a distraction for what I really wanted to be doing.

I reached for my phone again before I shoved it under one of my pillows.

No distractions.

# Chapter 3



*ETHAN*

I'D LIVED IN Chicago—or damn near close to it—for most of my twenty-nine years. It was where Mom had grown up before she'd moved to Japan and met Dad. That's where we'd lived until I was five, and Mom decided she didn't want to be away from her parents for her next pregnancies. I couldn't believe it when she'd finally sold the American experience to someone whose heart was so deeply ingrained in his culture, it was a miracle he'd even considered moving in the first place. The fact that he'd actually followed through… I hadn't understood the significance of it when I was a kid. Now, all I could think of was how hard Dad had tried to adjust in those early years—trying to fit in, trying to adapt to the lifestyle, trying to learn the new language he was expected to speak.

That was the only reason I knew exactly where I could find the review of the concert I'd attended the night before. Dad was still using the local papers to practice English, just like he had for all those years when we'd first moved.

Mom had always taught me English alongside my lessons in Japanese, and I'd been young enough when we'd moved to Skokie, one of the suburbs not *too* far outside the city of Chicago, that making the switch hadn't been too hard. I remembered the mornings, though, when we'd sit in the kitchen of our two-bedroom apartment and Dad would start speaking in Japanese only to have Mom remind him my two younger brothers didn't understand.

That's when he started reading the newspapers. Any and all parts of them. If he was going to learn something, so were we. And the news was as good as any place to learn. Most of it hadn't made any sense back then, but now I guess I could brag that I knew more details of the 2004 presidential election than most kids probably had.

I wasn't kidding, though. Dad read us *everything*. Including the concert reviews.

That's how I'd found my passion for music. Not that I was any good at it myself. I couldn't carry a tune for shit. But I'd fallen in love with the way the reviewers described the concerts they'd attended. Since my parents didn't particularly listen to anything modern, the reviewers had been the ones to help me discover some of my favorite artists. Then, when the Internet had started to evolve, I'd kept up with it myself, no longer needing Dad's morning readings.

By that point, we were on different schedules anyway. I was in school, and Dad was taking classes of his own while he worked on obtaining his citizenship.

I had to admit, it had been a while since I'd seen a review in an actual newspaper; I got most of my information from social media now. I still wasn't going to be reading a physical paper, I supposed. But I *was* going to read that Stray Land review.

I'd signed up for the free trial of the newspaper Heather worked for and everything, just so I could see if she'd actually been kidding when she'd said she would trash Stray Land. Something about her had screamed no-bullshit, and while it intrigued me, it also made me wonder if she'd *actually* been joking in her texts last night.

There wasn't much scrolling required, the top of the Music page boasting the headline: **Review: Stray Land demonstrates they have 'no boundaries' at first-ever Chicago show**

I chuckled at the creative use of the title of the album the tour was promoting. But it also made it seem like she was about to give my favorite band the credit they deserved.

It started out with the usual fluff that I expected: nice draw to keep any new readers continuing on followed by an introduction to Stray Land (looked like Heather had done her research) then going more into the nitty-gritty of the show. I didn't care so much about the stage set-up since I'd been there to witness it, but I had to admit Heather did a great job of describing that too.

Then I got to the good part.

> There's no better way to understand a band than through its fans, and the die-hards that follow Stray Land are no joke. The band commanded the audience, making them fall into the trance brought on by their synth-infused tracks that broke only when the venue lights came back on. Sold-out arenas couldn't hope to compete with the energy that radiated in the 200-person-capacity room Stray Land headlined. To keep it simple, the crowd-surfing, mosh pits, and beer showers were very appropriate.

I couldn't help but actually laugh at that one. My dumbassery would live on in infamy, forever on the website for the largest news outlet in the Chicagoland area.

"Whatcha laughing at, boss?"

Shit.

I jumped, my phone clattering out of my hand and landing with a *thud* on the top of the bar at Mellow Cat Kitchen. For some reason, I'd decided mid-inventory-check would be a good time to find Heather's article. I should have waited until

I was back in my office upstairs and employees who were early for their shift wouldn't catch me doing exactly what I told them not to do: be on their phones.

"I, uh—" I scrambled to pick my phone back up, showing the screen to Liam. "Just looking at some stuff from a concert I went to last night."

Liam chuckled as he joined me behind the bar, tossing his belongings on the unofficial-official employee storage shelf. "Post-concert depression. Classic." He pointed at my phone. "Who'd you see?"

"This small group called Stray Land? I wouldn't be surprised if you'd never heard of them."

Liam grinned as he leaned against the opposite counter, crossing his arms over his chest. "Heard them for the first time last night, actually."

"You were there too?" I asked, brows raised.

"Kinda," he said. "I work nights at The Sound Hall. When they have shows."

That explained his many requests for nights off. I'd always assumed he was in classes or something. He was still in his early twenties, so he was in his prime for earning a higher education.

"That's sick. How'd you land that gig?"

Liam shrugged. "Same way I got this one. I went in and asked if they were hiring."

I shook my head at him. "Hopefully you don't find as many

distractions at that job, eh?"

"Hold up," Liam said, pushing off the counter, wearing a new smirk. "*Who* did I find on their phone when I walked in here a few minutes ago?"

I gave the back of his head a playful smack before saying, "We're good with stock back here if you want to go check on the silverware. I wasn't here to double check that all the closing tasks were done last night."

"You were too busy rocking out," Liam said, throwing up a rock-n-roll sign with his hands. "I have to admit, you've got good taste in music, E. Mind if we put on a Stray Land playlist today?"

"As much as I'd like to—and trust me, I do—I don't think it's really the vibe people are coming here for."

Liam snapped his fingers in an *oh shucks* kind of way. "Thought maybe I could take advantage of that post-concert depression."

Knowing we needed to really start getting down to business, I nodded toward the kitchen. "Silverware," I repeated. "I'll be upstairs doing next week's schedule if you need me."

"Aye, aye, boss," Liam replied with a salute before he disappeared behind the swinging door of the Mellow Cat's kitchen.

There would, maybe, be three other people back there. We weren't usually too busy during the day, the main draw of the establishment coming in the nighttime. That's when our hired jazz bands came in, bringing in crowds of Chicagoans that still wanted to admire one of the genres that helped build the music scene in this city. Even though jazz wasn't my particular favorite, I knew as well as anyone that it was a type of music that anyone could appreciate, whether for its artistry or its aesthetic appeal.

Plus, it was one of the only types of music Dad actually liked. That meant he came to visit at least once a month. It depended on how many shows his favorite group was scheduled for.

I'd worked hard to curate the perfect environment for all types of jazz fans. The food, I had to admit, was pretty niche. Asian-fusion wasn't everyone's favorite, but it was what I knew the best. It was the perfect representation of how I'd grown up, the recipes that Mom and Dad had created as a compromise to enjoy their favorite dishes. Some of our menu items had been stolen straight from Mom's recipe box.

After an associate's-degree-worth of entrepreneurship classes at Northwestern, I dropped out and ran with the idea I'd come up with for one of my projects. Nothing like a half-way decent grade to kickstart a young man's ambitions. Then again, not many people could say they were operating a fully functional restaurant by the time they were twenty-four.

By twenty-nine, though…

I sat down in my worn-down desk chair with a groan. The

schedule I'd tried to start before I went to do inventory was right where I'd left it. As much as I really had needed to check if we had enough liquor, the task had been as much a distraction as anything else. Reading Heather's article was an addition on top of that. Anything to keep me from accepting the harsh reality that was sitting in front of me.

We had ten staff members. Ten. Three servers, a hostess, and a bartender, but usually I ended up covering that job. Then there were the three cooks, bus boy, and dishwasher. Even that seemed like more than I could afford as rent kept skyrocketing. It was criminal what these people thought they could charge for a space that could only fit a four-piece band, an array of tables that sometimes felt a little too close together, and the bar.

I'd already beaten the two-year odds that most small businesses succumbed to. But as I was approaching five…

That was the mark where more than half were known to close shop.

I refused to let Mellow Cat fall victim to the statistics. I *couldn't* allow it.

As much as this business was my labor of love, it was also my livelihood. Part of my family's livelihood.

And if there was one thing I refused to do, it was to let my family down.

✕ ✕ ✕

"SCHEDULE WAS POSTED in the group chat," I said by way of greeting to Liam when I finally emerged from my office a few hours later. I'd spent a solid twenty-minutes of that with my head down in my arms after I went over the budget sheet.

He nodded as he finished mixing the cocktail he was working on. One quick glance around Mellow Cat let me know it wasn't too busy, but we had a steady flow for a Thursday afternoon.

That was promising, at least.

I settled behind the bar so none of the customers could see when I pulled my phone out. From the corner of my eye, I saw Liam smirking and prepared myself for another comment about texting on the job. As much as I tried not to use the I'm-the-boss card, I probably would this time around as I read Heather's reply to my compliment on a well-written review.

> Thanks! Once I got going I realized it was
> gonna be hard to be ruthless lol

> Lmao! Told you they're great :)

"Who's the recipient of *that* text?"

My head popped up, my face probably looking like I'd just been caught with my hand in the cookie jar. "What do you mean?"

"You're grinning kinda funny," Liam said. "You got a new girlfriend or something?"

"Not even close." My romantic life had taken a pretty big backseat to keeping Mellow Cat running. I'd even pressed pause on the couple of dates I'd set up with girls I'd met on the dating apps. Needless to say, they'd ghosted me when I'd tried to start things back up again. Probably for the better.

But now that he'd brought it up...

"You said you work at Sound Hall?" I asked.

"Affirmative." Liam finished off the cocktails with a nice garnish. They looked fruity, perfect for the first warm-ish day that was hitting Chicago. Once the spring started to show signs of life, it was like everyone in the city came alive again.

Maybe that was another positive outlook to keep in mind for the future of my business.

"Do you get to know people who work the shows?"

"Kinda." I watched as he moved the drinks onto a serving tray. "You thinking of getting a job as a stage crew member or something?"

"No, no, nothing like that." I didn't have the time as it was. "I was, uh, more curious about the people who work the shows from external sources." When Liam raised his brow at me, I clarified. "Like news reporters."

Something about the grin that formed told me I didn't need to explain further.

"You met Heather, huh?" he asked.

"Uh… yeah."

"She's a firecracker." Liam lifted the tray. "I'll be right back, then we can talk more."

I watched as he walked over to his table, greeting the guests—two middle-aged women—with a big, toothy smile. Given how they smiled back at him, their bodies shaking with what I assumed was laughter, I knew Liam had worked his charm on them.

He had a way with people that I'd rarely met on anyone else, so it shouldn't have surprised me that he'd gotten to know Heather. Something about him immediately knowing who I was talking about, though, created a little bit of worry. *Firecracker* wasn't an adjective that was typically used to describe women I dated. In fact, it wasn't a word I'd use to describe anyone in my life at the moment. I tended to surround myself with people like me: calm and down for fun but not *too* much fun. Most of them were from my childhood, but some I'd met through my business program at Northwestern. At this point, though, many of them were settling down and starting families.

Hence why I'd been at a concert alone. At least in part.

When Liam came back, he got straight to work on entering the ladies' order into the computer system while simultaneously picking up our conversation back up. "So, can I assume Heather was the reason for that goofy grin I called out?"

"It wasn't a goofy grin," I defended. "It was just a regular smile."

"Yeah, but it was because you were texting her, right?" When I nodded he continued, "What did you do to grab her attention?"

"I, uh, might have spilled my beer on her."

"Nice work, Romeo," Liam said through a chuckle.

"For the record, I'm not trying to start anything with her," I said. I had too many other things going on at the moment to consider adding Heather into the mix. Even if I couldn't deny I was a little intrigued by her. "I was just genuinely curious if you knew her."

"We got to know each other about a year or so ago," Liam said. "She likes to come in for a drink before she has to get to work. Since I'm usually the bartender on weekday nights, we started chatting and became friends." He shrugged. "She's around frequently enough where I'd say I see her... maybe once a month or so?"

"That's it?"

Liam chuckled. "It's not like all the concerts in the city take place at Sound Hall, man. She's going all over the place. But I know she likes the smaller, up-and-coming stuff the most."

I nodded slowly. That was good to know.

"I saw her review this morning, and it looks like she's really talented," I commented.

"Honestly, I've never read her stuff," Liam admitted. "But

if anyone knows music it's Heather. I don't know, it's like it runs in her blood or something."

I smiled at that. "Does she do anything music-related? I mean, other than her reviews."

"Not that I know of. I've never thought to ask. Something tells me it's just passion, though. It's, like, her thing." A call came from the kitchen, and Liam groaned. "Fuck, I knew they'd be confused by that order. I'll be right back."

"Go do your job," I said. "We can talk when there's not as many guests. And let me know if you need me to be a runner."

"You've got it, boss."

Liam hurried away into the back, already in a conversation with the cooks by the time the swinging door flapped shut behind him.

I took it upon myself to check the system to see if any drink orders had been put in. The least I could do was help out if I was going to waste Liam's time with small talk that benefitted my personal agenda.

Maybe a relationship was out of the question right now, but I didn't see any reasons why I couldn't continue to talk to Heather. If our texts were any indication, she seemed interested in that too. She wouldn't have responded if she didn't want to talk to me after we'd left the venue. Truthfully, I'd been half expecting that outcome when I'd sent my selfie with Stray Land.

And Liam had given me some good information about how I might be able to find more time with her.

# Chapter 4

*HEATHER*

"WOW. BOUJEE."

I shook my head at Nia's initial evaluation of our destination for the evening: The Mellow Cat Kitchen. She wasn't wrong, though. Despite being a relatively small—but comfortable—space, the décor created an ambiance that made me feel like I'd walked into a swanky jazz club in the 1950s.

A three-piece band was already on the modest stage at the back of the room, the female singer in an evening gown crooning a song I was semi-familiar with. Frank Sinatra or Nat King Cole had probably sung it at some point. Or Michael Bublé. Or all three, honestly.

She wasn't performing for a crowd as big as any of those

names would have brought in, though.

A quick scan of the place told me that while warm and inviting with the ambient lighting and décor that kind of reminded me of a spa with all the nods to traditional Asian styling, only certain kinds of patrons came here. But one thing was for sure: given that most of the people in the room with us were easily over the age of fifty, the majority of guests were actual jazz lovers. The others were just masquerading like Nia and I. Trying to enjoy a nice night out with some fancy cocktails and trendy food.

Nia and I were definitely some of the younger in the sparse bunch, even though I did spot a few other girls, probably in their early twenties, dressed to the nines, posing for photos with their fancy cocktails. Otherwise, groups of adults were talking in politely hushed voices, the hum of their conversations distorting the lyrics of the song, but not enough to where the performance couldn't be enjoyed.

Instinctively, my head bobbed along with each pull of the double bass. I might have grown up on rock and roll, but I appreciated a good rhythm when I heard it. This band was delivering a clean performance, instantly putting me at ease. Not at all like the roaring sets I usually found myself listening to.

Like the name of the restaurant suggested, this was indeed going to be a mellow night.

"I like it," Nia commented as we waited by the host stand,

each of us taking in our surroundings. "Not the usual vibe, but I can get behind a night like this."

I chuckled, knowing just how far from Nia's *usual vibe* this was. Where I liked settling myself in a crowd at a concert, she liked being among the crowd at any one of the loud, club-like bars that were scattered around Chicago. It worked well, since I preferred the tamer, tavern-esque front portions of the bars, building a buzz strong enough to survive when Nia pulled me into the world of flashing lights, foggy rooms, and music so loud you couldn't hear yourself think.

A few seconds later, a young girl—probably a high-schooler—burst through the back door that I assumed led to the kitchen. She tossed a towel and spray bottle of disinfectant behind the bar and hurried over to us, her face still showing signs of being frazzled.

Come to think of it, she was the first staff member I'd seen since we'd walked in.

"Welcome to Mellow Cat Kitchen," she greeted. "Is it just the two of you?"

"Yes," I replied.

Having had some time to calm down, she put on a customer-service smile and grabbed two menu booklets. "You can follow me right this way."

We were placed at a table in the middle of the room with a great view of the stage. I found the cocktail models again and noticed how they eyed us with a hint of jealousy—or maybe it was judgement—at our superior position. Their seat in the corner by a large potted bamboo tree didn't quite compare.

"Please excuse any extended waits," the hostess said as she set our menus down in front of us. "We're a bit short-staffed this evening."

Well, that explained her earlier panicked look. She was likely covering for the bus boy or something. I'd worked enough food service jobs in high school and college to know that no matter what your primary role was in a restaurant, you sometimes had to pick up other skills too.

"No worries," I assured her. "We'll just listen to the music."

I wondered how much flack they'd been getting about slow service, because the relief that washed over the girl was visible. I watched as she hurried away to perform whatever task she was needed for next.

"Ya know," Nia said as she picked up her menu. She flipped right to the back where the cocktails were. "My cousin played trumpet in middle school band, so I was so nervous when you said this was where you wanted to go tonight."

"You seriously thought the entire Chicago music scene was built on something that probably sounded like—and no offense to your cousin—the musical equivalent of a dumpster fire?"

"He wasn't *that* bad," she amended. "His little jazz quartet tried so hard, but yeah. This is another level." Her eyes widened when she saw the cocktail list. "Okay, these are the cutest drink names ever, but almost twenty bucks?"

"Like you aren't paying that at your clubs for a vodka soda," I challenged. "I'm getting the Ella Fitzgerald."

"I'm leaning towards In the Mood."

"Bourbon?"

Nia's head shot up. "I know right? This ambiance is changing me."

I shook my head at her just as a server—a man probably a few years older than Nia and I—showed up at our table. We ordered our drinks, then took a quick glance at the appetizers before we ordered some seared brussel sprouts and tuna poke nachos, too. This was very much an appetizers-and-drinks-only place.

And if I knew Nia and I, we'd be inhaling Taco Bell at two in the morning when the bars closed anyway.

It was a rare weekend where I hadn't been assigned at least one show. It was made even rarer when I learned my best friend and world's best pediatric nurse—not that I was at all biased—had her monthly weekend off too. Considering the next week was about to be hell for me, I planned on making the most of my night off.

Not that going to concerts for free all weekend was necessarily *work* in my eyes. But being trapped at my laptop, trying to write my review while I knew my friends were out, having a good time like twenty-eight-year-olds should be, was.

This was a good compromise from the usual routine. I was still discovering a new act, albeit one I probably never would have sought out had it not been for Ethan's invitation.

We'd been talking enough where I contemplated visiting Mellow Cat Kitchen at all. Our conversations were friendly and entertaining, even if there were usually many hours between replies. If he was actually the manager here, he likely didn't have much time to be on his phone. Not to mention I was the world's worst texter.

But sometimes that friendly conversation teetered very close to an edge I didn't want to jump off. One that began with another f word.

I was about as good at flirting, though, as I was at responding in a reasonable manner. Still, it didn't mean it wouldn't work for Ethan. I'd met him once. I didn't know what he liked, what he disliked. For all I knew, he'd been swooning over my every digital word.

That's why I hadn't asked if he'd be working while Nia and I made our visit. If he did just so happen to be here, then that would be our second meeting, I supposed.

The part of me that kind of hoped that would be the case prevented me from stilling my bouncing legs and wandering eyes. Texting and communicating in person were two very different activities. I had time when we were messaging. I could think of witty remarks that wouldn't come off as too brash—as many a past date had told me I could be sometimes.

I couldn't help it. I'd grown up in a world that required me to stand my ground. Unfortunately, that same world was one that saw women like me and labeled them as a bitch without much reason. I was too far-gone to change my ways now, and it usually resulted in not getting invited to date two.

Oh well. Their loss. I wasn't always a hard-ass, but they'd never get the chance to see that. Which was exactly why I was nervous about Ethan. Spilling beer on me provided a temporary excuse for any attitude, and when I looked back to Wednesday night, I didn't think I'd been too harsh after that.

He'd kept talking to me. That was promising enough. But if we talked tonight, I wouldn't be afforded any sort of buffer.

"You seem very on edge for someone in possibly the most relaxed bar in this part of town."

My attention settled on Nia. Damn her for knowing my tells, though as much was expected after almost fifteen years of friendship.

"Just taking it all in," I lied.

Nia leaned back in her chair. "I'm ordering bourbon. You're enjoying something that isn't rock or some obscure music genre." She shook her head. "Sounds like we're both being changed."

I rolled my eyes, smiling, only paying half attention as a figure approached our table.

"Alright, I've got one In the Mood and one—Heather."

My head snapped up at the sound of my name. Well, that answered that question, I guess.

"Wait, your drink had the same name as you?" Nia asked, her brows furrowed, as she started to flip through the menu again.

"No, I ordered the Ella Fitzgerald," I said. "Thanks for bringing it over, Ethan."

My friend's eyes widened, and she stared at me from under her lash extensions at this new tidbit of information I'd given. I dutifully ignored her as I accepted the glass with my fruity-looking gin cocktail.

Ethan grinned back, his surprise from finding me at the restaurant worn off and replaced with a look of almost-ease. Something told me he was masking pretty hard, if the sweat on his brow was any indication. Probably the same sort of situation as the hostess.

"Okay, I see," he said. "Order the two most expensive cocktails because they're on the house?"

I lifted my glass in cheers. "Thanks for that." In all honesty, I'd forgotten he'd made that offer and was even more surprised he was holding to it.

My eyes slid to Nia when she set her glass down with a

heavy hand then cleared her throat. Clear interest—and curiosity—shone in her eyes.

"Ethan, this is my best friend, Nia. Nia, this is Ethan. He's the reason I came home smelling like a dive bar a few nights ago."

All other emotions on her face were immediately replaced by mischief.

"Oh, *you're* Beer Boy," Nia crooned then extended her hand with a polite smile.

"Apparently?" Ethan accepted her offering to shake as his eyes landed on me. I only shrugged. I couldn't help the nicknames my friends came up with for the people I met at concerts. It had become our thing in college—me recounting the stories and our friend group coming up with silly names to keep everyone straight.

But even as my best friend, I hadn't told Nia much about Ethan, mostly because I knew how she'd act if I went into detail further than *cute and a little shy.*

Kinda like this, with a clear intention of wanting to whisper-yell at me, but keeping on a calm, cool, and collected front while Ethan was still present.

I had to admit, I'd downplayed him a little bit. *Cute* could have probably been replaced by *hot.* I'd hear about it as soon as he walked away, I was sure.

Switching subjects, I said, "This place is nice. A good vibe."

"Thanks, that's what I was going for."

"You ever get up there and sing?" Nia asked, nodding towards the band on stage.

Ethan made a *pft* face. "Oh hell no. I leave that for the professionals. There'd be no one in here if I started to sing."

Nia and I chuckled politely, but as I watched Ethan, I saw that confidence he'd adopted fade slightly. It made my own smile disappear as I scrutinized him, then lifted my drink to my lips to try and hide it.

Him on the mic or not, this place wasn't packed by any means, and there was no way to disguise it.

Given the way he cleared his throat, a soft redness coloring his face, I didn't know that I'd done such a good job at hiding my observation. He was acting as though he'd just been caught, though for what, I didn't know.

"Well, you ladies enjoy the drinks," he said, wearing a shy smile. "If there's anything else you need, don't hesitate to ask."

He offered us a polite wave and we gave our muttered goodbyes, the both of us watching as he walked away. I had a feeling my reason was a little different than Nia's—my curiosity still at its peak over his sudden change in character. It wasn't like I knew Ethan all that well; a night at a concert and some sporadic texting didn't make us friends. But I knew people. And that was the look of a person who had something to hide.

Nia, on the other hand, hadn't seemed to notice. She placed her palms on the table, and I waited for the inevitable question in three... two...

"Okay, so you forgot to mention Beer Boy was freaking *hot*. And that means *a lot* coming from me."

Not a question, but definitely along the lines of what I was expecting.

I gave a nonchalant one-shoulder shrug as I picked up my drink and sat back in my seat. "I didn't think you would care, seeing as he's not exactly your type."

"Maybe not," Nia confirmed. "But I like to know when my best friend runs into absolute man candy. Woo." She stared off in the direction Ethan had gone as she fanned herself. "I might not be straight, but I'm also not blind."

I chuckled at that. "He's not bad to look at."

All prior theatrics were dropped as Nia leveled one of *those* stares at me. The kind that said she wasn't about to put up with my bullshit.

The unfortunate part of trying to play it casual with someone who knew you better than you knew yourself? She could pick out my lies—especially the ones I was telling myself.

"Girl," Nia said, absolutely calling me on my shit. "Do I need to go behind that bar and wing-woman you?"

"No."

"Don't tell me you're holding a grudge about the beer. I

know how you get about concert etiquette."

I shook my head. "No, not at all."

"Then what is it?"

I shrugged. "I don't have time."

"What the hell is that supposed to mean?" Nia grabbed her drink, mirroring my actions.

"It means I have my career to worry about," I said. "I know I hated it, but do you know how big that Taylor Swift gig was? Usually, the seasoned pros are sent to the big acts."

"You *are* a seasoned pro," Nia argued. "You know I've been telling you those assholes at your work don't give you the credit you deserve. They never have. You know music better than literally anyone I know."

I allowed a subtle smile for that. She had—ever since we'd graduated college and I'd gone from freelance writing for music blogs to reviewing for the largest paper in the Chicagoland area. Nia also wasn't wrong, but a job was a job, and I was doing what I loved. There were enough people out there who couldn't say the same. I knew I should be appreciative.

"Thank you," I said. "But that's not always enough to cut it in this industry. I have to build my reputation."

"And is being single part of that reputation?" Nia leaned forward again. She set her drink down and reached across the table, inviting me to do the same. "When was the last time you put yourself out there, Heather? Seriously. Work shouldn't stop you from living your life."

"I know that, and it doesn't," I argued. "I'll get back out there when I'm ready." I took a sip, then said, "Besides, I've been on dates."

"Correction." Nia held up a finger. "You've been on *a* date. Singular. As in, each person gets a single chance."

"Yeah, but there have been multiple of those, so therefore dates. With an 's'."

Nia rolled her eyes. "Semantics aside, I say you go for it. I mean, he's cute. Likes concerts. Has his own business that will give you all the live music you could ask for even if it's not your usual vibe," she finished, gesturing dramatically with a sweep of her arm towards the stage. "What've you got to lose?"

To that, I didn't have a witty remark. What was there to say? I had absolutely *nothing* to lose. But it wasn't starting to pursue Ethan that was the issue.

It was everything that followed.

And I wasn't ready for all the love songs to be a lie again.

# Chapter 5

🎵 Honest | The Band CAMINO



CONSIDERING OUR SOUNDTRACK was smooth jazz, there was nothing relaxed about Mellow Cat's staff that evening.

"Table eight asked for veggie poke not tuna poke."

"Are those rangoons good to go yet?"

"Anyone know if we have any more rolled silverware?"

I ran a hand back through my dark hair as I tried to remain calm. Level-headed. I was the captain of this sinking ship, and dammit I was going to do anything I could to make sure we made it back to shore.

The door smacked shut behind me as I made my way from the kitchen to the bar. At least the general ambiance of the restaurant was still calm, all the guests engaged in their conversations or listening to the music.

My eyes naturally found the table where Heather and her

friend were seated, the latter clearly trying to get the former to go along with something, given the enthusiastic eyes and table hitting going on.

I couldn't draw my eyes from Heather as she allowed her friend a small bit of laughter before she took a sip of her drink. Liam had been right. She *was* a firecracker, but more so with her words than her actions, I'd found. Nothing about her had screamed wild when I'd dropped off her drink—not knowing it had been her who'd ordered it, of course. I hadn't thought she'd take me up on the offer to visit Mellow Cat. But something about her actually coming…

She looked like she belonged here, in that chair, surrounded by people who simply appreciated music—or wanted a good Instagram picture. I wasn't stupid. I knew that was half the draw of my restaurant. Still, I saw the way her foot tapped gently under the table. Not just anyone did that.

"Ethan."

I was jolted from my very obvious staring when Garrett rushed up to the bar.

"What's up, man?" I asked, trying to act like I'd been surveying the whole room, not one patron in particular.

"I don't know what the hell Brad's been doing, but drinks are so behind tonight. Would you mind getting the order for table four ready?"

"Sure… can…" I drawled as I punched buttons on the computer system, trying to pull up the order he was talking about. There were no tickets printed. No wonder Brad wasn't doing his job. He didn't know there was a job to do. "Looks like we might need to leave written tickets again."

Garrett groaned. "Still not fixed?"

"Apparently not." Even though I'd been assured the new machine would work loads better than the last. Considering the price, I'd believed it.

"Would you still be able to help out with this one? I'll go let the others know so we don't get too far behind."

"Will do."

Garrett rushed away after giving me a relieved I-owe-you-one look. Yeah right. I owed my staff a lot more than they owed me lately. It was the least I could do to jump in and help them when they needed it.

I was so engrossed in the work, focused mostly on keeping the cocktail shaker shut—because wouldn't it be my luck for it to fly open on me—that I didn't notice the new person who'd slid up to the bar until they spoke.

"Is this where I get a refill?"

I startled and almost dropped the shaker, but tried to play it off like I was done mixing. Heather really needed to stop popping up if I wanted to keep my focus.

She stood there, her cocktail glass grasped gingerly in her fingers, a mischievous grin on her lips. They were some shade of light brown tonight. At the concert they'd been burgundy. Not that I was paying attention.

I tried to channel the same energy I'd used when I realized I'd gone to her table. Something to match her, at least a little.

While Restaurant Owner Ethan knew how to assert himself, be pleasantly conversational, Regular Ethan sometimes didn't.

Someone like Heather—with her quick wit and an exterior that I could only think to describe as badass—made it even more intimidating. Texting had been easy so far. I had time to think about how I wanted to respond. Face-to-face though…

"That's risky. I'm not sure the bartender knows yours are on the house."

I'd meant it as a joke, but her eyes widened. "You're giving me free drinks all night?"

"Well… yeah?"

Heather set her glass on the bar top, her hard exterior cracking a little to reveal some concern. "Ethan, I can't let you do that."

"It's my treat," I assured her. "You took the time to come here, so that's the least I can do to thank you."

"One drink was more than enough for that." One of her eyebrows lifted, challenging. "But I can pay for that round too. I was happy to come here tonight."

I didn't want my relief to show, but I had a feeling it did when she gestured to the rest of the room behind her, and asked, "You get a steady crowd here?"

Tonight, I was lucky. It wasn't like the space was huge, but enough tables were starting to fill where I could respond, "Yeah, it's not bad," without prompting any further questions.

Still, it seemed like Heather saw straight through me.

She nodded slowly. "So you're all Stray Land and smooth jazz?"

I chuckled. "I'm more Stray Land. The smooth jazz comes from my dad."

"Oh." Her surprise was evident. "Is he the owner of this place?"

"No, no—I'm the owner." I shrugged. "My dad... I don't know. Jazz has always been his thing. It's how we bonded when I was younger, so I thought I'd pay tribute to that."

I didn't miss the subtle shift in her eyes. "Does he come here a lot?"

It wasn't like she would have been able to pick my dad out of a lineup. She'd likely just been searching for someone who resembled me. "Uh, sometimes?" I replied. "He lives out in the burbs, so it's hard for him to come out sometimes. But when my little brother is available, he'll drive him then stick around to help out."

I regretted that last detail the second it was out of my mouth, and I knew Heather had picked up on it by the way her brow scrunched.

"You need extra help?"

She did that room glance again. I hated that room glance. It made me want to duck down behind the bar and crawl away before she could ask me any other questions.

I'd dug myself into this hole, though. Oversharing at the wrong times. I'd been doing it over text too, so it didn't exactly surprise me it had happened in-person either.

There was just something about this woman.

I shrugged. "From time to time." In truth, I could definitely use a few more heads on payroll, but that was the problem: I'd have to pay them. "Kai stepping in helps."

"But that doesn't solve the issue?"

Damn her and all her correct guesses.

"Not entirely."

I went back to the drink I'd been preparing, using the work as an excuse not to elaborate. Not even Heather, as little as I knew her, seemed like a person who would interrupt a man doing his job. Or Brad's job, actually. But she didn't need to know that.

From the corner of my eye, I watched as she settled herself into a barstool. Only one other was occupied. Jerry. He was here almost every night. Had been since he'd retired almost a year ago.

I placed the finished cocktail on the tray for Garrett to take to his table, and when I turned around again, let myself glance at Heather's table. Her friend—Mia?—quickly busied herself with the plate of nachos.

Had she been watching us?

"She really wanted a refill," Heather said, as if she'd known where my attention had been. "Thought it would be faster for me to come over here myself."

"The Ella and In the Mood, right?" I asked, already pivoted to start the order.

Heather made a face and flicked her wrist twice, brushing away the question. "She can wait a few more minutes."

"Shouldn't you get back—?"

"How's this place doing?"

My eyes widened. Sheesh. I hadn't thought she'd be subtle, but that was about as blunt as it could get. And bold.

But it wasn't an accusatory look in her eyes. It was concern. Not at all like she was calling me out on being a failure—not that I was; Mellow Cat *was* still open—but more of a question from a friend who wanted to make sure I was doing okay. That my business was doing okay.

And while I was, for the most part, able to answer yes for myself, when it came to discussing Mellow Cat…

I sighed. "It's been steady."

She quirked a brow. "Which means?"

"I have customers."

"You keep saying things that should follow with *but*."

Caught red-handed.

"But they usually only filter in at night." Her brow rose even higher. "On the weekends."

"Can't you just close during the day?" she suggested.

"I know I have some regulars that only come in at that time. We have less staff here, so it's not much of a cost in that regard to open for lunch."

"But general operation costs?"

"Aren't you a journalist?" Asking the right questions was part of her job, of course, but how the hell did she know so much about running a restaurant?

She shrugged. "I worked in a bar in college."

"Had to pay for those concert tickets somehow, right?"

A slow grin curled her lips. "Nice try, changing to my favorite subject."

Damn. She was good.

"We were doing really well when I first opened," I started. "A few of those new business kinks—finding good staff, getting steady acts booked, perfecting the menu. But something about the last few years has been…" I shrugged. "I don't know. We went from being the cool new restaurant in the neighborhood—wait lists every night—to being lucky if we had half the tables filled at a single time."

I didn't know why I was telling her this. All in all, Heather was still practically a stranger. Hell, I hadn't even admitted this to my siblings yet.

Maybe it was because she didn't know anything. She didn't know the struggle of getting Mellow Cat started, or the grander reason why I had in the first place. Or maybe it was because she wouldn't be able to relay the message the same way someone I knew better would.

Or maybe it was because I'd learned that most people with an exterior like Heather had a softer interior. Someone else had made them build up that armor. They were usually looking for the person who could see beyond it.

She'd already shown a little bit of the person hiding behind it. Maybe she'd allow a little more.

The way she pursed her lips made me think that was going to be the case, but then they flattened out again, whatever deep thought she'd been lost in, gone.

She didn't say anything, though. What was there to say, really, after some random guy you met at a concert started venting about his struggles? Even if it was encouraged.

But the door had been opened, and now I was curious.

She sat back in her stool when I leaned forward on the counter, resting on my elbows.

"Be honest," I prefaced, even though I didn't doubt for a moment she would be anything but. "What do you think of this place?"

That seemed to catch her off guard. Not that I blamed her. I was hardly so blunt with most of my good friends, but I needed to hear it from someone who was going to be tell the truth. Not someone who knew what would hurt my feelings and what wouldn't. The time for sugar-coating was over.

Knowing a challenge when she heard one, Heather leaned

forward on the bar, mirroring me. Our faces were level, and I couldn't help the way my eyes darted to her lips before they quickly rose back up to meet her stare.

"How honest we talking?"

Okay, now I was scared, but in an attempt to hide that from Heather, I said, "Do your worst."

Her smirk grew, and I couldn't tell if it was in a way that told me she was impressed by my bravery to accept criticism or in a way that would result in me crying in my office after she ripped me a new one.

Heather leaned back a little and jerked her head to the side. "They the only band you have here?"

"No, but they come here a lot."

"What's *a lot*?"

"They're on the schedule every other week." And it had taken great effort to get that deal in place. The Chroma Groove Project were blowing up on TikTok after a few viral covers. Somehow, I'd convinced them to perform for free with the promise of growing their audience even more.

Heather's following slow nod worried me. "Do they ever play something—you know. A little more upbeat?"

"They're a jazz band."

"Yeah." Her eyes drifted to the trio on stage. "But my grandpa listens to songs with a better tempo than this."

In her defense, they *were* currently in the midst of covering *Moon River*. Even Jerry had stopped his foot tapping. "I see your point," I agreed. "What else?"

"You've got a good ambiance going in here. Very relaxing, which makes sense. There were some girls taking pictures here, so you can pretty much bet those are going on some form of social media."

"Free marketing is always nice," I added, nodding along.

"Exactly. But they're no longer here."

"So?"

"What do you mean *so*?"

What did she mean what did I mean? "They finished their meal and left. That *is* what happens at a restaurant."

I jumped back, surprised, when she reached across the bar and lightly hit my arm with the back of her hand.

"Dude," she said. "That's what they do at a *regular* restaurant. It's Friday night in Chicago, and this place is essentially a glorified cocktail lounge. As soon as I saw the menu, you wanna know what I thought?"

"Isn't that how we got into this whole conversation?"

Heather shook her head, and this time I knew her smirk was proud, not annoyed.

"Apps and cocktails. All night," she said. "That's how you enjoy this place."

Now this was a take I hadn't heard before. "Go on."

She leaned forward again, a new eagerness lighting her face. "I'm not here to tell you how to run your business," she started. "But if you ask me, this is the kind of place that's perfect for groups that want to linger. Sip a few cocktails. Eat some finger foods. Get a little entertainment. But we're in the third largest city in the country, my friend. There's a lot of places around here that are perfect for that. So how do you stand out?"

"I have a feeling you're going to tell me."

"Right you are," she confirmed before she pointed her thumb back over her shoulder. "That group up there is talented. I'm not denying them that. But they're a snoozefest. And what's the point of staying out if someone could be in sweatpants on their couch sleeping instead?"

"Ouch."

"You know I didn't mean it like that," she amended. "I'm just saying, there needs to be a balance. Jazz, but also… not jazz. Something to make you unique—and that can liven this place up. You can appeal to the middle-aged crowd earlier in the night, but keep things going for the younger crowd as the night continues."

"Does anything come to mind?"

"You trying to get free ideas from me?"

I grinned. "Ideas in exchange for drinks."

"Now we're talking," she replied, smiling back. Then she glanced down at her wrist, to the smart watch that had lit up. "Looks like Nia is officially past her limit of waiting for the next round."

"I'm on it."

Heather sat quietly in her seat while I got to work on the cocktails. But as I went through the routine, I couldn't help but keep repeating what she'd said in my head.

She wasn't wrong. I knew I attracted a certain kind of clientele, but I supposed I'd never thought that could change. Or that someone who'd hardly been here for an hour could pick out exactly what could be done to adjust the business model.

That wasn't to say I was going to do a complete switch of everything I'd worked towards because one girl made one suggestion. Mellow Cat was still *my* project. It was *my* passion. I didn't want it to lose any of the heart I'd built into it.

Still, that wasn't to say there couldn't be some adjustments made. I only needed to think of what could be done with the limited resources available.

"One Ella and one In the Mood," I announced as I turned around and slid the finished cocktails to Heather.

She hopped out of the chair and grabbed both the glasses. With her body half turned away from me, she said, "You'll think of something, and if not, you've earned yourself a repeat customer tonight. Free drinks or not."

With that, she walked away.

# Chapter 6

🎵 Don't Go Breaking My Heart | Elton John



I TRIED TO concentrate on the text I'd just gotten over the cacophony of sounds coming from the stage. Experimental indie. Sometimes, my boss introduced me to my favorite shows when he assigned me this genre. Other times, I went and told him we'd be better off not running a piece.

This was likely going to be the latter.

Still, I tried to keep a straight face. The crowd was small, and some were clearly into this sort of stuff. Others, it seemed, were in the same boat as me.

I tried not to laugh when I saw a girl a little bit ahead of me in the crowd physically cringe when a shrill—but intentional—screech erupted from the speakers. The shoulders of everyone in the sparse crowd went stiff as the totally unaware aspiring producer continued his set on stage.

Yup. Definitely letting my boss know this one was a bust. I wasn't about to risk my credibility in order to save some feelings. I'd just tell the producer we'd decided to run something else. Besides, the three other show reviews and interview with the architect of an up-and-coming venue I'd done over the last week would be enough to satisfy my quota.

"Sheesh. I think my left eardrum just burst."

My eyes widened—and it had nothing to do with my shock over the producer mixing a reverbed alien spaceship sound with an angry cat.

Ethan was at my side, face scrunched as he rubbed his ear. "W-what are you—?"

I didn't bother finishing the question before I lifted my phone to finish reading the text. It had been from him, but nowhere in the conversation about our evening plans had he said anything about coming here.

"What?" he asked, turning to me. "A man can't enjoy his Thursday evening at a local open mic night?"

"This isn't an open mic night," I corrected. "This guy's on tour."

Ethan's attention turned back to the stage where he found the aspiring producer with wide eyes. "Oh. Well, that explains the twenty-dollar cover."

That time, I didn't hide my smile.

"You didn't mention it was so… unique," he added.

"I didn't think I had to." Ethan showing up hadn't been in my bingo card for the evening. "Shouldn't you be at the restaurant?"

"We close at nine on the week days," he said. "Friday and Saturday are our only late nights."

I nodded. "And you chose to enjoy your freedom here?"

"Eh." He shrugged. "Didn't have anything better to do. Plus, someone I thought I trusted to give music recommendations said she was coming." He tilted his head, side-eying me. "The trust is waning."

I shook my head at him. Given our conversation the last time we'd seen each other in person a few weeks before, I thought he might have been mad at me. It wasn't until I got home that I realized maybe I should have been a little softer. He'd asked for honesty, but it had also been his small business I was roasting.

Nothing had changed, though. In fact, the texting had gotten more energetic. More frequent. I often found myself smiling down at my phone due to some witty remark or another. Every now and then I got a story about a funny customer. They were becoming some of my favorite parts of my day. A nice break from the usual.

And it seemed his physical conversation had warmed up just as much as his digital ones.

"They can't all be Stray Land," I retorted. "Which, truly, are you stalking me now or something?"

"Aren't you the one who showed up at my restaurant unannounced?"

"Unannounced, but not uninvited."

Ethan placed his hand over his heart, his face contorted in mock pain. "She wounds me." When he opened his eyes, he added, "But not as much as this guy."

When I laughed, a few of the surrounding audience members turned to me. Bad timing, maybe, since a new mix of a jackhammer and dog barking had just started up, but the main act was way too into his element to notice.

"Why does this remind me of Ross from *Friends*?" Ethan said when I'd calmed myself.

"With an electronic backtrack," I added.

"And too much bass," he finished, and that time we both laughed. This time the crowd reaction was less curious and more annoyed.

I offered a polite "sorry" to someone who glared for a particularly long time before they turned around and started bobbing their head again.

There was something out there for everyone, I supposed.

"I can't believe this is real," I said.

"And you have to write about it?"

I shook my head. "Nah. I decided about three minutes before you showed up this one wasn't worth crushing this guy's dreams." Pretentious hipsters liked to argue, and this guy fit that label to a tee.

"So what are you still doing here?"

"I don't know. I felt like I should stick it out." And I'd met the guy before he started. Sure, I was lost in the semi-sparse crowd—and he was more than lost in his music—but leaving felt wrong. There was still a chance he'd notice my absence if he ever snapped out of his artistry-induced trance.

Even Ethan seemed to catch on to my weak excuse.

His brow lifted. "Is it worth the damage to your ears? I mean, how will you be able to do your job if all you ever hear from this moment forward is a high-pitched ringing?"

I mirrored his actions. "What are you suggesting?"

"I feel like there are better places we could be."

"Such as?"

"Such as the karaoke bar I saw down the street from here."

My head tilted a little. Not enough where Ethan would likely question it—he'd question my hesitation to answer more—but in a way that definitely hinted at my curiosity to his motives.

"All fun, I promise," he added. Yes, he'd noticed.

And I couldn't deny that I wanted to accept.

I shrugged. "I guess I'll take bad drunk singing over this."

× × ×

A SNORT SNUCK out of me when a large bearded man dropped it low while singing a diss track originally performed by a female country artist. My hand instinctively went up to my mouth to prevent any of the beer I'd just taken a sip of from escaping. Thankfully, it hadn't come out of my nose either.

Ethan's eyebrows were practically in his hairline as he watched. I couldn't tell if it was due to shock or wonder.

"Looks like someone missed his calling," I joked.

"Apparently," he agreed.

He was smiling as he turned in his chair to face our table again. All the good seats had been taken by the time we'd gotten here, meaning all the tables that allowed us to both view the stage at all times. This place was packed for a Thursday night, which made me believe karaoke night was a weekly occurrence.

We'd walked in to the tune of two thirty-somethings belting Beyoncé off-key. Truth be told, this concert was far more entertaining than the last one. I loved a good show put on by an Average Joe who was fueled by liquid courage.

The guy on stage was definitely living up to my expectations.

"How many more times do you think he can do that before his jeans rip?" I asked, gesturing to the stage as the man dropped again then did a full, seductive body roll as he got up. The crowd in the bar went wild.

"I was more worried about that last girl," Ethan countered. "Aren't you ladies supposed to look out for each other?"

"Hey, that dress was hot on her," I argued. "If I had her curves, I would've been working it, too."

Ethan's pause made my attention drift back to him—just in time to watch his throat bob. Like he was swallowing words he wanted to say, but had decided not to.

"I'm just saying, if I was her friend and I saw her dress riding up like that, I would have stepped in *before* we saw what was underneath."

"Or lack thereof," I amended.

Ethan grinned. "I've never seen a bouncer move so fast."

"The girl needed to go home if she wasn't even aware it was happening." I took another sip of beer then said, "But yes. I agree she should maybe go into the market for some new friends."

"At least she has one of those stories she can look back on in a few years and hopefully laugh about."

The song finished, and Ethan and I joined in the cheering as the emcee for the evening announced the next song. The disco instrumental started up as a group of middle-aged women took the stage.

"I love this shit."

I hadn't realized I'd said it out loud until Ethan turned to me again. "Oh yeah?" He nodded backwards. "You gonna add your name to the list?"

"Oh, hell no," I said, and he chuckled. "I just like watching. Like, how often do you think these people come out of their shells like this?"

"Well, that last guy didn't seem like he had a shell at all."

Sure enough, when I glanced at said guy, he was chugging a pitcher of cheap beer while his friends cheered.

"Okay, so this is another day that ends in 'y' for him," I agreed. "But look at these women." Ethan did as I'd instructed before I continued. "See the one to the left of the mic? You can totally tell she's just doing this because her friends roped her into it."

"How?"

I leaned across the small round high-top where we were seated, stretching out a pointed finger so Ethan could follow.

"The other ones? They're all swaying and confident à la fashion faux pas girl." Another chuckle rumbled out of Ethan. "The one I'm talking about is just kinda bopping along to the beat. She hasn't taken the mic from the stand. She hasn't strayed from that spot. But she's up there all the same, doing her best."

I watched him sidelong as he nodded, taking in what I'd said. "So you're saying you love analyzing people?"

"I love seeing them embrace another side of themselves because of music."

"Is that why you got into the field you're in?"

I sat back and Ethan turned away from the stage so we could keep our conversation going.

"Yes and no," I said. "I grew up around concerts. My

parents were… well, they were groupies, so before I could take care of myself, they'd drag me along. Or when I was *really* little I'd stay with my aunt and uncle while they did their thing. Then when I was old enough, their thing became my thing, and it never really stopped." I shrugged. "I was never great in school—probably because I was taken out so often—but I could write well enough and, like you said, knew how to analyze music and crowds, so I got a journalism degree from my local community college and worked my way up."

Ethan let out a low whistle. "Now you're working for one of the largest news outlets in the Chicagoland area?" When I raised a curious brow, wondering how he knew that, he shrugged. "I've read some of your reviews, remember?"

Right. None of my articles came without my employer's name at the top center of every web page. Or printed paper if that was Ethan's vibe. Considering he ran a jazz club, it might have been.

"I'm one of the lucky ones, I guess." My hands wrapped around my half-filled pint glass. "I'm in a career I'm passionate about. Plus, it doesn't hurt that I get paid to go to concerts, instead of the other way around."

"Who's the coolest act you've met?" Ethan asked.

"Stray Land," I replied instantly, and he threw a crumpled napkin at me. Smiling, I added, "It's always the names no one knows who are the best, honestly. Seems lame, but… I don't know, they're more humble? More willing to engage with their fans and not be all annoying about it and whatever. Like, I can't tell you how many big-name acts I've met that act like I'm the help. Like my words don't matter because they've already got this massive following and multi-album deal."

"That's bullshit," Ethan said. "Don't they know how big cancel culture is nowadays?"

"Nothing they say or do to me is *that* extreme," I assured him. "And I'd never write anything to intentionally harm an artist." Case in point, the piece I'd decided to forgo earlier that evening.

"But you're honest," Ethan concluded.

I nodded. "Yeah, I try to be." I took a sip of my beer. "Which, speaking of, I hope you know I thought your place was cool as hell. I wasn't trying to bash it the last time we saw each other."

It was obvious he hadn't expected me to bring it up, and the closed-off Ethan I thought I'd finally managed to get past was back.

I watched as he lifted his glass to his lips, taking a drink, buying himself time. I watched his throat bob—watched his strong hands clasp his glass—and I didn't think I'd ever found myself thinking sexually about a throat until that moment.

His fingers flexed when he set his pint back down and released his grip. Suddenly, my mind shifted there, wondering what else they'd held—*who* else. Out of all the topics we'd covered over text and the few times we'd seen each other in person, past relationships had never been one of them.

Why that thought was coming to me now, I didn't know.

"I asked you to be honest," Ethan finally said. "You only gave me what I asked for."

"Yeah, but I didn't need to be a bitch about it."

His brow furrowed. "I didn't think you were being a bitch. You gave your opinion."

"Sure, but—"

"Heather," Ethan said through a chuckle. He reached across the table and placed his hand over mine. I ran my tongue along my teeth, trying to prevent any other reactions from passing over my face. "You're fine. In fact, I've already started thinking of some ideas."

"Oh." I wasn't expecting that at all. "Can I get any teasers?"

"Well, they're still in the works. It's a drawing board situation right now."

I gave a one shoulder shrug and nodded. "Makes sense. I can't wait until everything's ready to be unveiled."

He smiled, but it wasn't nearly as convincing as I wanted it to be. Something about Ethan made me believe he was a chronic worrier—that no matter how much fun he wanted to have, there were little demons in the back of his mind reminding him of everything else he should or could be doing. What he'd admitted to me about his business probably didn't help. I'd be worried, too, if I noticed a decline in visitors.

Before that conversation could go any further, though, the disco music ended and the crowd offered some polite cheers for the group of women as they left the stage. I smiled when I saw the others hugging their shier friend, and the joy that radiated from her in response.

"All right, let's give it up for that great performance," the emcee said into the mic. "We've got room for a few more tonight and no one on the line up. Who's going to be our next singer?"

Before I could think twice about it, my hand shot up in the air.

Ethan's apparent shock was probably similar to my own. Never before in my life had I done karaoke. Well, scratch that. Never before in my life had I done karaoke without having at least three shots of tequila beforehand. Right now, I was running on the steady buzz of a few beers. It was hardly enough to warrant the courage involved with going on stage.

Yet, there I was, volunteering to do just that.

"We'll go," I called out, earning the attention of the emcee as well as most of the other crowd. I'd have bet a lot of them were regulars. I was the fresh blood in the room.

"Wonderful!" the emcee shouted. "Come on down and

pick your song."

"What are you doing?" Ethan hissed from across the table, his eyes wide. "Who's 'we'?"

"Us, stupid," I whispered back. "You've gotta know at least one duet."

"Yeah, but I don't sing."

"Neither do I."

"So why did you volunteer?"

I hopped out of my chair and moved around the high-top, grabbing Ethan's arm as I went to force him to join. There were some surprising muscles hiding under his chambray button down.

"We're gonna be the lady."

"What?"

"The lady who was afraid," I explained. "We're gonna go up there and have the time of our lives singing horribly."

For a second, I thought he might pry my hand off him and leave me to deal with the consequences of my choices alone. But then the worry lines faded, his face softening.

"Alright," he said. "Let's do it. But we're not singing that Lady Gaga song everyone does."

✕ ✕ ✕

WE SANG "DON'T Go Breaking My Heart" and by the time we got off the stage, we were all smiles, running high on the adrenaline of the performance and the audience's enthusiasm. Apparently, the bar regulars really engaged with newcomers. Who knew?

The smiles still hadn't worn off after a few beers—courtesy of Bearded Guy—and most of an Uber ride later. We sat in the back seat, holding fake microphones and singing bits and pieces of the songs playing on the radio. It was a miracle our driver hadn't turned it off yet to shut our tipsy asses up, but I was thankful for it. This was the most fun I'd had in ages, and I was pretty sure Ethan could probably say the same.

I hadn't even noticed the car had stopped until the driver said, "Is this good for the drop off?"

Somewhat disoriented, my head swiveled as I took in our location. Definitely my street. Ethan must have put my address first when he'd set up the ride.

"Yeah, this is good," I told the driver then turned back to Ethan. My hand found his knee, and I grinned. "I had a great time tonight. Thanks for singing badly with me."

"Always happy to make people cringe with my singing abilities."

I chuckled while I shook my head at him.

This should have been the point where I made the driver the happiest man in the world and left the car. Instead, I lingered, not quite able to draw away from Ethan yet. From his smile. From the happy glow in his eyes. From the warmth of him beneath my palm.

That warmth extended through my whole body as I lifted my other hand to his face and leaned in to kiss him.

He was tense under my touch, but a moment later, his hand found my hip and his lips moved with mine in a soft, tender dance. It had been so long since I'd been kissed like this—in a way that made me believe I could get lost in it. Like it could go on for seconds or hours and I wouldn't know the difference.

I had a feeling it had been the former when the driver cleared his throat.

Ethan and I pulled back from one another, and it was only then that I realized what I'd done.

"I, um—" I cleared my throat. "Yeah, uh, goodnight!"

And before Ethan had the chance to say anything in response, I bolted from the car.

# Chapter 7

♪ Older | Sasha Alex Sloan



SHIT.

Shit shit shit shit SHIT!

I clicked the lock of Nia and I's apartment shut, leaned back against the door, then slid down it until I hit the floor. My face found my waiting palms almost immediately after.

What had I done?

Why had I kissed him?

No. I knew exactly why. It was because he'd just been sitting there all attractive and smiley with his hidden muscles and sexy neck and strong hands. And heck had I been right about his hands. The second he'd grabbed onto my waist, I'd wanted him to hold me tighter, pull me closer, touch places that hadn't been touched in *way* too long—by someone other than myself or my vibrator, that was.

*Ugh.*

My head tilted back until it hit the door a little harder than I'd intended. Good thing I'd decided to skip the write-up for that disaster concert. I might have given myself a minor concussion. Combined with my distractions, there was no way it would have gotten done.

I'd made plenty of stupid decisions in my lifetime. Growing up with parents that hadn't exactly parented did that to a girl. I'd learned the hard way for a lot of life lessons, which by this point meant I was pretty good at avoiding said stupid decisions. That included drunken mistakes like kissing boys in the backs of Ubers when there was supposed to be a very strict line drawn.

This was Ethan. The guy who lit up when he was comfortable, but shut down the second he wasn't. My choice tonight… it could have ruined everything that had built up over the last few weeks of us talking. For the first time, I'd thought I'd actually managed to keep a friendship from a concert, and here I'd gone and ruined it with one not-thought-out, alcohol-addled decision.

Then again, his grip hadn't been one of someone who was mad about what I'd done. Nor was his kiss.

God, his kiss. Women would kill for the experience I'd just had in the back of that car, even if it had only lasted a few seconds. A minute, max. And if that's what he could accomplish in that short time, I didn't want to think about what could have been done with more.

Or maybe I did.

I had no fucking clue anymore.

My phone vibrated in the pocket of my coat and I pulled it out, only to find a text notification from the very man I'd been thinking about.

Just got home! Thanks for a fun night ☺

I read it again and again, trying to find some sort of hidden message, but there was none. It was just another text from Ethan, no different than any of the others in our message string. Like the kiss hadn't even happened.

My arm was like jelly as it lowered and the back of my hand slapped the floor. My phone was still in my grip, the screen still lit with the text.

Huh. Well, that wasn't what I'd expected. I hadn't expected anything at all, actually.

I'd thought for sure Ethan would go silent. He didn't strike me as the face-conflict-head-on type—not for his personal life. Silly me for thinking the shyness would win over the other, hidden outgoing side of him.

The side that I, of all people, had somehow managed to bring out.

But maybe that had been the key. Maybe, against all odds, we'd actually managed to build a true friendship from that one chance encounter. And maybe, that was why he was willing to keep whatever this was we had going despite what I'd done.

If Ethan could do it, I could do it. No problem. Except for the moment when I next saw him and inevitably remembered how his lips felt—

No! There would be no more thinking about lips or hands or necks or anything even remotely sexual. From here on out, everything would be strictly platonic as it should have remained from the start. It would be easier that way. Less attachment meant less disappointment.

And I was, unfortunately, way too accustomed to that.

Our line needed to stay drawn. With a marker. In black. And bolded a little bit. I wasn't ready to give up the surprisingly witty texts that made me laugh quite yet, but I'd try my best to forget my other feelings, as complicated as they were.

× × ×

NIA WAS ASLEEP after her shift at the hospital, and I hadn't texted Ethan back before I'd gone to bed, so it surprised me when my phone lit up on the coffee table the next morning— and stayed lit up.

Oh no.

I brushed the everything bagel residue off my hands and finished chewing before I reached for the phone. The name and contact picture staring back at me confirmed my suspicions as to who was trying to reach me.

"Hey, Mom," I said after I accepted the call and pressed the speaker button.

"Heather! Honey! Hi!"

Say that three times fast.

I could barely hear her over the noise in the background. One glance down at the phone screen again told me it was seven-thirty in the morning. Something told me she wasn't in Wisconsin at the moment. Not even us cheeseheads started the parties that early, even if it was Friday.

"What's up?" I asked before I took another bite of my bagel with cream cheese.

"Oh, just checking in on my favorite girl!"

"I'm your only girl," I deadpanned.

The laugh was too excited, too loud, even if she was at some sort of party. My heart sank hearing it.

"You're too funny, baby girl! You get it from your daddy!"

"What's up, Mom?" I repeated, wanting to get this over with as soon as possible. I didn't need to hear her when she was like this, and I'd told her plenty of times to leave me alone when she was.

"I jus' wanted to tell you how proud I am of you! Writing about big pop stars! Hey, hey, hey—I told Gary about it, and you know what he said?"

"What?"

"The fucker didn't believe me! Said there was no way someone like me coulda made someone like you. I told him you're all your daddy and—Tim! Hey, Timmy, come here! It's our baby!"

Oh, for the love of God.

"Mom, I've gotta go. I have work—"

I reached frantically for my phone to turn down the volume when Mom erupted in a cheer on the other line. She wasn't alone, the noise from before having grown ten times what it had been when I first picked up.

"You'll never believe it, baby!" Mom shouted over the noise. I could just barely make out what she was saying. "Marty just jumped off the roof into the pool and—oh, there you are! Say hi to your little girl!"

"Heather!" Dad's shouted greeting came across a little clearer than Mom's. He, for the most part, sounded normal. Then again, he'd never been into anything hard. He'd just never stopped Mom. "How's my girl?"

I rolled my eyes. "Good. Hey, I really gotta go finish getting ready for work. I can call you back after—"

"Oh, we'll be busy, honey!" Mom said. "But hey—"

I listened as the noise in the background grew softer, meaning Mom was probably walking away from the commotion.

"Hey," she said again, her voice softer now. Hushed. "Your dad and I wanted to stay one more night with all the others, but I checked our accounts and we're running a little low. You don't think you'd be able to… you know. Send us a little something?"

I shut my eyes and sighed through my nose. I knew it. I knew my parents didn't actually want to call and check in. I couldn't think of the last time that had been the case. There was always some hidden agenda attached to them reaching out.

"How much?"

"Just a couple hundred. Two-fifty maybe? I can check with your dad and let you know."

The words were on the tip of my tongue, waiting for me to finally say them. *No, Mom, I'm done sending you money.* But the words that came out instead were, "Yeah, just let me know."

"You're the best, baby girl!" She made a dramatic *mwah* sound, like she was kissing my cheek over the phone. "I gotta run now! I'll talk to you later!"

She hung up before I had the chance to say anything back. My phone beeped three times, letting me know the call had been disconnected then went black.

I reached for it and went to my tracking app to see where I'd be funding an extended stay.

Miami. They were at a party in a time zone only one hour ahead of me.

I glanced out the window where the sun had just barely finished rising then back down at my bagel. I'd hardly taken three bites, but suddenly I wasn't very hungry anymore.

# Chapter 8

♫ Trouble | Never Shout Never



MY PHONE WAS silent. *Too* silent. Normally, I loved not being contacted; it gave me less to worry about—less stressing about the right thing to say. But this time, I hated the silence.

I was jittery for all the wrong reasons as I hung clean martini glasses behind the bar. Only a few tables were occupied, and the act for the evening, an older trumpeter named Leo, was helping the rest of his band set up on stage. Maybe once he started playing, I'd finally relax a little bit.

It wasn't that I expected my phone to show notification after notification from Heather. But it had been *all day*, and considering what had happened last night...

I curled my lips in, remembering the feel of the kiss. It

had been a long time since a date had ended like that for me—not that we'd been on a date. That hadn't been my intention when I'd asked her to join me at the bar. I'd just wanted to spend time with her. I'd been thinking about how that could happen for the whole week between when she'd visited Mellow Cat and last night. I would have sat through that whole damn mess of a concert she'd been at if it meant just being there with her.

Thankfully, it hadn't come to that. The karaoke bar had been a blast, and she'd been right about conquering my stage fright. Though I wasn't sure if I would have let loose with any of my other friends the way I'd let myself go with her. Maybe it was because my friends were, for the most part, a lot like me. Reserved. Cautious. Practical.

For someone who claimed she didn't like being on stage, Heather had gone at the song with an energy that put the bearded country singer to shame. Once I'd seen that, it had been easier for me to let my guard down. To have a little fun.

Looking back on it, maybe it had ended up feeling a *little* bit like a date.

I swore under my breath when I missed the stemware rack and the martini glass I'd been trying to hang landed on the counter then rolled off and onto the floor where it shattered. Every head in the restaurant turned my way, and I offered an apologetic wave. Appeased, they turned back to their meals or the stage set-up.

"You doing alright?"

Liam appeared with a broom and dust pan before I even had the chance to think of what to do next.

"Yeah, thanks," I said as he got to work cleaning up my mess. "I'm just distracted."

"Don't blame you." He nodded toward the stage. "Wasn't that the guy who walked off midway through his set the last time?"

"Yeah." Apparently, it had been because of a dispute with the band, but Leo's personal drama was the least of my worries.

"Don't sweat it, boss," Liam said as he finished sweeping. "The odds of that happening again are slim."

I offered him an appreciative grin, as I got back to work with the non-shattered glasses. As much as I liked Liam, he didn't need to know my personal business. Especially not when he also knew—

"Heather!"

A second glass nearly met its demise when he called out her name, and sure enough, when I glanced back over my shoulder, there she was. Her red hair was tied up in a bun, and her make-up was noticeably lighter than I'd seen it in the past. Namely, her lips weren't painted. A big change from the bright red I'd found smeared on my own lips when I'd gone to brush my teeth the night before.

"Liam?" she called back from where she stood at the host stand. She said something to Sarah, who glanced back our way, probably seeking permission to let this person through.

When I gave my nod of approval, she gestured toward the bar and Heather made her way over.

"*This* is your second job?" she asked as she took up a seat in one of the barstools. I couldn't help but notice she hadn't looked at me yet.

"Server three days a week," Liam confirmed with a nod. "Four this week. I took a shift tonight when the show at Sound Hall got cancelled."

"Cancelled?"

"Lead singer lost his voice," Liam explained with a shrug.

"Shit that sucks," Heather said. "But that works in my favor. Having a bartender around who knows my drink of choice is always nice."

Liam chuckled. "Single or double?"

"Is triple too dramatic?"

"A little."

"Double."

"You've got it," Liam said with a broad smile then got to work.

Heather's eyes tracked him for a moment as he moved, then they finally found me. Immediately, I knew she was stressed. The request for a third shot in her drink could have clued me into that, but there was a… *something* in her eyes.

A lackluster shine. Defeat, maybe?

"Long day?" I asked.

She shrugged. "Just another day in paradise." I wondered if she'd noticed me scrutinizing her because a small smile formed on those lips. "Hi," she whispered.

It wasn't seductive. Not at all the voice of a person who'd surprised me with a kiss in the back seat of our Uber.

This was a friendly hello, but testing. I'd been sure to text her as soon as I got home to make sure no awkwardness fell between us, but maybe it had missed the mark. I'd been worried she'd see right through it, and maybe this was her way of hinting that I'd been right to be nervous.

How the hell else was I supposed to act? Even now, I was thankful the bar was between us. If we were any closer there was no telling what line I'd cross, and she'd just made it abundantly clear with her tone that last night shouldn't have happened. What we'd enjoyed had most definitely not been a date, and the ways I'd thought about the kiss—and what else I would have loved to do if I hadn't been so hyper-aware of the Uber driver watching us—were meant only to be a fantasy.

"Hi," I said back. Her grin widened at the nerves that snuck into my voice, raising it a half-octave higher than usual. I cleared my throat. "How was the rest of your night?"

"Good. I went to bed pretty early. Work and all that."

"Your boss was okay with the piece from the concert being nixed?"

"Yeah, I showed him a clip I recorded on my phone and he actually thanked me for making that call." I chuckled, and she leaned forward, resting her arms on the bar. "He gave me a new assignment for next Wednesday. Country concert over by Goose Island. You in?"

My brows rose. "In?"

She nodded. "In other words, are you coming with?"

"Am I allowed to?" I stepped out of the way as Liam walked past to get a glass for her drink. "Isn't this for your job?"

"So was last night," she said. "I figured I'd skip the surprise appearance and go straight to the invitation."

Touché. "I don't know," I said, for a lot of reasons, but the one I voiced aloud was, "I'd have to check the schedule here and see if I could make—"

"I'm free next Wednesday," Liam interjected as he slid up beside me and passed Heather her drink. "Want me to step in for the night?"

My whole body tensed, and if I was a stronger man, I might have told him 'no' on the spot. I'd be lying to myself, though, if I said I wasn't at least a little bit interested. I'd thought for sure after last night Heather and I would be limited to visits at Mellow Cat and text messages from here on out. Yet here she was inviting me to a concert.

Which was, of course, a very platonic thing to do. Not at all anything I should read too much into.

"The concert's cheap enough where I can probably convince my boss to pay for a second ticket," Heather added. "He sometimes lets me bring a guest. So I'm not going to all these things alone all the time, or whatever."

Between the two of them, Liam and Heather were really making it hard for me to find a reason to say no.

I shrugged. "I suppose I can join. What time?"

Heather smiled. "I have to get there around six to interview the headliner. Opening act goes on at seven. I was thinking we could grab a bite to eat before? The venue is in the back of a pretty good barbeque restaurant."

Dinner *and* a show?

Still platonic. Still very, very platonic.

"Sounds good. Then I can save us a spot in the crowd?"

I startled when Heather actually started choking on the sip she'd just taken. "Are you kidding me?" she asked when she'd recovered.

"…No?"

"You're meeting the headliner too. I'm not leaving you in that crowd alone if I don't need to."

My eyes widened. "Are you serious?"

"Hell yeah, I am." This time after she took a sip, she set her glass down with a sigh. "Get your best dancin' boots ready, partner. It's gonna be a wild ride."

I laughed and might have said more had I not noticed who walked in.

Nia called out Heather's name, and she turned in her barstool, waving to her friend before holding up a one-minute finger.

"I already warned your hostess she'd be coming," Heather said when she faced me again. "I'll catch up with you later?"

"Yeah. Sure thing." When she stood and reached into her purse, I added, "Don't worry about it. That one's on the house."

Heather narrowed her eyes at me, looking like she wanted to argue, but then Sarah brought Nia past.

"Hi, Beer Boy," she greeted, wiggling her fingers in my direction.

"Hi, Nia." I'd learned her name through Heather and I's texting conversations. Even though I wasn't sure she knew me as anything other than Beer Boy.

Heather threw one more smile my way before she wrapped her arm around Nia's shoulders and Sarah guided the girls to their table. I didn't stop watching, even after they'd been sat.

A low whistle came from behind me. "Wow, you've got it *bad.*"

I turned on Liam with a scowl. "I don't know what you're talking about."

Liam gave me an "Are you serious?" face before he said,

"I don't blame you. She's a lot of fun. Pretty."

That was putting it lightly. "Why don't *you* go for her then?"

"Because *I* am happily taken. But I don't believe *you* are."

He wiggled his eyebrows at me, and I rolled my eyes. "We're just friends."

Friends who kissed in the backs of Ubers and had a somewhat embarrassing obsession with the other person's lips. But friends nonetheless.

"Whatever you say, man."

Liam laughed when I shoved his shoulder in response. "Get back to work. We have drink orders coming in."

He didn't argue any further, thankfully. I didn't know how many more ways I could have said the same thing over and over again before I sounded like I was extremely in denial.

With my employee aptly distracted again, though, I took the chance to steal a glance at Heather's table—only to find her looking back.

My whole body heated and I ducked into the kitchen faster than just friends would when they were caught.

× × ×

LEO LIFTED HIS trumpet into the air and bowed for the remaining crowd. Jerry set down his drink and two-finger whistled, while the rest of the audience clapped politely.

It was just past ten. Only three tables remained. We didn't close until midnight on Fridays.

I'd already cut Garrett and Sarah, opting to handle the seating by myself. Liam said he could handle any other tables that came in, and I didn't doubt it. Plus, I'd seen him stopping by Heather and Nia's table on occasion. I figured I'd give him a chance to chat with his friend when at least one of them wasn't working.

From down the bar, Jerry groaned, downed the rest of his drink—scotch, neat—before he replaced the glass on the counter.

"Same time tomorrow, Jer?" I asked.

"Wouldn't miss it," he replied. "Who do we have on the lineup?"

"Clara Calloway." Whose real name was actually Emma Smith, which didn't have quite the same ring as the one she used on stage.

Jerry's smile widened. "We're in for a treat. She's a real talent."

I didn't disagree, but the fact that he was already asking about tomorrow night's act instead of commenting on Leo was strange. Jerry tended to chat about any act that came in the door, his favorite, of course, being Chroma Groove Project, just like everyone else lately.

Staying quiet about Leo was concerning.

He left with a quick wave, and another body immediately

filled the space he'd vacated.

"When can I be introduced to that guy?" Heather said, nodding in the direction of the door. "He seems chill as hell."

"Next time you come in. Jerry's always here."

"I'm gonna become his friend," she said. I didn't doubt for a second that she meant it—and that she would succeed.

"Speaking of, where's the other friend?" I glanced back at the table to see if Nia was still there, but it was completely empty. Liam was busy cleaning up the empty cups and plates.

"Bathroom," Heather explained. "Thought I'd come keep you company until she came back."

The way her eyes lowered as she finished speaking made me think there was something else she wanted to say.

"And?" I prompted.

When she met my waiting stare again, she smirked. "Damn. Someone's getting to know me. Should I be worried?"

I only chuckled, not sure what to say to that. "So what is it?"

"I want to do a write-up on the restaurant."

It would have been impossible to keep my eyes from widening in surprise. "Seriously?"

Heather nodded. "Yeah." She shrugged. "I really don't know how I didn't think of it before, but it seems like the perfect solution doesn't it? I can add to my quota for the year, and you get the exposure."

Exposure was an understatement. Not that I had any idea how Heather's articles actually performed, but having the name of the biggest news provider in the Chicagoland area talking about my restaurant? It definitely couldn't hurt anything.

"If you want to, that should be okay."

"Anyone you recommend I start with?"

I quirked a brow. "Start with?"

"I was thinking this could become a series. Give Chicagoland a glimpse of the jazz scene in the city. I'm sure you get the big acts, right?"

I gave a one-shoulder shrug. Chroma Groove Project was my biggest act by far, but there were some others on the list that local jazz-listeners might recognize.

"Are you free tomorrow?" I asked. "We have a female singer who'll be here."

Heather smiled. "Sounds like now I will be too."

The sight of that smile, the enthusiasm in her voice, made my heart skip a beat. That, and the fact that we would officially be seeing each other three days in a row. I wasn't sure our texts would be able to compete after this weekend.

We both turned when Nia came around the corner and sidled up to the bar beside her friend. "You ready to go to the next stop?"

I couldn't help but grin at the pained expression that crossed Heather's face. "What time does it close?"

"Four A.M., lady! Get ready!"

I didn't want to know where these women were headed, but I was very happy I wasn't joining them. Though, from the way Heather cast me a desperate side-eye, it seemed like she was contemplating inviting me along.

"You could help with closing," I suggested as an alternative. "I've got silverware that needs rolling."

For a moment, she looked like she might actually accept, but then she groaned. She got out of her seat and fell under Nia's arm. "I'm not doing shots, though," she said. "My liver can't take so many nights out in a row."

"Just one?" Nia tried.

"We're *old*, Ni. Shots are *scary*."

Their weak argument faded the further they walked away. My attention strayed from them to where Leo's band was still working on taking down their equipment. Their fearless leader was nowhere in sight, and it was evident, even from across the restaurant, that none of them were happy about it.

"Heather!" She paused just before the door and turned back over her shoulder to see what I wanted. "What did you think?" I asked with a nod toward the stage.

She followed my eyes, then when she found me again, she shrugged. "I can sleep for free on my couch."

# Chapter 9

♫ Yours | Russell Dickerson



I'D THOUGHT GOING back to Mellow Cat Kitchen for a work project would make tonight easier. Put up some sort of boundary. Of course, I'd been serious about giving Ethan the exposure; he deserved it, and I believed the job had been done when the piece was published online on Tuesday. Not to mention the act he'd recommended had truly been talented—a modern day Marilyn Monroe with a pop-star stage presence.

Yet as we sat across from each other at our little high-top table, sharing some cheese curds and fried pickles before I went to interview the headliner of tonight's show, it was like we were back at the karaoke bar.

And every time I thought of the karaoke bar, I thought of

what had happened afterward.

I was practically drooling as I watched Ethan take a swig of his beer. His tongue ran over his lips after he swallowed, licking away something that had been left behind there.

Necks, hands, lips. At least the list was getting relatively more normal.

"Heather?"

I snapped out of my trance. "Huh?"

"I said should we close out?" he apparently asked for the second time. "It's almost six."

"Oh, yeah, no, we're good. Press perks."

I did, however, dig into my purse and pull out a twenty for the server who'd taken care of us. That should more than cover tip for a couple appetizers and some drinks.

I didn't cover country concerts often; it wasn't really my vibe. But I could appreciate a good venue atmosphere when I saw one.

If I hadn't known better, I might have believed we were in a country-themed restaurant, what with the cowboy hats, rustic metal beer signs, and cow skulls hanging on the walls, combined with the twangy music that had been playing since the moment we entered.

Once we walked a little further back, though…

The makeshift box office entryway illuminated the faces of fans already in line, awaiting the moment the back doors would open and the mad dash for the front row would start.

In my peripheral, I caught Ethan watching them, but I simply flashed my press badge for the bouncer on guard.

"He's with me," I added, throwing a thumb over my shoulder at Ethan.

The bouncer didn't ask any more questions than that before he pushed open the door. The fans all began to murmur the same way they always did. *Who is she? Why does she get to go in first? Is she part of the crew? Did you catch a glimpse of him back there?*

The last one was actually warranted.

A messy drum beat, some electric guitar, and a bass being tuned echoed around the venue space from the stage. The lead singer, a young guy named Jaxon Baker, stood at the mic reciting the classic, "Check, check. One-two. One-two," before he went into what I assumed was a chorus. His drummer and guitarist joined in while the bassist continued to work on tuning.

It actually didn't sound bad. More pop than twang, which was a nice change from what we'd been subjected to outside in the restaurant.

My smart watch vibrated on my wrist, and I looked down as Ethan and I made our way closer to the stage, him trailing a little bit behind as he took in the pre-concert routine. Even though he had acts in Mellow Cat all the time, it was always a little different watching bigger names prepare for a show.

A text message waited for me.

Baby girl did that money ever go through?! The hotel declined your dad's card!!!!

It was a third day in a row I'd gotten a text from her, and even though they hadn't all been copies of one another, the message was still the same. They needed the money. I hadn't sent it.

Their lifeline was waning, and the persistence meant they were getting desperate.

I lifted my watch to my lips, ready to vocalize my reply. "I get paid on Friday," I muttered. I glanced at Ethan to make sure he hadn't heard. The noise of the soundcheck helped. "I'll send it then."

I tapped the screen, making it go black again, before I plastered on a smile and stopped right in front of the stage.

"Jaxon Baker," I announced with all the confidence of someone greeting an old friend. "You're already sounding great."

He gave me a big smile filled with southern charm before he motioned for his band to cut the noise. With one big hop, he was off the stage and standing on the floor beside me.

"You must be the newspaper lady," he said and extended his hand for me to shake.

"Heather Hansley," I introduced then nodded toward Ethan. "And I brought a guest, if you don't mind."

"The more the merrier," Jaxon said. "What's up, man?"

I nudged Ethan with my hip, bringing his attention from the band members to Jaxon. He quickly accepted the lead singer's waiting hand, and I smiled when I noticed a blush tinting the tips of his ears.

"It's great to meet you," he said. "I'm really looking forward to the show."

I didn't doubt that. Neither one of us had heard of Jaxon before I'd been assigned his concert, but Ethan told me he'd been listening to his music all week in preparation. At least one of us would look like we belonged in the crowd later.

It was better when I went in blind anyway. Naivety led to a more honest review.

"You not with the paper?" Jaxon asked. His eyes slid to me briefly before they went back to Ethan. By now he'd probably noticed I had the press badge; my companion didn't.

"Ethan's a friend," I replied.

The smirk that found its way onto Jaxon's lips was more than suspicious. "Got it…"

He winked, though I didn't know what for. When I turned over my shoulder to Ethan he appeared just as confused as I felt, but neither one of us said anything further.

"So, uh, why don't we get this interview started?"

JAXON OWNED THE stage. For a man who couldn't have been shorter than six-five and weigh more than one-hundred-sixty pounds, he commanded everyone's attention from the moment he put the microphone in his hand. Maybe it was the result of the two tequila shots he'd insisted we take together after the interview—the first one just between the two of us, the second with Ethan and his band invited to join—but something told me it was simply him.

And the crowd was absolutely eating it up.

We were packed like sardines into the smaller venue space. I'd guess Ethan and I were two of three-hundred in attendance for the sold-out show. Jaxon had offered to let us watch from the VIP balcony that the rest of his party was enjoying, but I'd quickly declined. Being elbowed in the general admission pit was half the experience.

On the stage, Jaxon held his mic out and the crowd shouted the final line of his song back to him. When the music cut out, they erupted into cheers.

"Woo!" the singer half sighed, half shouted into the microphone, earning a fresh wave of hoopla from the audience.

"Alright, alright—you guys are absolutely wild out there tonight, Chicago!"

I shook my head as I smiled at the near deafening roar. Man knew how to give the people what they wanted.

"I know the party's just getting started," he continued,

taking a moment to wipe the sweat from his forehead. "But is it alright with y'all if we slow it down for a second?"

The crowd cheered again, albeit with less enthusiasm. It was clear they wanted to keep the energy up, but I didn't blame Jaxon for adding a few breaks into his setlist. The man had been bounding around the stage for close to forty-five minutes now.

"Awesome." A soft acoustic guitar melody started to play. In a new, low voice, Jaxon said, "This one's for all the lovers in the crowd."

My eyes cut to a woman standing a little bit ahead of Ethan and me. She clung to the man standing beside her with excitement in her eyes.

"This is it!" I managed to hear her say over the softer music. "This is the part I was telling you about! Oh my gosh, I hope he picks us!"

I had no idea what she was talking about. Probably something she'd seen on social media, but I didn't have much time to dwell on it before the drums picked up and the rest of the band joined the guitar.

"I don't know if I'm allowed to say this to a concert reviewer," Ethan said. He'd bent down so his lips were right beside my ear, and my whole body went tight and loose simultaneously as his warm breath caressed me. "But he's really good."

"Yeah. Very," I agreed.

Around us, people turned on their phone flashlights and lifted them into the air, swaying them back and forth in time with the music. The room was the brightest it had been since the lights went off for showtime, and it was only then that I realized how close Ethan and I actually were.

We'd bumped into each other a few times when the crowd got rowdy. He'd been there to steady me each time, but even now, I caught how his hand hovered at the small of my back, ready to catch me if I got pushed. I'd mistaken it for the person behind me standing just a little too close.

A part of me wanted to lean back into his touch, remember what it had felt like to have his hand on me, if only for a moment. But a stronger, louder part of me told me not to take the leap. Professional boundaries had been set—or at least I was trying to set them. It was my own fault for giving into temptation before. If I hadn't been so reckless, I wouldn't have even been tempted.

That Ethan wasn't actually touching me, said enough about how he felt on the matter.

How could he do it? How was he so damn good at just standing there, acting like nothing had happened? Texting me the same as we always had in the month since we'd met?

Maybe I'd mistaken his reaction to the kiss. Maybe… maybe he hadn't reacted at all. Maybe my brain had wanted to believe so badly that he was at least a little interested in me too. That he *had* kissed me back.

Fuck.

As if I didn't know this song and dance by heart already.

"Alright, ladies and gents."

I turned back to the stage where Jaxon wore that same smirk he'd directed at me before the interview. The girl in front of me, clung tighter to her partner and jumped a little in her spot. This must have been the thing she'd been talking about.

The band continued to play an instrumental backtrack as Jaxon went on. "The only thing greater than the love I have for all of you wonderful people here tonight, is the love y'all have for each other."

The crowd cheered some more, and at this point, it was evident more people—particularly the women—were picking up on what was about to happen.

Maybe I *should* have done a little more research, because I felt terribly out of the know.

"How about I show y'all some of the wonderful lovers I've seen here tonight?"

The screen behind Jaxon changed from the generic backdrop of his stage production to a shaky camera view. In a wave, every hand in the room went up as people tried to catch a glimpse of themselves as the camera panned across the room.

"Do you see it?" Ethan leaned down to ask me.

I shook my head. Try as I might to locate where the

camera was coming from—clearly somewhere above us, if the angle was any indication—I couldn't find it.

"Show some love, Chicago!"

As soon as Jaxon finished speaking, his band picked up the volume of the instrumental and the picture on the screen went from the whole room to a narrowed view of a single couple in the crowd. After a brief moment of recognition, the man pulled his partner in for a dramatic kiss, earning plenty of applause from everyone else.

A lesbian couple was next, and they kissed before one of them proudly waved around their baseball cap, on which a pride flag pin was attached.

A middle-aged couple followed after that. Somehow, they managed a kiss—albeit a sloppy one—while the woman nearly toppled over in the process. Someone had clearly been enjoying the bar.

I was still chuckling to myself when the next couple appeared on the screen.

My face dropped.

That… that was me—and Ethan.

Apparently, we registered what was happening at the same time because we both turned to face each other. The look on his face could only be described as horrified, though I wasn't sure mine was any better.

"Don't be shy!" Jaxon's taunt came from the stage.

Holy shit. That's what the smirking and winking had been

about. He'd thought… he *still* thought Ethan and I were together.

And now he was putting his assumption on display for the whole venue.

That son of a bitch.

Not that Jaxon had any clue about what was going on. The guy probably thought he was doing something sweet— a nice little surprise for the woman who'd interviewed him.

Well, he'd gotten the surprise part right. That was for sure.

The slow chant started with the guy in front of us and spread through the room like wildfire.

"Kiss! Kiss! Kiss! Kiss!"

The steady beat of the bass drum joined in, followed by Jaxon in the microphone.

All eyes were on us. Even the main act had surrendered his attention to Ethan and I, eager as anyone else in the crowd to see if we'd succumb to the peer pressure.

Ethan's eyes were waiting for me when I finally returned my attention to him. It didn't take long after that for his hands to find their place on either side of my face and his lips to crash against mine.

A small part of me wondered if Jaxon was jealous of the eruption that came from the crowd as soon as it happened. I knew, even from behind closed eyes, that people had thrown their arms in the air, cheering like they would if their favorite football team scored a game-winning touchdown.

But the rest of me was too engrossed in Ethan to think much further on that.

I'd thought the backseat kiss had been it, but now, I realized, that had been absolutely nothing.

My arms snaked around Ethan's neck. One of his hands moved, his fingers tangling in the hair at the back of my head as he tilted me back, angling me just right to deepen the kiss.

His tongue swept across my lips in the gentlest caress, and I opened for him, relishing in the taste, the touch, the feel of everything that was Ethan Morimoto.

It wasn't until Jaxon joined the band again, going in for the final repetition of the song's chorus that I remembered we were in public.

I pulled away from Ethan, absolutely breathless. When I opened my eyes, I saw his chest rose and fell with heavy pants. We'd yet to tear our gazes away from one another, and should we want to, one small movement would allow our lips to touch once more.

"Woo!" Jaxon said as he finished the song. "I don't know how we're gonna top that!"

You could say that again, man.

# Chapter 10

♪ F*ck Up The Friendship | Leah Kate



I NEEDED TO get home. I needed to write my review. I needed to drink some water and eat something that hadn't been cooked in gallons of grease.

Instead, I was sitting in the passenger seat of Ethan's parked car.

The faint sounds of a Stray Land song came from the speakers, preventing the complete silence I was worried about. We'd only been like this for a minute, max. Still, that was plenty of time to make it shift from a comfortable quiet to one that clearly came from our inability to figure out what to say.

We hadn't known each other all that long, and yet we'd never fallen into this sort of situation before. Ethan had always been easy. Comforting. Like I could tell him anything and no judgement would be passed. He'd just be happy to sit there and listen, if that's what I needed.

That's what had happened for most of the car ride here, in fact. I'd been too chickenshit to talk about what had happened at the concert that I'd just started word vomiting. And Ethan, bless him, had listened to every nonsensical bit of it.

Now, though, time had run out. And I was sitting in his passenger seat like an absolute weirdo.

One glance across the street told me Nia was home. The light in our living room was on, and the changing glow of a TV show illuminated what it didn't reach. I had every excuse to leave—to go in there and carry on like any other night post-concert.

Except this time, I was afraid there wouldn't be a got-home-safe text. The moment I left this car, if we had things left unsaid, I had a terrible fear they would remain that way forever.

I sucked in a deep inhale through my nose, ready to spit out my feelings, the same time Ethan said, "I like you."

My breath caught and I held it for a moment before I allowed myself to exhale. My eyes slid in his direction.

"I like you too," I whispered.

He clutched the steering wheel in both hands, his head tilted back, eyes on something in the distance. "In what way?"

This was the most middle-school conversation I'd ever had about feelings. Even then, I hadn't bothered with this sort of talk. Either I liked a guy or I didn't. He liked me or he didn't. Simple as that. Once we established some equal measure of likeness, we started dating. Or, lately, going on a single date and calling it quits.

But thinking back on the time I'd spent with Ethan so far, we might have unwittingly already passed the second date mark.

Still, I didn't know what to say back to him. Had he seriously not been able to tell tonight how desperately I'd wanted that kiss to keep going? I didn't think I could have made it much more obvious—at least in a public setting.

"I like you in a way..." *In a way that's really fucking confusing.*

When the words didn't come out, he finally turned to me. His eyes were shining with the same emotion they'd held at the venue.

I swallowed. "Can you kiss me again?"

That had to be enough. Friends didn't ask other friends to kiss them. That had to tell him enough about what I was feeling without needing to actually voice it. Right?

For a moment, I wasn't sure. I watched the battle rage in his eyes—softening, hardening, narrowing, considering— before they landed on my lips.

"You always have them painted."

My brow furrowed at the random statement. "Huh?"

"Your lips," Ethan clarified. He released the steering wheel and turned just enough so he could reach one hand out, his thumb running over my bottom lip. "They're always a different color."

"I… I guess you're right."

Putting on lipstick was such a mundane part of my routine at this point that sometimes I forgot about it entirely. No man had ever pointed it out before, let alone admitted they noticed the variety of colors I sported.

"I love your lips," he said, his voice lower, huskier. "And I will kiss them anytime you'd like me to."

My insides were officially lava.

"Then hurry up and do it."

Ethan was shy. Him taking charge at the concert had been surprise enough, and I figured it might take a little work before he gained enough courage to do something like that again.

But as soon as the man had express permission—oh boy did he follow orders.

We met each other over the center console, both of our seatbelts unbuckled to allow for easier movement. I'd gone as far as to sit on my knees, my hand cupping his face as our lips moved in tandem.

I felt like a teenager again—high on the adrenaline of finally kissing the boy I'd been crushing on before I snuck back into my aunt and uncle's house. Sure, Ethan and I had done this before, but this time was different. There was no driver nonchalantly clearing his throat to get us out of his backseat or concert-goers cheering us on.

This time we were alone.

I moaned as one of Ethan's hands tangled in the hair at the back of my head and his lips moved from mine to my neck. His other slid down my side, to my hip, then finally to my ass. The gentle squeeze he gave me doubled as a tug, an encouragement.

He didn't want the console between us any longer. Neither did I.

Very ungracefully, I climbed over to the driver's seat. A soft hum filled the space as he moved his seat back.

"Careful. Careful," he warned as I tried to navigate onto his lap.

"It's Chicago," I countered. "You think these people have never heard a stray car horn before?"

He only chuckled as I finally managed to situate myself—no accidental honking necessary—so I could straddle his lap. Even through my jeans, I could feel how hard he already was and couldn't resist grinding my hips against him as I grabbed his face in both my hands and kissed him again.

"Fuck, Heather," he moaned when he pulled back, and his hands found their way to my ass once more, holding me against him, coaxing me to keep going.

I kissed along his jawline until my lips were beside his ear. "I've wanted you to touch me like this since we were in that stupid Uber."

He pulled back, and I stilled, worried I'd said the wrong thing. "Really?" was all he asked.

My thumbs stroked his cheeks. "Are you surprised?"

"I… yeah, a little."

"Why?"

He shrugged. "I feel like… I don't know. I feel like I'm not your type."

My head tilted to the side, curious, as I asked, "And what do you think my type is?"

"Someone more dominant?" Before I could inquire what the heck that meant, he added, "Someone who can match your energy. Not some quiet little nerd."

"You're a nerd?"

He nodded, eyes wide like he'd just admitted his deepest, darkest secret without meaning to. "Big time."

"For, like, everything?" Admittedly, I wasn't much of a pop-culture girl, so he could have said anything and I would have likely had no idea what it was.

Instead, he said the one thing I knew was high on the nerdiness list. "Anime."

Alright. He had me there. He definitely wasn't my usual type.

But knowing that didn't change that fact that it had been

him who'd made me smile with his silly selfies and innocent humor. It had been him who I couldn't stop thinking about when we were away from each other. Him whose smile gave me butterflies and whose kisses left me craving more.

Ethan Morimoto might have been the exact opposite of every guy I'd ever had a crush on before, but he was proving he was far better than they'd ever been.

"Wanna know a secret?" I asked. When he nodded, I leaned in close to his ear again. "I've always heard it's the nerds you have to look out for."

His reply of, "Oh yeah?" came out as hardly anything more than a breath as I nibbled on his earlobe.

"Mhm," I hummed as I picked up the rhythm with my hips again, eliciting another squeeze from him. "They're the ones hiding the dirty little secrets." I grabbed his chin with my thumb and index finger, forcing him to meet my eyes when I pulled back. "Tell me a secret, Ethan," I whispered.

For a second, his face twisted in a way that made me believe he was thinking, *What have I gotten myself into?* Fair question. I knew I was a lot to handle. Many men I'd been with had asked the very same thing—most of them out loud, to my face.

But then his expression grew serious, his eyes never leaving mine as he said, "The night we sang karaoke, I got off thinking about you."

He lifted his hips as soon as he finished talking, pressing

into me. I bit my lip to stifle my moan before I asked, "What were you thinking about?"

"Your lips," he said, unsurprisingly given what he'd told me not too long ago. "And all the places I wanted to feel them."

Yup. I was right. The quiet ones were the dangerous ones.

"Your turn," he continued before I even had the chance to fully compute his last statement.

"I did the same thing." There was no use hiding the truth now that I knew we were even. "You hardly touched me, and still, I couldn't stop thinking about it."

Those very same hands I'd imagined that night in bed shifted to hold my hips, his fingers brushing the skin where my shirt had risen up.

I whispered, "I kept imagining it was you. Touching me," then lowered my lips down to his once more.

This time, we could be described as nothing but absolutely ravenous, our desires out in the open. There was a clear shift in the way Ethan kissed me now. Hungry. Desperate. As if my revelation had been exactly what he'd needed to hear in order to release the tether he'd put on himself.

There was nothing holding him back now—especially as he found the front of my jeans, undid the button, and his hand slipped inside.

I broke our kiss, too distracted by this new form of

pleasure. There was no way to ignore him touching me right where I'd wanted him to, right where I'd imagined, his fingers working me with expert precision.

"You like this?" he asked, less dirty talk than actually making sure I was enjoying myself.

I nodded and bit my lip. Words weren't an option. My brain was narrowed in on one sense and one sense only: touch. Until I was away from Ethan again, I wasn't sure I'd be able to form a single coherent thought. In that moment, he was my entire focus.

My hips grinded against his hand, increasing the friction. How he was managing to make me feel like this while my jeans were still on, with hardly any room to work, I didn't know. I didn't think I'd ever know. But what I *did* know was I was building. Higher and higher until I arched my back and came—

And set off the car horn with my elbow.

Ethan's hands—even the one that had just been in my pants—were on me in an instant, pulling me away from the steering wheel. My whole body trembled as he held me, and I could tell from his tension that he was nervous. I'd just set off an alarm for our location, and if anyone in the neighborhood decided to come investigate, our current position would make it pretty obvious what we'd been up to.

I didn't care one bit, though. I lifted my head from his

shoulder as I came down from the orgasm and met him with a content smile.

"Your turn," I said.

He grabbed my hands as soon as I reached for his belt. "Maybe another time when your neighborhood hasn't been put on high-alert."

"No one's watching," I tried, but as if it wanted to prove his point, a dog barked—a little too close for comfort.

I glanced over my shoulder to my apartment's front window. Nia was completely visible and clearly trying to inspect where from and why a car horn had blared at nearly midnight. Thankfully, the headlights were still on to prevent her from seeing through the windshield, and she had no idea what kind of car Ethan drove.

She would, however, be happy to hear that I'd gone for it. Leave it to my best friend for knowing what I needed more than I did.

Ethan chuckled at what I could only imagine was my visible disappointment. "Another time," he repeated as his hand lifted to cup my cheek.

All I could do was offer him a small smile in return, clinging to that little promise he'd given me.

He wasn't ready to leave.

Not yet.

# Chapter 11



*ETHAN*

WHEN I FELL, I fell hard. Fast. Which was why I was surprised that I'd allowed myself to go so far with Heather. Kissing was one thing—I'd kissed plenty of girls, even though it sometimes took me a bit to work up the courage to do it.

That had surprised me too. I couldn't remember the last time I'd been so bold. I hadn't even checked if she'd *wanted* me to kiss her in front of an entire concert crowd. Then again, she hadn't asked me in the back of the Uber either, but I'd wanted it. Just like she'd clearly wanted it.

It had only been a few days, and I still was trying to figure out a way where the two of us could be alone together again. That always seemed to be the problem. Between my work at the restaurant and hers at concerts, there were very few times we'd actually been by ourselves—or where we could find a day that worked with both our schedules.

Even now, I watched as Heather sat at the bar, drink lazily grasped in her hand as she chatted with Jerry. She'd gotten right on that promise of becoming his best friend, and he'd unsurprisingly reciprocated. She was like a magnet to everyone she met. Once they started talking to her, it was impossible to pull away.

Since I'd gone many steps beyond talking, I had it even worse. It took every ounce of willpower in my body not to join them, just to be near her. Instead, I was awkwardly hovering between tasks, which wasn't much better. But hey—something was better than nothing.

Heather laughed at something Jerry said, then lifted her drink to her lips. Bourbon—neat. Apparently the foofy drink from her first visit had been a fluke. I'd seen her order nothing but dark liquor or craft beer ever since.

When she brought the glass down again, she ran her tongue over her upper lip.

My hand clenched the edge of the bar. Dammit—I was like a teenager who'd just seen boobs for the first time. Maybe I shouldn't have put my romantic life on the backburner if this was the way I was reacting after touching a woman for the first time in…

Shit. Had it really been *that* long?

Chroma Groove Project ended their song, and the soft

clapping from the select filled tables brought me back to reality. Heather and Jerry joined in, the latter leaning over to whisper something in her ear. I couldn't make out what it was, but she nodded, her lips pursed, face serious. Assessing.

So far, Heather had seemed more interested in the setlist than the last time she'd seen the group on stage. They'd changed it a bit, probably after I made a gentle suggestion to liven it up. They'd just finished a rendition of "Sway", which was better than usual.

For a group with *groove* in their name, they really did keep these sets mellow.

My eyes moved to the stack of cocktail napkins beside me, where the Mellow Cat Kitchen's logo—a smiling cat with sunglasses and a fedora—stared back. They were just sticking with the vibe I'd set, I supposed.

"Oh-ho, there he is!"

I was thankful for the band being in between songs—Ronnie, the lead singer, gave me a very pointed look at the outburst that echoed around the small space—when the middle child of our family, Eric, strolled through the door, tattooed arms spread wide. My youngest brother, Kai, followed behind with Dad.

"What are you guys doing here?" I asked, as I waved them forward past the host stand. Poor Sarah. With all the special guests lately, she was hardly able to do her job.

"Visiting you, obviously," Eric replied. Per usual, he

walked behind the bar as if it was him, not me, that owned the place and gave me a hug. He followed it by going right into the mini fridge and removing a bottle of whatever IPA I had in stock at the moment.

He'd always been the more extroverted of us Morimoto boys, as was evidenced by the way Kai quietly took up a seat with Dad at the bar. Not wanting to make it seem like I played favorites, I got a beer for my youngest brother—a pale ale—before I got to work on Dad's drink. Usually, he'd stick to a gin and tonic, but I liked to keep a bottle of saké on hand for surprise visits like this. I knew he appreciated it, even if he didn't say anything.

He smiled as I placed the small sipping glass in front of him. "*Doumo arigatou*," he muttered.

"*Kinishinaide*," I replied, and Dad's smile widened before he took a sip. It had been years since I'd held a full conversation in Japanese, and my skills had weakened some, but I still remembered the basics enough to hold small talk with Dad.

He appreciated that *much* more than he did the saké, especially since neither of my brothers had learned the language at all. Perks of being born overseas.

"This isn't who that music reviewer was talking about, is it?" Eric asked, still behind the bar, before he took a swig of his own drink.

"Would you go take a seat like a normal person?" I, like any loving brother, smacked the back of his head and gave him a light shove to get him going. He laughed, but obeyed. "Also, what are you talking about?"

"The music review said there was some woman who sings here and sounds like a modern-day Marilyn," Kai clarified. "This doesn't sound like that, though."

No, it did not. Chroma Groove had officially turned on the *groove* and was performing a jazz cover of "24K Magic" by Bruno Mars. Try as she might, Ronnie stood at the front of the stage clapping, trying to get the audience to join in. A few at the front of the room, thankfully did. They were probably Chroma Groove fans. The rest of the room remained engaged in their private, hushed conversations.

I sighed. "No, that's Clara."

"How'd you get such a big paper to come here anyway?" Eric asked next.

"Dad nearly toppled out of his chair when he saw your restaurant in the reviews." Dad nodded along as Kai spoke.

"Not even the food reviews. In the music!" he added, his accent still heavy even after two decades in the States.

"Speaking of, do you have those pot stickers on the menu still?" Eric asked. "The ones with that spicy chili dipping sauce?"

Kai took his turn to hit Eric, opting for a backhanded tap to the shoulder. "You're obnoxious."

"I'm hungry. Sue me."

I rolled my eyes but walked over to the tablet to punch in

the order. I threw in some shishito peppers too since I knew Kai liked those, and I doubted he'd eaten much either. He was still in school, getting his Master's degree in biomedical engineering at Northwestern. The kid hardly had time for sleep, let alone food. It was a miracle he was here at all with all the studying and research he was doing.

"Seriously, though, how'd you get that hookup?"

I nearly choked on my brother's choice of words, and my eyes slid to where Heather was now very obviously listening in, her head turned just right so one of her ears faced our conversation. It wasn't a very long bar. She was only two seats away from Kai. My brothers'—mostly Eric—inability to maintain a regular, indoor volume didn't help.

"I, uh, got lucky, I guess." I shrugged. "Right place, right time."

"Did the paper contact you or did you contact the paper?"

I knew it was only a matter of time before she stepped in, but I'd thought Heather would at least remain inconspicuous for a little longer.

"A bit of both," she announced as she turned in her seat, earning the attention and surprise of my brothers and Dad. "Hi. Heather Hansley. Music reviewer."

The way she spoke made me smile. Even the extension of her hand, like this was an important business meeting instead of an introduction to my family, was so *Heather*.

Kai, being seated the closest, accepted her invitation to

shake. She didn't bother reaching further down the bar for Eric and Dad, opting to offer them a casual wave instead. I couldn't help but watch Eric's eyes widen as he took her in. The surprising jealousy that overcame me as a result faded when, in turn, Heather showed no interest. Or she'd just gotten very good at ignoring full-body once overs from strange men. Probably a bit of both.

"This is embarrassing," Kai said through a nervous laugh. "We, uh, didn't know you were sitting right there."

"Couldn't resist coming back for more?" Eric asked.

When Heather's eyes slid to me, I became very interested in checking the status of food orders in the system.

"Something like that," she said. "I'm doing a bit of a series. Covering the repeat acts here at Mellow Cat Kitchen to help give the place a little more exposure."

"That's really nice," Kai said, almost sounding incredulous. "E, why didn't you tell us?"

I gave a one-shoulder shrug. "It's sort of a new thing."

My brother was forced to lean back in his seat as Dad reached forward. Heather didn't hesitate to give him her hands, which he shook with great enthusiasm.

"Thank you for writing such kind words about my son," he said.

Heather's entire face softened, and even though she was smiling, the light in her eyes was dimmer than usual. Like no one had ever said something like that to her before.

"He's running a great business here," she replied. "You should be very proud of him."

"I am," Dad assured her, and when he turned to me, he added, "and his mother would be too."

I busied myself again, my eyes down, to avoid Heather's following stare. It bore into me, but I couldn't bring myself to look up. Mom hadn't come up yet. I hadn't been sure that she'd *ever* come up. Talking about your dead parent seemed like a downer, and since we were, in my opinion, still in the getting-to-know-each-other phase, downers were forbidden.

Talking about how my mom had died of breast cancer when I was fourteen was a conversation for a more established friendship.

It wasn't like Heather had told me anything about her family either. She'd mentioned she was an only child, but I knew nothing about her parents.

This conversation, courtesy of a surprise visit from my brothers and dad, was the closest either of us had come to divulging any sort of information about familial relationships.

Heather, probably sensing my unease, changed the subject entirely. "And you must be... brothers? Cousins?"

"Brothers," Kai confirmed.

"I'm Eric—the handsome one." I rolled my eyes at his lack of humility. "That's Kai—the smart one. And you already know Ethan."

Heather nodded once, her eyes once again on me. "I do,

but I'm curious. What *one* is he?"

Eric shrugged. "I don't know. He's just… Ethan." He took another swig of his beer then nodded the neck of the bottle at Heather. "After talking to the three of us, what do you think?"

"Hmm." Heather lifted her drink to her lips, her eyes narrowed like she was actually considering what she'd say.

As far as my brothers and Dad knew, Heather and I had seen each other once—maybe twice, if they assumed we'd talked prior to her first review of the restaurant's acts—before this. She'd written one review, now she was back for another. Eric was asking because he wanted to be entertained by what a supposed stranger would say about his big brother, not because he thought she'd have an actual answer.

"I think you've got it wrong," she said to Eric. "I think *your* descriptor should be loud." Her head tilted and she smirked at me. "I think Ethan is the handsome one. Though, I can see where he gets it," she added, using the compliment of Dad as a cover.

Still, I couldn't stop the heat from crawling up my face, all the way to the tips of my ears.

Dad blushed too as he patted Heather's hands then released them to give an *aw-shucks* wave.

One thing to know about Dad? He thought everyone was in love with him. His dentist complimented his gums? Obviously in love with him. The check-out lady at the grocery store threw in an extra coupon? Obviously in love with him. The woman he accidentally rear-ended on his way home from church didn't call the cops? Obviously in love with him.

All three of us boys knew he'd never consider dating anyone. He, much to the supposed misfortune of the millions of women he was leaving heartbroken, was still too in love with Mom. Dating someone else, he'd admitted to me once, would feel like a betrayal. So every time he recited a new story, Eric, Kai, and I just smiled and went along with it. What was the harm in letting the man live with some wholesome delusions?

The audience clapped as Chroma Groove transitioned into their rendition of "Cheek to Cheek", Dad among them.

"Oh, I love this song!"

"Why don't we go take up a table?" Heather suggested. I gave my nod of approval when she glanced at me. "I should be listening to the band anyway."

"We'll meet you over there," Kai said.

"Yeah, we wanna catch up with our big bro," Eric added. He planted his feet on the metal bar near the bottom of his chair and lifted himself so he could pat my shoulder across the bar.

I brushed him off. "I'll have Garrett bring over some water, Dad."

"And a gin and tonic," he added. "And another drink for

your newspaper friend."

Heather grinned, but shook her head at me, letting me know she didn't need another round, before she hopped out of her chair. Dad followed and offered her his elbow to take, ever the gentleman, as they made their way over to an empty table. They hadn't made it far before she looked back over her shoulder wearing an expression that made me believe she thought her current situation was both sweet and entertaining.

Eric punching my shoulder wiped my own silly grin off my face.

"What the hell was that for?" I asked, rubbing the spot he'd hit.

"You're fucking the music reviewer," he accused, and Kai nodded along.

"I am *not* fucking the music reviewer." Not technically. I'd only made it to third base.

"*Pft.*" Eric made a face before he mocked, "*Ethan's the handsome one.*"

"No one ever says that, man," Kai added, and Eric pointed his thumb at our little brother, nodding his agreement.

"Gee, thanks," I deadpanned. Nothing like some brotherly love to boost a guy's ego.

"You know that's not what we mean," Kai tried.

"Can't more than one of us be handsome?"

"No."

"Don't make me cancel the order for your pot stickers."

Eric's face softened into something like an appreciative puppy. "Aw, you ordered me pot stickers?"

Kai elbowed him in the side. "What we're saying is she was pretty flirty."

Eric slapped his hands down on the bar top. "Yeah, because they're *fucking* and our big brother is *lying* about it."

"If you must know," I started, and my brothers' faces lit up like two kids' on Christmas. The little gossips. "We met at a concert last month and stayed in contact. We're friends."

"With benefits," Eric finished.

"I will seriously never give you pot stickers again."

"You didn't deny it."

"Because there's nothing to deny," I said, perhaps a little too loudly, as I threw my arms up in exasperation.

From a little further down the bar, Jerry turned and dramatically shushed me before he returned to his foot tapping and general enjoyment of the music.

Traitor.

Surprisingly, Kai and Eric said nothing more, but the way they stared at me with raised, expectant brows said enough.

I sighed.

"I'm… interested in Heather. I'll give you that."

"And?"

"And we might have hung out a few times outside these little reviews she's doing for the restaurant. But it's nothing serious." Or at least that's what I was telling myself. I refused to let myself believe anything more in case Heather didn't feel the same way. Falling hard and fast meant the rejection stung twice as much. "It's casual."

"She's cute," Kai said with a shrug. "What concert did you meet at?"

"Stray Land. I, uh,"—I rubbed the back of my neck—"might have spilled beer on her."

"Smooth," Eric said with a smirk.

I rolled my eyes. "It worked, didn't it?"

"And so you thought to ask her to do the reviews once you learned what she did?" Kai continued, not bothering with our antics. He was *definitely* the smart one out of the three of us.

"That was her idea, actually. She thought it would help out Mellow Cat."

"Does Mellow Cat *need* help?" Eric glanced around the restaurant. "Looks like an okay crowd."

He would say that because he hardly ever visited, but Kai, with his experience helping me out on occasion, knew better. Eric was right—the crowd was fine. But then it needed to be put into consideration that Heather and Dad were taking up a table. Jerry hardly counted anymore; his presence was a given. Only five other tables were filled otherwise. And three of the no more than thirty bodies in the room were going to have their food and drinks comped. I'd never let my dad and brothers pay before. Making them start now would be a clear admittance of my failure.

"It's been steady," was all I said in reply.

"It's early spring in Chicago, man," Eric added. "Once the weather stays consistently warm, more people will be out and about. People are still too scared of the cold to go outside right now."

I might have believed it if it hadn't been fifty-five and sunny that afternoon. In classic Chicago fashion, people had already started to break out their shorts and tank tops like it was the middle of summer, not a week where the ten-day forecast showed perfectly fine weather like we'd seen today followed by potential snow flurries.

"Yeah, you're right," I said.

"Finally, you admit it." Eric lifted his bottle to his lips one more time to finish off his drink. "Can I have another one of these? I'm gonna go sit with Dad and meet this girl you're sleeping with."

"I'm not—" I shook my head. "Yeah. Sure. I'll have Garrett bring it over with Dad's drink."

He hopped out of his chair and saluted me before he strolled over to the table where Dad and Heather had set up camp. Garrett must have known the order I'd put in had been for my family, because the pot stickers and shishito peppers were already waiting at the table when he sat down.

"Did you see I got you some food too?" I asked Kai. He'd yet to show any signs of going to join.

My youngest brother nodded. "Yeah. Thanks."

Kai and I were very similar. Quiet, keep-to-ourselves kind of people. Not very good at expressing our feelings. So when he leaned forward on the bar, his expression intense, I knew whatever he said next was going to be serious.

"You'd tell us if you needed help, right? With the restaurant, not your actual life. I know you're okay there, and I know Eric gives you shit—he gives me shit too. But if I need to come in more, I can shift some classes and—"

"You're not doing anything with your classes," I said, my voice stern. "You have—what? A semester and a half left?"

"Just about."

I shook my head. "No. You're going to graduate and become a scientist or whatever the hell you wanna do with that giant brain of yours. You don't need to help around here."

"But you know I will, right? Free of charge."

I did. I knew Kai—and Eric, for that matter—would drop anything and everything to come help me if I ever told them that's what I needed.

But they had their own lives—Kai with his school, and Eric at the autobody shop he managed out in the burbs. We all had our own things going on. Besides, I was the big brother. I needed to lead by example, and that started with proving I had my shit together.

"Thanks," I said. "I'll let you know."

Kai gave me a smile that told me he didn't quite believe me, but he wasn't going to press any further.

"You've got this, E," he said. "You always know what to do."

While I appreciated the sentiment, I wasn't so sure.

# Chapter 12



*HEATHER*

"YOUR DAD IS the sweetest human being on this planet and must be protected at all costs."

Ethan spun around in his chair. The thing took up most of the tiny office space in the upper quarters of Mellow Cat Kitchen. What wasn't occupied by the chair, was filled with milk crates of manilla folders and an L-shaped desk. At least, I thought it was a desk. I couldn't actually see any blank space under all the papers that were skewed on it.

It was clear he hadn't expected me in here.

"How did you find this room?"

"Eric told me this was probably where you were," I said. When we'd gone to leave and Ethan was nowhere in sight, I'd felt weird knowing I hadn't said goodbye. His family hadn't held any qualms, but they did let me know that Ethan sometimes got distracted in his office. I wondered if he even realized the restaurant had closed for the night.

I reached into the pocket of my black faux-leather blazer and tossed him a set of keys. "He gave me these in case the door was locked," I explained when Ethan caught them. "They were behind the Malört bottles, if you need to know where to put them back. I don't know how many spares you have stashed around here."

"Dammit," he groaned. "I really thought he wouldn't find them there."

I smirked. "No one ever goes for the Malört."

"Exactly."

I chuckled as he tossed the keys onto what I could now, in fact, confirm was a desk and not a giant stack of disorganized papers given the *thunk* they made when they landed. That meant I had found my new seat.

Ethan didn't look up from what he'd been reading as I hopped up onto the desk mere inches from where he worked, my hands clasped around the edge and my legs crossed at the ankles. I, in turn, never took my eyes off him.

He was stressed.

"I wanted to say goodnight," I said. "Before I went home."

That finally earned his attention and he tapped his phone screen. The time glowed back up at us. A quarter past midnight.

"Did Dad leave?" he asked.

I nodded. "Kai hopped in an Uber around ten-thirty, but Eric and your dad stayed with me until the end of the set."

"Ugh, I'm sorry."

"Why? Your dad's wonderful."

"He's not who I was apologizing for."

I smiled. "Eric's not bad either," I said. "If I had to pick favorites, I'd go with Kai, though."

"Not me?" I was grateful for the playfulness that had returned to him.

"I told you you're the handsome one, didn't I?" I reminded him, and he laughed.

Ethan's hand cupped the back of my calf like it was the most natural thing in the world for him to touch me. His attention returned to whatever paper he'd been reading—it looked like some sort of spreadsheet—yet he'd still found me. His thumb caressed me over my tights, the gentle strokes sending a shiver up my spine. If he hadn't done that, I would have left immediately. But now, a part of me wanted to stay. Even if we weren't saying anything, his acknowledgement that I was sitting there with him made me believe he wanted the company.

Unfortunately, I wasn't one for prolonged silence.

"I'm sorry," I whispered. "About your mom. I had no idea."

Ethan's thumb stilled, and for a moment, I thought that would be it. Then, he shrugged. "I didn't tell you. How were you supposed to know?"

"I don't know. I just… I don't know."

He was right, obviously. I supposed I'd never thought about it before—how he'd mentioned his brothers and dad in our daily text conversations, but his mom had never come up. Then again, it wasn't strange for me. I never talked about my mom with other people. Even with Nia, I guarded what I said. She knew everything, but that didn't mean I enjoyed talking about it.

Knowing Ethan had lost his mom… I felt for him. I really did. And a very twisted part of me almost wished we could trade fates.

I tried to dismiss the thought as soon as it came. As horrible as my mom was, she *was* still my mom. That was part of the reason I still dealt with all her bullshit. She hadn't given me a lot—far from it, actually—but she had given me what mattered: my love of music, and my freedom to embrace it. I didn't know where I would have been without that.

Certainly not in this tiny office space with Ethan.

He pushed himself back from the desk and swiveled in the chair to face me. His face was understanding, his smile soft, as he rubbed his hands from my knees to my thighs and back again.

"It was a long time ago," he said. "I sometimes forget that not everyone knows she's gone."

"Were you two close?"

Ethan nodded. "Very. She helped me adjust when we moved from Japan back to the States, and was… she was always there. For everything. Until she wasn't."

I placed my hands over his, wishing I had something to say. It would have been empty—a speech that he'd probably heard hundreds of times before.

So instead of suffering through it once more, Ethan went on.

"This place was my gift to my dad," he said. "If it was hard for *me* to adjust, it was ten-times as difficult for him, and when Mom died… he was so defeated. She was the reason he came over here in the first place. They'd moved so that we could be closer to my grandparents when I was little—and then when Eric and Kai were little too. Extra childcare and all that. So when she died, it was like a light went out for him. And I wanted to bring that light back."

If I hadn't already thought Ethan was the kindest soul I'd ever met, I definitely did now. The dimness in his eyes told me he didn't feel the same way, though. Maybe it was a blessing that I'd grown up the way I had. Seeing some of the worst of humanity made it easier to see the good.

My hands shifted, grabbing ahold of his to give a gentle squeeze.

"I think he loves it," I said. "He had so much fun tonight."

"He does," Ethan replied. "He doesn't get to visit often, but when he does, he has the time of his life. The man loves his jazz," he added with a wistful smile.

I couldn't help but mirror it. "It's amazing you did this for him, Ethan."

"But it's why I can't let it fail." A chill replaced where his hands had been when he swiveled back to his spreadsheets. "The numbers have been declining for months. I already let two servers go. All our acts are volunteer—by some miracle. The menu was scaled back last fall to help with inventory costs…"

He shook his head before it landed in his waiting palms. I watched him stare down at the papers—the numbers that showed this dream he'd had was turning into a nightmare.

I hopped off the desk and pushed his chair back enough so that I could stand between him and the source of his stress. He didn't protest, but he didn't react the way I wanted him to either. Ethan looked so… so *sad*. Stressed. Beaten down. It made me wonder if he'd been feeling this way the whole time I'd known him, or if his family visiting had awoken it all.

"You're not going to fail," I said, matter-of-factly. "Mellow Cat isn't going to close."

It might have been bold to sit on his lap, but it got more

of a reaction from him than anything else had since I'd showed up in his office.

"We're going to keep this place alive," I continued. "You understand?"

"We?"

I nodded. "I'm going to start with the review series, but then we're going big. We're brainstorming. We're doing anything we can to make sure these doors don't close."

"Heather…" He appeared torn between stopping there and finishing what I knew he wanted to say. "You don't have to help. The reviews are more than enough. This is *my* mess."

"I know I don't *have* to, but I *want* to," I assured him. I ran one of my hands back through his dark hair. "Maybe if you'd quit being so handsome and nerdy, I wouldn't feel so obligated."

Maybe if he stopped kissing me like he did after I said that, I wouldn't feel so obligated either.

But I was never going to tell him that.

I didn't want the kisses to stop.

# Chapter 13

🎵 Chicago | Frank Sinatra

*ETHAN*

WHEN HEATHER HAD said she wanted to help, I'd thought it would stay pretty contained. The reviews. Some more of her brash—but often correct—opinions.

So when she showed up mid-day at the restaurant the following Tuesday and slammed a file down on the bar, it was safe to say I was more than a little surprised.

"Don't you have a job?" I asked.

"It's remote," she replied. "At least for today. Told my boss I was doing research."

"You lied to your boss?"

"No, I just stretched the truth," she retorted. "I'm doing a review series here, aren't I? Familiarizing myself with the venue is important to tell an accurate story."

I guess she wasn't wrong. But still… "What's all that for then?" I asked, nodding to the folder.

Heather wasted no time flipping it open and began to leaf through the papers upon papers inside. From what I could tell, it seemed like a collection of newspaper articles, flyers, and printed versions of web pages.

"Did you know that after New Orleans, Chicago is the largest city for jazz in the United States?" she recited.

"I did." I'd needed to know it, since Mellow Cat Kitchen originated as a school project. Demographic interest and all that.

"Okay, smarty-pants," she continued, and I grinned. "Well, did you know that there are approximately nineteen-thousand and five-hundred cities in the United States?"

"I did not."

She seemed proud that she'd figured out a stat I hadn't been aware of, though I didn't know why it was important.

"Out of all those cities, we're number two for jazz." Heather held up that same number of fingers, and for emphasis repeated, "Two. Do you know what that means?"

"We're in the right place?"

"Yes, but also, oversaturation."

She gestured to the folder again, and this time when I took a peek at the various headlines, I saw what they read.

Jazz concert. Jazz festival. New Jazz Club Opens in River North. New Jazz Club Opens in Lincoln Park. In West Loop.

In Humbolt Park. In Uptown.

Pages upon pages were filled with announcements where the people of Chicago could go to find jazz entertainment—many of which I'd visited to do research for the project that had inspired Mellow Cat.

Then I got to the bottom of the stack where, below the more positive—albeit slightly frightening—announcements, came the headlines that made my heart sink.

Jazz Club To Close After 30 Years. Jazz Clubs Struggle To Stay Afloat. Jazz Club Regulars Disappointed To Hear About Closure.

"Well, this is depressing," I said as I picked up a press release about a club closing after almost sixty years. Its ownership spanned three generations, and here I was wondering if Mellow Cat would even make it past me. "Why did you bring these?"

"It's easy to read about success," Heather said then leaned forward to jab her finger once, twice, three times at the paper in my hand. "What you should really be reading about is the mistakes. Why did these places close their doors?"

"Sounds like the owner died and no one wanted to take it over," I recited from the press release.

"Because?" Heather asked in a sing-song tone.

I skimmed further until I found my answer. "Because they felt jazz is a dying genre." My face scrunched. "That's bullshit."

"Number two," Heather repeated. She snatched the paper from me. "It's not dying. There wouldn't be so many success stories here if it was. This city has and always will love jazz. But do you remember what I told you that first night I came here?"

"That you could sleep on your couch for free?"

She shook her head. "Not that. The other thing."

I tried for the life of me to remember, but even though the conversation had occurred only a month ago, nothing in particular came to mind. She'd thought Chroma Groove's set had been boring. She liked wearing sweatpants and drinking for cheap at home…

"I've got nothing," I admitted, which earned me a playful smack to my shoulder.

"You've got to go for something unique," she said. "Jazz, but not jazz." She reached across the bar and grabbed a cocktail napkin from a stack. "Look at your name versus all the names on these papers."

I wasn't going to spend the time going through probably the couple hundred pieces of paper in front of me, so I glanced over the few at the top of the good news piles, as well as a few in the bad news stack. One word was prominent in all of them.

"They all say *jazz*," I said.

"I can't believe Kai is considered the smart one," she replied, and I smiled. "What word are you missing in the name of your restaurant?"

"Jazz."

"Ding, ding, ding." She leaned forward on the bar, her weight resting on her folded arms. Something about the way she smirked made me think she was very excited about what she was going to say next. "Remember that trash experimental concert?"

"How could I forget?" Instead of a normal ear ringing, I was sometimes haunted with the sounds of cats and jackhammers.

"That was my inspiration."

Out of all the things she might have said next, I never would have guessed that. "How in the hell was *that* your inspiration?"

"You know music. Do you honestly think that guy was signed to any label?" she asked.

I shook my head. No. No, I did not. Plenty of labels—especially of the independent variety—were more diversified with the acts they picked up, but I didn't think any executive would be crazy enough to sign whatever that guy had been attempting to do.

"How often do you go out in Logan Square?"

"I live there, so pretty often."

Heather opened her mouth to say something more, but quickly shut it. That's when I knew she'd pieced it together. I knew where she lived since I'd dropped her off twice, but she'd never visited me. After the karaoke night, I'd done that by design. Not because I didn't want her to visit, but because I didn't want her to know what I'd done.

"You mean," she said, "you took an Uber with me all the way to Lincoln Park just to turn around and go back to Logan Square?"

I chewed on my bottom lip as I nodded. "I wanted to make sure you were safe."

The way she gaped at me made me wonder what the people in her life were like. How many would have done what I'd done. Wasn't that girl code, or whatever, to make sure your friends got home safe? There was no way she and Nia didn't have some sort of checks and balances on each other.

Besides, it wasn't like what I'd done was anything monumental. Our neighborhoods were twenty minutes away from one other with traffic. At midnight on a Thursday? I'd gotten home in record time.

Thank god for that. Any longer and that driver might have dropped me off on the side of the road. Maybe *that's* why he'd been so irritated, come to think of it. A back-and-forth trip probably hadn't been fun.

Finally, Heather blinked and shook her head, like she was coming out of some trance. "You're insane," was all she said before she got back to business.

"Logan Square has all sorts of open mic nights. I bet that keyboard artiste extraordinaire built his following just doing that. It wasn't like the room was packed, you know?"

"But there was a decent crowd—all things considered."

"Exactly." She jabbed her index finger at the cocktail napkin with Mellow Cat's logo. "You can do that, too."

"You want me to hire the keyboard guy?"

"Ethan." Heather reached across the bar and took a hold of my hand. Her face looked like she was consoling me after the loss of a loved one, not like we were talking business. "I want to help these doors stay open, not close immediately. No—don't hire the keyboardist. But use the lack of *jazz* in your name to your advantage. Start diversifying your acts."

"What?"

"Mellow could mean anything," she continued. "Poetry, singer-songwriters, spoken word. Oh! Or you could always do art showings with local artists. A gallery-type situation. Of course, the regular jazz acts could always remain in rotation, but this way you're not limiting yourself. It's still mellow, as the name suggests, but you're opening the door to so many other people with varying interests."

It was pretty brilliant, actually. Never before had I thought of Mellow Cat Kitchen as anything more than what I'd originally intended it to be, but Heather was offering a plan that would make it that and more. The space, of course, couldn't hold all types of performances, but the ones she'd suggested weren't out of the question. And in a city like Chicago, none would be hard to find.

"I have to ask," I said.

"What?"

"Did you sleep at all the last two days or were you working on this?"

She grinned. "I told you I'd do whatever I could to help you keep these doors open."

"Yeah, but that doesn't mean losing sleep."

"I'm a night owl anyway. It wasn't a big deal," she assured me. "But what do you think?"

"It's fantastic," I said. "And I'm a little upset I didn't think of it myself."

"Great. So, we'll get started tomorrow."

"Wait, what?"

"A lot of small, local acts will open for the bigger names that come into town," Heather explained and leaned back in her chair. "Lucky for you, you know someone who can help you meet them."

"Lucky me, indeed," I replied, my voice dripping with sarcasm.

"Oh, please—like you aren't absolutely thrilled to be spending even more time with me."

She was right, of course. I'd been trying to think of excuses of how we could hang out without coming across as too desperate. I wasn't even exactly sure what Heather and I were anymore. Moments like these—uncomplicated and lighthearted—felt like ones between friends. Then there were the times where she'd sit on my lap or we'd kiss like that was exactly what we'd been brought together to do.

Those indefinite distinctions meant asking her out for a cup of coffee or a few drinks could be interpreted in multiple ways.

This. This was the excuse I'd been looking for. The chance I'd needed to finally see her outside of Mellow Cat—even if it was, technically for professional purposes.

"Give me the time and venue, and I'm there."

Heather's answering smile could only be described as beaming.

"Get ready, baby!" I knew she didn't mean it as a pet name; she was just excited. But hearing myself referred to like that by her made my heart skip all the same. "We're going on tour!"

# Chapter 14

♫ With Somebody | Public Library Commute



OKAY, SO MAYBE my intentions weren't entirely pure when I'd come up with my plan, but—hey. Ethan had bought it. And, realistically, it was a really good fucking idea. It's only that my motive wasn't only to save Mellow Cat Kitchen from closing.

I'd made the suggestion with the knowledge that I could spend more time with Ethan.

Seeing him every week at Mellow Cat had been fine. I understood there was a level of professionalism he needed to uphold at his restaurant, but I'd been craving Wild Ethan. Not Boss Ethan—although Boss Ethan had his appeals too.

I appreciated a man who had his shit together. Even if he saw himself as a failure—and I was desperately trying to change that—I'd witnessed the way he rallied his team. How he handled the acts when they sometimes turned into divas. How he wasn't afraid to pull his weight for any of the positions. I wouldn't have been surprised if he secretly helped cook the food, if that's what was needed of him.

And seeing him so dejected in his office had broken my heart.

This restaurant meant everything to him, and even more it meant something to his family. For that, I'd truly do anything in my power to help.

Getting some bonus Ethan time was just a nice perk if anyone—Nia—asked.

"Remind me again who we're seeing?" my partner-in-crime asked as I flashed my press badge and we were let in the back door of the mid-size venue.

"The headliner is some chill house singer." Whose name I'd honestly forgotten—and would need to find out quickly if I didn't want to embarrass myself during the pre-show interview. "The opener, though, is exactly what we need."

"Which is?"

"Singer-songwriter. Indie pop."

I caught Ethan nodding in my peripheral. "Local, I'm guessing?"

"Technically, he's the opener to the opener," I explained. "This is the only show he's doing for this tour, as far as I could tell." Which usually meant local. At the very least, it meant they had family in the area.

"That's promising."

I knew he wasn't just thinking about the act we were trying to scout. I'd received some distressed texts from Ethan once my plan of action had some time to culminate. To be honest, I'd wondered why he hadn't asked more questions right off the bat. He was a worrier. That's what worriers did. Maybe the first sign of hope he'd been given helped put that off for a bit.

But close to midnight, he'd made it very clear what his top concern was.

Do you think these people will want to be paid?

I'd told him no, but in hindsight maybe I shouldn't have said anything at all. I had no idea, and wouldn't until we actually met the act. I'd done a bit of research on some upcoming shows I'd been assigned—or would push to attend now that the plan was in place—and none of the openers seemed overly pretentious. Online presence, however, could very easily be a ruse. I'd learned early on in my career that a good PR team could make the devil look like an angel.

I hoped we didn't run into that on night one. Ethan's spirits would be crushed before we even began.

Backstage buzzed with pre-show energy. The stage crew rushed around, making sure everything was set up properly for the openers, while various members of various people's teams spoke tensely about what their respective acts required.

"This is way more intense than Jaxon Baker," Ethan said

in my ear.

I only nodded, not wanting to admit that maybe I'd made a mistake. Shit. Granted, these diva-like requests could have been from the opener or headliner. There was nothing to guarantee that the guy we'd come to see would be the one who *needed* six purple hand towels and room temperature Fiji water in order to put on a good show—

Ethan's arms wrapped around me, pulling me to a stop before the dressing room door had the chance to knock me out. I might have been inclined to lean into him, enjoy the warmth of his hold, had I not been such a busybody.

"Holden! Wait, I'm sure we can fix this!"

No freaking way…

A kid who couldn't have been more than twenty-years-old stormed out of the room, followed by a flustered, slightly older man with wire-frame glasses.

"Leave me alone," the kid seethed. "I need time to breathe."

The man did as he was told, though he didn't look happy about it. He watched from mere feet away as the kid disappeared down the hallway, his fists clenched at his sides.

Well, that had been him. Holden Young—opener to the opener.

"Wow," Ethan said once the coast was clear. "That was dramatic."

I nodded, but my attention was still on the guy in glasses.

He must not have known we were there because he cursed and kicked the nearest equipment case with a gusto that didn't match his lanky frame.

"Excuse me?" I said as I stepped away from Ethan. The other guy startled. Yup—no idea he had company.

He did little in the way of professionalism, his frustration winning as he groaned and rolled his eyes. "Yes?"

I lifted the plastic badge attached to the lanyard around my neck. "Heather Hansley. I'm here to cover the show."

That little tidbit of information flipped a switch in the guy. He went from annoyed to personable in a matter of seconds. Crazy how people reacted when they knew your only job was to critique—and that you'd just seen one of the night's acts storm off.

"I'm so sorry," he said, then gestured down the hall. "Normally Holden isn't like that. He's just a little stressed."

"Pre-show jitters?"

Glasses Guy shook his head. "No, no—he's a pro when it comes to performing. Truly. What you just saw was completely out of character."

"That must mean you work close enough with Holden to know?" I inquired with a quirked brow.

The guy extended his hand. "I'm Cal—Holden's older brother and manager."

I accepted his waiting hand and shook. "So what's the problem?" Indecision flashed on Cal's face, probably about whether or not he wanted to divulge his act's issues to the very person who could use the information to tear him down before he'd even really begun. "I want to see if I can help in any way."

The sentiment seemed to stir enough ease that Cal sighed. "Holden and I were here earlier today getting some studio time in, so he didn't bring all his equipment. Most of it's here, but he still lives at home. Out in the northwest burbs if you're familiar?" I nodded, even though I wasn't really, being from Wisconsin and all. "Our parents were going to come to the show, so they said they'd bring the rest."

"I'm assuming they canceled?"

"They got a flat tire." He nodded in the direction Holden had gone again. "We just got off the phone with them. He's stressed because his soundcheck was supposed to start soon."

"Where are they coming from?" Ethan asked as he stepped up to my side.

Cal regarded him with suspicion, and I didn't miss the way his eyes darted down to where a press badge would have been hanging.

"He's with me," I said.

That did the trick. "Palatine."

Ethan's grimace said enough. "Yeah, that's a rough drive even without a flat tire. The traffic alone is brutal."

Cal nodded, then sighed. "He really doesn't want to

cancel," he said of his brother. "The kid's been working for years for something like this. It's not a headliner gig or anything, but the exposure would be great, you know? He's got a decent enough following as it is—numbers are good on socials and streaming—but there's always room to grow."

"And what is it he's missing, exactly?"

"His guitar."

Yikes. Yeah, that would be enough to need to cancel. From what I'd seen of this guy in the few YouTube videos I'd looked up as part of my scouting research, he utilized his guitar for most, if not all, of his set.

"He didn't need that for the studio?" Ethan asked.

Cal shook his head. "We were doing vocals and some engineering today. All the instruments had already been recorded, and we figured it would have been easy enough for Mom and Dad to handle."

"And none of the other acts have one he can borrow?"

"They're all electronic, so they have keyboards. One of them has drums, I think?"

I kept my mouth shut about it probably being a good idea to make sure the most vital pieces of equipment were with the act. What was done was done, and the more Cal spoke, the less likely it sounded like we'd be able to find a solution that would allow Holden to play.

"What kind of guitar does he use?" Ethan asked.

"I don't know what model he's been into lately, but if I can find him, I can ask—"

"No, like, electric? Bass? Acoustic?"

"Electric."

Ethan nodded. "I might be able to help."

I think it was safe to say that Cal and I met him with equal levels of shock and confusion. I could have sworn Ethan had told me he wasn't musically gifted. Our karaoke night had proven singing wasn't his hidden talent, but had he been holding out on me about guitars?

"I run a restaurant," he explained, and when Cal quirked a brow, he clarified. "A jazz club—well, kind of. It's going through a bit of a revival at the moment. But it's mostly jazz. Other singers can go there too, though. And it—"

"He has a stage that people perform on," I summarized.

Cal nodded as he pieced together everything he'd just been told, then shrugged. "I'm not sure how that helps us."

"When I first opened, a lot of the acts I hired were just getting their start. Some didn't have the proper equipment, so I did what I could with some extra cash and bought random instruments. Technically, what I have is a jazz guitar, but it's a form of electric. Maybe Holden would be able to use it?"

Holy shit.

My expectant eyes drifted to Cal who didn't appear to be one-hundred percent confident in the idea, but he obviously hadn't dismissed it either.

"How fast can you get the guitar here?" he asked.

Ethan shrugged. "If I leave now, maybe thirty minutes? We aren't too far from the restaurant."

I held my breath as we waited to hear what Cal would decide. Honestly, I didn't know why he was even taking so long to consider. Either he went with Ethan's offer or Holden didn't play that evening. Or maybe it was the matter of the kind of guitar. As a musically challenged person myself, I had no idea if there was a difference between a regular electric guitar and a jazz guitar. Maybe there were less strings? More strings? The chords were a little different? Though from what Cal had said earlier, it sounded like Holden liked to switch up his guitar of choice.

Cal nodded furiously as he whipped his phone out of his pocket. "Go. Hurry," he instructed Ethan. "I'll tell Holden to be ready in thirty. Hopefully they can push off his soundcheck that long."

He was speed-walking down the hall, his phone at his ear, seconds later. All business. No thank you. Classic showbiz.

I, however, turned to Ethan, and an incredulous laugh escaped me.

"I don't know how the hell you pulled that off, but oh my god—that was amazing."

"I don't either," he admitted. His stress was already evident.

I grinned as I lifted myself onto my toes and kissed his

cheek. A faint, burgundy outline of my lips was left behind. "You'd better get going. You're on the clock."

He didn't waste any further time before he jogged back down the hall, ready to save the day.

× × ×

TWO HOURS LATER, we were clapping alongside Cal as Holden finished his set, holding Ethan's guitar triumphantly in his fist as he thanked the crowd and bid them goodnight. He could be described as nothing short of a crowd-pleaser, with his fresh face and wavy hair; trendy clothes and beaming smile. But the moment he left the stage and knew he was out of sight of the audience, that smile turned into a face that said *I can't believe that just happened.*

Ethan and I stood to the side, watching as the two brothers embraced after the near catastrophe. Cal had been right—Holden was a professional. The second Ethan returned to the venue with the guitar, he'd gotten straight to work, making sure it was tuned properly and worked with the PA system connections. His little hissy fit truly had been the result of panic. As soon as he was back in his element, feeling comfortable with the new instrument, everything had run smoothly.

As was evidenced by the fantastic set he'd put on.

It was Ethan who earned the performer's attention next.

165

"Dude, I—" He huffed a laugh and shook his head. "I can't thank you enough. You seriously saved my ass tonight."

"No kidding." Cal ruffled his little brother's hair. After our initial meeting, it was interesting watching them act so casually. "We'll cover your rides—or whatever you needed to get to and from your place to get the guitar—but if there's anything else, you let us know. We owe you. Big time."

A slow grin spread across my lips, and I gently elbowed Ethan in the side. This was it. No grand speech about why performing at Mellow Cat would be a great opportunity necessary.

"Well, uh…" Ethan rubbed the back of his neck, his nerves showing. "You know how I mentioned the restaurant was going through a bit of a revival?" he asked, and Cal nodded. Holden, having been absent for the conversation, thankfully seemed intrigued to see where this was going. "You would be a great addition to the lineup of acts we're putting together. To perform at the restaurant, I mean."

It was a good call to not mention that he would be the first member of this so-called revival. Musicians were already wary about that, but their managers? No chance in hell they'd be the first to take that risk—owed favor or not.

The brothers exchanged a side-eyed glance. I tried to decipher the silent conversation as best I could, but these guys were good. I couldn't tell what they were thinking about the whole situation.

Then, Holden shrugged and extended the guitar back to its owner. "I'd love a chance to play that instrument again. Sign me up."

FOUR DAYS LATER, Mellow Cat Kitchen was packed. As packed as the narrow restaurant could be, anyway.

"Whoa," Nia said as we walked through the door. One of Holden's songs I recognized from his show earlier in the week greeted us, as did the noise of the crowd around the stage.

The tables had been pushed back to make room, all of them filled. There were hardly any seats at the bar, either. I was able to pick out Cal, though, seated at a four-person round table with a middle-aged man and woman. Those must have been the parents. I'd have to thank them; they didn't know how much their flat tire had helped lead to this.

"This is way different than the last time we were here," Nia commented.

"It's amazing," I replied, then turned to Sarah the Hostess. "You wouldn't happen to have room for two more?"

She smiled. "Ethan said you'd be coming. He reserved a table for you."

"Hopefully we can get to it," Nia commented. She stood on her tip toes, trying to see to the front of the space. Holden was hardly visible on the stage between the bodies, both seated and standing, filling the room.

We followed behind as tiny Sarah politely shoved her way through the crowd. The whole way, I couldn't help but smile—half at the outcome, half at Nia's absolute awe over how the place had seemingly changed overnight.

I wasn't naïve. It helped that Holden had just performed not too far from here only a few days before; those new fans were still motivated by the post-concert high to come see him again. His already-existing local following helped too.

We'd gotten lucky. This was an easy stepping stone on the road to keeping Mellow Cat alive. The pressure would be on to find other acts that could compete.

"Here you go," Sarah said when we got to the table. "Garrett will be right with you."

"No Beer Boy tonight?" Nia asked as she sat down.

While still standing, I took the chance to scan the room again. "No, it doesn't look like it." Ethan wasn't even in his usual spot, hiding behind the bar. "I have to use the bathroom. I'll see if I can spot him."

"Want me to order you anything?"

"Double whiskey sour," I said. "Oh—and let's get the pot stickers too." Eric had been onto something with those. That dipping sauce had occupied my thoughts since I'd last had it.

With the order confirmed, I made my way back through the dining room. There was no way Ethan hadn't shown up to work today, of all days. He'd texted me he'd been nervous, but playing hooky wasn't an option.

I pulled out my phone and shot him a quick message. Where are you?

Upstairs, he replied right away, followed by, Are you and Nia here?

I didn't bother sending him a text back, nor did I think twice about walking straight into the kitchen and up the stairs that led to the office.

The door was unlocked, and I pushed it open slowly. Ethan had swiveled in his chair to see who was breaking in, and seemed surprised to find that it was me.

"Someone's getting comfortable," he remarked, and I grinned.

"What are you doing up here?" I asked. "It's a party downstairs."

"I know. I came up here to call a few other servers to see if they could come in and help out."

"And?"

"Liam will be here soon. The others already had plans for the night."

"Great, so you can come down and join everyone." I did a little shimmy as I said, "Reap in the benefits of your success."

"Which are?"

I shrugged. "No one can get mad at the boss for having a few celebratory drinks, now can they?"

He chuckled, but the moment of happiness was short-lived. I watched as his energy drained back down and his shoulders slouched.

"Don't tell me you're up here staring at those spreadsheets again too," I reprimanded.

"No," Ethan said, shaking his head. "The only spreadsheets I've been looking at are inventory."

"Then why are you sad?" I pointed to the floor, below which the muffled sounds of an on-going concert could be heard. "Listen to how much fun people are having down there. At *your* restaurant."

"I'm not sad. Trust me I'm—" He huffed a laugh. "I'm fucking ecstatic that so many people are here tonight. I'm just… recharging."

I opened my mouth to ask what that meant, but quickly shut it again. In all the excitement and planning, I hadn't thought about what the increase in business might mean for Ethan, personally. In fairness, I didn't think he had either, but now that the time had come…

I offered him a soft, understanding smile. "I can leave you alone," I said, then turned to do just that.

"No," Ethan said, just as my hand brushed the doorknob. I turned back over my shoulder. "I mean—" He cleared his throat. "You don't have to, if you don't want to. But if you do, I understand."

"I'm not a detriment to the social battery?"

"Not anymore."

I couldn't help but laugh at the honesty. "Aright, then," I said when it faded. "Anything you want to talk about?"

Ethan shook his head. "Not particularly. I suppose I just… I didn't want to be alone." He pointed to the floor. "It felt kind of lame."

"But necessary," I added.

"Very necessary."

I nodded as my eyes scanned the room. It was the first time I'd really gotten a good look at it. While nothing had changed in terms of the sheer amount of paper on the desk, that now wasn't my focus. I knew to expect that messiness. This time, I took note of the little touches Ethan had put around his office: the picture of him and his brothers on what looked like Eric's college graduation day, and old picture of him and who I assumed were his parents—I recognized the younger version of his dad and deduced the woman was his mom—standing in front of a Japanese temple, a signed picture of teenage Ethan and a singer I recognized from an annual

Christmas TV special. There were even a few pictures of anime characters. Not the pervy, underdressed women kind, but what looked like miniature posters from his favorite shows.

"I forgot when you said you like anime, that you used to live in Japan," I said as I ambled across the room to take a closer look at the old photo.

"Stereotype much?" he retorted and I shot him a look over my shoulder.

Not bothering to answer—mostly because he was right—I leaned in toward where the picture was thumb-tacked to the wall.

"Your mom is beautiful." I refused to use the past tense. Even though I hadn't known her, it didn't seem right. "You look a lot like her."

"Seriously?" He pointed to his face. "Most people see my eyes and immediately say I look like my dad."

"And you just accused *me* of stereotyping?" I shook my head as I returned my attention to the picture. "No. You're definitely more like your mom." With a smirk I added, "Minus the eyes."

Ethan rolled said eyes as he chuckled, and I moved onto the next picture. The one with the Christmas-special singer. "You should add your picture with Stray Land to the collection."

"That's not a bad idea."

"I'm not sure if you've noticed, but I have loads of great ideas."

"I have," Ethan said. After a moment of silence, he added. "Thank you, by the way. All of the stuff that's happening downstairs—it wouldn't have been possible without you."

I shrugged. "It's no big deal. It's been fun."

"It has," Ethan agreed, nodding. "All of it."

Those three words. That one little distinction. He wasn't just talking about the concerts or the sarcastic texts or attempts to work on the future of Mellow Cat Kitchen. No—that look in his eyes let me know Ethan was talking about the times we'd spent together that went beyond that. The deeper conversations. The moments of vulnerability. The moments of trust.

I'd hardly known this man for a few months, and here we were together in his office, holding a chaotic yet heavy conversation while a concert—and my best friend—waited downstairs.

He hadn't wanted to be alone, and I was the person he'd chosen to be his companion. Me—who'd always been told I was loud and brash and unfiltered. I couldn't deny that yes, I sure as hell was all those things. But knowing I could also be someone's peace on top of that…

"Heather?"

I hadn't realized I'd zoned out until Ethan said my name. He watched me with concerned eyes, his brow furrowed like he was afraid he'd said something wrong.

He was always worried he'd said something wrong.

Yet, he was probably one of the few people in my life who always knew exactly what I needed to hear.

And fuck if that didn't turn me on.

It took two strides for me to get to him. I settled onto his lap the same way I had in his car. After that, the office chair was no issue to maneuver. In fact, it was easier in my mini skirt. Ethan's hands, which immediately found their place on my ass, helped. Especially as I grabbed his face in both of mine and brought our lips together.

The last time I'd kissed him in this chair, it had been tender. Frankly, I hadn't even realized I'd done it until it was over. It had just seemed so... natural. Just like when I'd kissed him on the cheek before he'd gone to get the spare guitar for Holden.

But this? This was hungry. Passionate. His confession had broken a tether on the both of us.

*All of it* also included these moments. The ones fueled by heat and lust. By the attraction I'd tried so hard to deny.

There was no doing that now. Not a chance. Not with the way he sucked my lower lip into his mouth as we kissed. Or how his hair felt tangled between my fingers. Or how I couldn't help but moan as he broke away and ran his tongue along my neck—up, up, until he found that sensitive spot just below my jaw and sucked.

"Fuck, Ethan," I moaned, my mouth hanging open, my back arched.

Then we were moving.

The chair squeaked as he stood, bringing me with him. My legs wrapped around his torso on instinct until I was placed on the flat surface of the desk. His damned spreadsheets crumpled under me, but if he didn't care about them, I certainly didn't. Not as he nudged my legs apart, settling comfortably between them, before he brought his lips back to mine.

I locked my ankles together behind him, forcing him closer. His height put him at just the right spot, and his hardness pressed into me under where my skirt had ridden up.

This time, I wasn't going to let the night end without making up for our last time together.

He didn't stop me as I fumbled blindly with his belt buckle until it came undone. The button of his jeans followed after that.

That was as far as I got before his hands moved from my hips to the hem of my shirt. I lifted my hands over my head, giving him permission to remove it. Thankfully, I'd chosen a good bra—the black, semi-sheer lace one that made my B-cups look like C's.

Ethan appeared to appreciate it, too—so much so that he didn't even bother taking it off me, and instead pushed the fabric aside to expose my peaked breasts. Then, he lowered his head and his lips closed around my nipple.

One of my arms shot back, my hand pressed flat against the wall to keep myself upright. Admittedly, this wasn't my preferred form of foreplay, but fuck—I could learn to love it. Especially if it was Ethan doing this to me.

No. Ugh—no. I wasn't supposed to be the one enjoying this sort of pleasure right now. I'd gotten what I'd needed the last time. Now, it was Ethan's turn.

As much as it pained me to do so, I grasped his chin with my index finger and thumb and forced him to lift his head. One of his hands still remained on my breast, my nipple pinched between his fingers. I bit my lip, my selfish side tempted to let him continue, but ultimately brought his lips to mine before I hopped off the desk.

"Your turn," I said, repeating the sentiment I'd given in his car, as I lowered onto my knees, watching him from under my lashes.

This time, he didn't stop me as I grabbed the waistband of his jeans and briefs and lowered them with one, swift downward tug. I suppressed a gasp as his erection sprang free.

"You like what you see?"

I tore my eyes away from it to stare up at Ethan and his smug grin.

"Nothing I can't handle," I replied, wrapping my hand

around him then doing exactly what he'd told me he'd been imagining.

His whole body trembled when I took him into my mouth, and the moan that escaped him was nothing short of melodic. I didn't think I was *bad* at pleasuring men, per se, but this—Ethan was making me feel like a star with the way he reacted to each stroke. Soon, his hands tangled in my hair, keeping me close as I worked him.

It was enough to make me immediately crave the feel of him filling me elsewhere. My body wrapped around him while we—

"Hey, boss! Just wanted to let you know I'm here before— holy hell!"

I reared back, Ethan's cock slipping from my mouth with a *pop*. My hand was still wrapped around him as I stared wide-eyed at Liam. Ethan's hand left my hair, but his eyes were still lust-clouded, his face still showing the after-effects of growing pleasure. Despite that, he hastily pried my hand away, and with great difficulty tried to re-tuck himself inside his pants.

"I—shit," Liam tried. One hand was over his eyes as he turned to face us again. "I didn't see anything."

"Go downstairs and help cover the bar," Ethan instructed. I smiled at the way he tried to use his boss voice, but it came out more strained than he'd probably intended.

"Got it. Going. Carry on."

The office door shut with a solidifying *bang*, and the room was silent—aside from the rumblings of Holden's on-going set—once more.

"I, um—" Ethan cleared his throat then adjusted the front of his pants. "I'll meet you downstairs in a bit, okay?"

I smiled and rose onto my feet again as I adjusted my bra. "Okay," I agreed. I knew when he was this flustered not to push, even though I would have been more than happy to pick up where we'd left off. "I guess now we know for the future, though."

Ethan quirked a brow. "Huh?"

I smirked as I lifted myself onto my toes and kissed him quickly. "We'll lock the door next time."

× × ×

LIAM WAS BEHIND the bar, in the midst of making a drink when I finally strolled out of the kitchen, the door slapping back and forth behind me.

"Hey, how's it—?"

"Nope," he was quick to interject. I grinned when he shut his eyes and shook his head. "No, no, no. I need to wash my eyes out with holy water before I can look at you again, my friend."

"I'm decent, I swear."

"Not taking any more chances."

I chuckled. "Come hang with Nia and I if you get a chance."

He muttered something that sounded like a hesitant commitment. Deciding that was good enough for me, I made my way back to the table where an untouched drink, two pot stickers, and Nia waited for me. Thankfully she didn't seem too peeved that I'd left her alone. In fact, she appeared plenty entertained by Holden's set. I imagined he'd probably break soon, but he was on the schedule to perform until the restaurant closed at midnight.

A quick glance down at my watch told me it was nearing nine-thirty. The crowd was still going strong.

"Nice of you to join," Nia sassed. "Your drink might be watered down at this point, but—oh my god."

I paused, glass at my lips, to see what had made my friend get so excited.

"I take it you found Ethan?" she said.

"What makes you say that?"

"Your hair." She pointed animatedly at me. "That's I-just-got-fucked hair."

Shit.

I set my drink down then got straight to work trying to smooth out the long strands of red hair at the back of my head. I'd thought I'd done a pretty good job in the bathroom considering I didn't have a brush with me, but apparently not.

"I didn't just get fucked," I replied.

"But?" Nia pressed, her smile expectant, eyes widened with interest.

"But after seeing his dick, I desperately need to."

"Girl!"

I laughed as Nia lifted herself out of her chair and reached across the table to give my shoulder a playful slap. A few people seated around us stared, clearly wondering what had caused such a reaction.

"You're *going for it*," my friend said when she sat back down. Her whole face glowed with pride. "You're really going for it."

I shrugged. "He's nice to be around."

Nia rolled her eyes. "Would you get off your high fucking horse and just be honest? Ethan's *amazing*."

"You hardly even know him." They'd met a few times at the restaurant, but it wasn't like I'd invited Ethan into our apartment or anything. Not to mention Nia's preferred name for him was still Beer Boy—though she *had* just used his given name. That was definitely something.

"No, I don't know him," she agreed. "But I know my best friend, and you haven't stopped smiling since you've come back to this table."

"It's the lust wearing off."

"Is that what the kids call it these days?"

"Oh my god." Now it was my turn to stare incredulously

at her. "I've known him, like, two months, Ni."

She placed her hands over her chest and gave me a puppy-dog pout. "The heart knows no limits."

"Ew, you're disgusting." I shook my head at her before I took a sip of my drink—then grimaced. It was indeed as watered down as Nia had warned.

And then, because the universe hated making things work in my favor, I heard the door to the kitchen slap open then closed. Ethan appeared from behind it, calm, cool, and collected. His head turned on a swivel, taking in the sights of the restaurant before he settled into his normal location behind the bar.

Liam made a face and side-eyed his boss as he walked past.

"You were right about the drink," I said. "I'm gonna go get another."

"You know we have a server, right?"

"Yeah, I know."

She grinned. "I love horny Heather."

I rolled my eyes as I stood, but said nothing more before I made my back through the crowd towards the bar. I owed Nia for all the times I was ditching her, that was for sure. At least she was playing along for now. I knew the night would end with an invitation to a club, and I wouldn't be able to deny it.

"Hey," I called across the bar as I slid between two young girls. They gave me looks, but I didn't care. My eyes were on the guy behind the counter. Ethan smiled as soon as he located me. I set my glass on bar top and slid it his way. "Can I get a refresh?"

"Leave this one sitting for a little too long?" he asked as he took the drink in question.

I shrugged. "I got distracted."

"Please go back up to the office if this is how you two are going to act," Liam said.

Ethan chuckled and nudged his employee with his elbow as he turned to begin preparing me a fresh drink.

"Holy water," Liam said when I opened my mouth to try to speak, the quickly walked away to serve the two drinks he'd just finished garnishing.

Oh, I couldn't *wait* until I showed up at The Sound Hall next week.

Figuring I had a couple minutes to kill while Ethan finished up, I settled into one of the few remaining bar seats. My glowering young friends no longer remained, but one familiar face did.

"Isn't this great?" I asked Jerry, leaning forward in my seat so I could be closer to him. Between the crowd and the music, it was definitely a shouting kind of night.

He shrugged in reply. "Who is this kid?"

"Holden Young," I said. "Up-and-coming local musician. He has a great sound, doesn't he?"

Jerry took a long sip of his drink. "Weren't Chroma

Groove supposed to play again this weekend?"

"They agreed to move to next weekend, and Carla is skipping a week now."

Our proximity and the end of Holden's song allowed me to hear his hummed response.

Weird. Jerry had chatted with me like we'd known each other our whole lives a few weeks ago. Maybe he was pissed he wasn't the only one at the bar. I had to admit the fresh-twenty-ones that appeared to occupy most of the Mellow Cat Kitchen—probably friends of Holden—were pretty pushy.

"One, fresh whiskey sour," Ethan announced when he returned. I raised a brow at him. "Double, of course."

"Perfect." I reached for the glass and my fingers brushed up against his. They might have lingered a little longer than what was considered normal.

Then, our attention was drawn to the stage.

"Thank you everybody!" Holden called out. "I'm going to take a quick break. In the meantime, be sure to refill your drinks and keep the kitchen busy because how amazing is everything here at Mellow Cat Kitchen?"

I watched Ethan sidelong as the room filled with cheers. Many of these people, I knew, were first-time visitors. Ethan probably knew it too. Still, his smile at their response was enough to make my heart flutter.

It was short-lived as joy turned into fear.

"I'll text you later?" I said quickly, before the stampede of young adults trapped me.

Ethan nodded, his expression having taken the same turn mine had. He had a cocktail shaker in his hand before the first standing-room crowd member even started speaking. Him, Liam, and Brad were in for a wild half-hour.

Drink in hand, I turned to leave.

"See you next time, Jer—"

But my thought went unfinished.

Jerry had already left.

# Chapter 16

♪ Anime Eyes | Kacey Musgraves



I'D NEVER BEEN so excited to see the inside of my studio apartment.

The moment I kicked my shoes off at the door, I sighed. That had been the craziest night I'd seen at Mellow Cat since—well, since ever. Or at least since the first few weeks. That new-restaurant buzz always did wonders, but it had worn off as quickly as it had come. Tonight was the closest I'd ever come since then to having a full house. Hell, it was probably *better* than opening week.

Who knew all it took was a pretty twenty-something-year-old boy with a guitar to absolutely pack the place?

Actually, any young female probably could have told me that. Unfortunately, I didn't think like one of those. But thankfully, Heather did.

Speaking of…

I pulled out my phone and shot her a text. She'd sent me one already—some blurry picture that I assumed was taken wherever she and Nia had ended up after they'd left. It came with the message HELP ME.

As much as I'd wanted to, I hadn't been able to leave Liam and Brad alone behind the bar. Young people could drink. I couldn't remember a time I could consume so many sugary cocktails and not worry about waking up with a hangover that would last the whole day. Maybe they just didn't care. I missed that feeling too.

Before I did that, though, I needed to work on the feeling in my feet.

Just as I sat down on my couch, prepared to enjoy the latest episode of my favorite anime—So what if it was nearly one-thirty in the morning? I deserved this, dammit!—my phone buzzed with a new notification.

Glad you made it home! Great work tonight ☺ wish I could be laying on a couch too lol

So she was still out, then.

You could always join me ;), I texted back.

Normally, we weren't so openly flirty with our messages. They'd teetered on the line of platonic for a while now, but crossing that boundary finally felt okay. Maybe it was because we were seeing each other practically every day now.

Or maybe it was because she'd had my dick in her mouth a few hours ago.

My hand went to my crotch to adjust the impending hard on. I'd been battling them all night. Every time I'd so much as looked at Heather while she'd been at Mellow Cat, I couldn't help my thoughts from wandering to us in my office. Her perfect tits in my mouth. Her hand on me. Her *lips* on me.

God, those lips. They'd been just as incredible as I'd imagined.

My phone buzzed again. What's your address??

Exhaustion be damned. I'd never sat up faster, my phone clutched in my hand, eyes wide and staring at her last text.

My address? Heather wanted to come *here?*

I knew every detail of the five-hundred square feet of rented property, yet knowing someone was coming here made me take a closer look. No, not just someone—*Heather.*

Telling her I was a nerd was one thing. I knew she'd seen the posters in my office, we'd just become preoccupied before she had the chance to say something. Having her here, however…

I couldn't just tell her no. Not after tonight. Shit—why had that happened *tonight?* If I declined her offer, that would *not* go over well. Plus, what would that make me? The guy who got some head then cut things off?

No. I was not that asshole. I'd seen my brother be that

asshole too many times to make the same mistake.

I texted my response to her question, no pomp, no circumstance. Just a street, building number, and instructions to buzz my unit when she got here.

Heather was going to come over.

And I needed to clean up some evidence.

× × ×

MY PROBABLY TOO-excited smile—considering it was two in the morning—betrayed the way my heart beat frantically inside my chest when I opened the door for my guest.

"Heather! Hi!"

Rightfully so, she eyed me with a quizzical expression. "Hi?" It turned into a grin as she ducked under my arm and said, "Weirdo."

Then she was in my space.

I closed the door softly, watching her over my shoulder the whole time as she took everything in. I'd managed to get most of my collection put away between when I'd sent my text and when the buzzer announced her arrival. I hadn't wanted it to look like no one lived here, but I also didn't need the embarrassment of her seeing the memorabilia I'd collected from the plethora of conventions and collectable stores I'd visited over the years.

I'd established myself as a sexy, successful business owner

in her eyes. I wasn't about to ruin that now.

"I like it," she said when she'd finished her evaluation. "Very—"

The grin returned, bigger than it had been before, as her eyes landed on something that clearly entertained her. When mine followed, my heart dropped into my stomach.

Shit.

Heather made her way over to the pile of blankets next to my TV stand, on top of which sat a plush of my favorite Pokémon. It was one of those things I'd had lying around for years, separated from the spots dedicated to my other collectables. While those had all been replaced by normal things like candles, old DVDs, and books, Gengar had gone unnoticed.

Until now.

Heather picked up the oversized plush and held it out for examination. Between Gengar's round body and pointed ears, it was nearly as big as her entire torso.

Seriously—how in the hell had I *not* seen it?

"Who's this?" Heather asked. She hugged the plush to her chest as she continued to grin at me.

"That's, uh,"—I cleared my throat—"a Pokémon."

"So, I know I'm not super into nerdy things, but I'm pretty sure these usually come with names. And I know it's not Pikachu."

Why was hearing her say the name of a Pokémon such a

turn on?

"It's Gengar," I explained.

Heather held it out again, her lips pursed as she scrutinized the stuffed purple creature in her hands. "It looks mean," she said, probably in reference to the red eyes and mouth that was sewn on in its signature grin.

"It's a ghost type." When Heather quirked a brow at me, I continued. "There's different types of Pokémon. Pikachu is an electric type. Charmander is a fire type," I recited, listing names I hoped were common enough. "Then there's Eevee who's really cool because it can—wait, you know what? Never mind."

"What?"

I crossed the room and took Gengar out of her hold. "You didn't come here to listen to me talk about Pokémon."

"Oh yeah?" she challenged. "What *did* I come here for then?"

Wow, I'd really dug myself into a hole with that one. Obviously, given how earlier parts of our night had gone, I assumed that's why she'd responded to my text the way she had, but I wasn't going to force anything. If we slept together, we slept together. If we didn't, we didn't. I wouldn't be disappointed either way. Just knowing she wanted to spend more time together was enough for me.

Even if, by her being here, she was figuring out a lot more than I'd intended to share.

"What happened to Nia?" I asked, changing the subject.

"Smooth." Heather snatched Gengar back then went to take a seat on my couch. She didn't seem apprehensive at all about making herself at home, not that I'd thought she would.

I tried not to stare as she shifted into a cross-legged position that made her mini skirt ride practically up to her hips. If not for how she held Gengar in her lap, hugging him, nothing would have prevented me from seeing what hid beneath.

"Seriously," I said. "Weren't you two out together?"

"Yeah, but she found someone at the bar and it was clear where her night was headed." Heather shrugged. "Figured I owed her the privacy to repay her for all the times I ditched her tonight."

"Such a good wing-woman."

"The absolute best, actually." I laughed when she flicked her hair back over her shoulder with some flair. "I stuck around as long as I could, but once I started getting hit on by too many women, I figured it was time to head out. You had perfect timing with that text."

"What I'm hearing is it's actually me who Nia should be thanking, then?"

"It might be enough to get her to permanently stop calling you Beer Boy."

"She still calls me that?" I asked as I took a seat on the

other side of the couch. It was probably pretty pathetic how jealous I was of Gengar—the way Heather was holding him—but I needed to make it clear that my text had not been intended as a booty call. No better way to do that than to keep a respectable distance in place.

"From time to time," Heather admitted. "It means she likes you."

"In that case, I'm honored."

Heather chuckled then her attention strayed to the TV. "Were you trying to watch something before I intruded?"

"You aren't intruding if I invited you," I argued, then shook my head. "I—no. I was going to try and relax a bit, but it wasn't anything in particular."

I'd been fiddling with a loose string on the couch, so it took a bit longer than normal to notice that Heather had gone quiet. When I looked up, I found her watching me with That Look.

"What?" I asked.

"You saying it was nothing in particular means it was, in fact, something in particular."

"That logic is completely insane."

"What were you going to watch?"

"It doesn't mat—"

"Oh my gosh," she suddenly said, smiling. "You were going to watch your nerd shows."

"It's called anime," I corrected. "And I plead the fifth."

"Why? We can watch it."

"We?"

"You, me, and Gengar," Heather clarified, hugging the Pokémon tighter. "It'll be fun."

I quirked a brow. "You *really* want to watch anime?"

"Why not?" She shrugged. "There has to be a reason so many people like it."

"Yeah, I mean, it's good, but…"

"But what?"

"I don't know. It doesn't seem like your thing?"

"No, but it's yours." Setting Gengar to the side, she hopped onto her knees and reached for the TV remote. "C'mon. Which one are we watching?"

I didn't bother to fight her as she started to scroll blindly through the anime streaming app that opened up right when she turned on the TV. I didn't do anything, honestly. Watching this woman—this beautiful, wild, firework of a woman—pretend like she was even remotely interested in all this was mind-blowing. It was what every guy like me dreamed of.

This was my waifu moment.

No. *Nope.* Too far.

By the time I came out of my thoughts, Heather had probably already been staring at me for a while.

Her eyes darted to the TV. "Which one?"

"Um…" My mouth hung open as I watched the screen,

sidelong. She was only one off from the show I'd wanted to watch. "Really, we don't have to. I'm sure there are better things we can do with our time."

"Which once again leads me to ask, like what?"

Damn, she was good.

Heather sighed when I didn't respond.

"Ethan, if there's one thing you must know about me, it's that I don't do anything I don't want to do." She spoke with her usual confidence, but still I saw something flash in her eyes. A hesitance, almost. But it was gone so quick, I couldn't be sure I'd actually seen it or if it was a figment of my imagination. "I don't care if you think this stuff is too dorky for me. I can promise you it's not. So pick a show, let's watch it, and try not to get too annoyed with all my questions because dammit—I'm going to leave here knowing every fact about every character."

There was no chance of me winning any sort of argument after that.

I grabbed the remote from her hand and went to the show I was in the middle of watching. Heather retrieved Gengar, but this time, when she settled into the couch it was right beside me. No more boundaries.

Heather had a way of doing that, I realized. From our first kiss to this, it was her who had initiated most of our contact. It wasn't like I wasn't thinking about doing the same thing, it was only that I was more reserved. I was worried that crossing lines would ruin things, whereas it was like she knew that crossing them was exactly what I wanted but had been too nervous to do myself.

Once she set the stage, though, I opened up like I'd never opened up for anyone before.

My arm naturally draped over the back of the couch, allowing her the chance to curl up into my side if she wanted to. To my relief, she did. Of course, she did. You didn't just go over to the apartment of the person you'd been hooking up with earlier and *not* cuddle.

She fit against me so perfectly, her head on my collarbone, one arm wrapped around Gengar, the other on my leg. The heat of her palm seared into my knee. I'd become so hyperaware of every place our bodies touched, that I didn't realize she'd asked me a question until she nudged me.

"Huh?" I asked.

"Why does that guy have that mouth on his cheek?"

"He ate a cursed finger and now he's possessed by a thousand-year-old demon."

"I'm sorry—*one thousand?*"

"I feel like it's pretty early on to remind you none of this is real. Also, why aren't you more concerned about the eating-a-finger thing?"

"Oh, who's the white-haired one? He looks fun."

"Of course, you'd like him."

"Wait, did he just—oh my god! He exploded!"

"Shhhhh." My arm fell down from the back of the couch and wrapped around Heather instead, pulling her closer. "Watch. It'll make sense. I promise."

Heather opened her mouth, a soft sound that should have been the start of her rebuttal escaping her. Then, she closed it and I'd be damned—she listened.

Her legs curled up, and she snuggled into my side. "This is already better than the reality stuff Nia watches," she mumbled.

I chuckled and it wasn't until my lips lifted from the kiss I'd placed on her head that I realized what I'd done.

Heather didn't stir.

I smiled.

# Chapter 17



*HEATHER*

I'D LAST CHECKED my watch around two-thirty in the morning, which meant I'd been out for at least an hour. This time when I lifted my wrist, it read four in the morning. Ethan was still dozing beside me.

My eyes only opened a crack, the fluorescent light of the anime on screen still shining bright in the darkened room. Given the change in animation style, it appeared the next show had started auto playing.

At some point, Ethan must have turned off the lights too, because those had definitely been on. How he'd managed that without me knowing, proved how tired I'd been. I'd honestly thought about ignoring his suggestive text all-together and calling it a night. But I'd meant what I'd told him about Nia; my friend deserved some fun. Besides, it sounded like he wanted to partake in that same sort of fun. A pick-up-where-we'd-left-off situation.

Seeing as we were still fully clothed and curled up on his couch asleep, that obviously hadn't been his intention. At all.

Somehow, this was better.

I lifted my head only to grimace at the kink that had formed in my neck. Sleeping at awkward angles was not something near-thirty-year-olds should be doing apparently.

As if, even in his sleep, he knew I was awake, Ethan's arm tightened around me. At the angle I was at now, it was obvious he'd gotten up at some point. We were currently majorly failing at big-spoon, little-spoon. At least I thought that's what he was going for. All I knew for certain was Gengar had at some point become my pillow.

Forget Pikachu. That mean purple creature was now my favorite.

I looked down at Ethan when he stirred. His face scrunched, then his eyes opened in the same manner mine had—slowly, confused, and fighting against the light of the TV.

A smile spread across my lips as I watched him try to figure out where he was, then, probably, why he was on his couch instead of the bed ten feet away.

Then his eyes settled on me.

"Hi," I whispered.

"Hi," he replied, then groaned as he sat up on his elbows. "What time is it?"

"Probably around four fifteen at this point."

Ethan's brow scrunched for a whole new reason. "What are you doing up?"

"I'm not sure. It just happened."

"It's not time to be awake yet."

Ethan extended his arm towards the coffee table and grabbed the remote. The light from the TV disappeared and we were left in complete darkness. That was probably part of the reason for my surprise when his arms then snaked around my waist and pulled me flush against his front.

I had to admit, I was significantly more comfortable now that my head rested flat on his chest. There was no way he was okay, though, lying on his back without a pillow.

"Do you want Gengar?" I asked. Ethan lifted his head, and with my eyes adjusted to the lack of light, I was just able to make out the way he lifted a brow. "For a pillow."

"You can keep using him."

"Ethan, you can't tell me you're comfortable."

I felt his shrug. Okay, that was it.

"C'mon. We're moving."

I wiggled in his hold, trying to break free. It was only when a sudden pressure pressed into my abdomen that I realized what I was doing.

I'd practically been dry-humping him.

Ethan must have realized what was happening too because he was quick to move. I was off him in seconds and not even the darkness could hide his embarrassment over the situation.

"We, um, maybe we can move to the bed?" I suggested. When he stared wide-eyed at me, I amended, "So we're both comfortable."

"Oh, yeah. We can do that." He gave me a once-over. "I have some sweatpants and stuff you can borrow. If you want."

I nodded. "That would be great." I'd slept in many a miniskirt in my life, but that didn't mean I enjoyed it.

We were off the couch and in the bedroom section of his studio in a few steps. He flipped on the lamp on his bedside table, and I stood at the end of his bed, watching as he went through the drawers of his single dresser, trying to find some spare clothes for me to borrow. When I knew he wasn't looking, I took the chance to survey his space a little more. Once Gengar had been spotted, I'd gotten distracted.

It was a nice place—perfect for a single guy. A small-but-updated kitchen; the space we were in now, which was big enough for a queen-size bed; the living area we'd spent most of our time in so far, and a bathroom. Even though everything was pretty confined, Ethan had done a good job of making each section feel like its own room with his furniture's layout.

My head tilted when I caught sight of a small figurine sticking out from under the bed. It looked like the mouth-cheek guy from the show we'd been watching.

I grinned and wondered how many others were hiding around here.

All evidence of my discovery was erased from my face by the time Ethan turned around, a stack of neatly folded clothing in his hand.

"I didn't know if you ran hot or cold, so there's some options," he said.

"Thanks," I said as I took the offering.

"The, uh, bathroom is over there. I should have a spare toothbrush under the sink too if you want to freshen up."

"Aren't *you* the host with the most," I teased with a wink, then made my way to the bathroom.

It was clean. Not that I expected anything less; Ethan's whole place seemed pretty well-organized, but it was always scary walking into a guy's bathroom for the first time.

Unable to help myself, I snooped through the colognes on the counter. There was some skincare stuff mixed in too. I was finally getting all the answers to the questions I'd been nervous to ask. Why he always smelled so dang good. Why his skin was always so soft under my touch.

A man that took care of himself could be appreciated.

I used the bathroom, but opted not to brush my teeth. Taking his spare toothbrush felt intimate. Way too intimate.

That would become *my* toothbrush, and it would be at *his* place. Knowing Ethan, he'd probably keep it around for any future visits that happened—which why wouldn't there be future visits?

I didn't think I'd be able to handle the sight of my toothbrush next to his in the little cup on the counter, though.

My pearly whites could wait until I got back to my place.

I settled on sweatpants and a t-shirt. That seemed like the most modest combination that would also prevent me from overheating. Men—they were like freaking space heaters.

The shirt caused me no issues, but when I went to remove my skirt…

I tugged at the zipper, begging it to go down, but nope. It was definitely stuck.

"Mother fucker," I muttered as I tried again. Turns out cussing wasn't the cure to make things work again.

Okay. I could figure this out. Maybe if I sucked in my stomach and tried to wiggle out…

The high-waisted skirt got as far as my hips before it refused to go down any further.

Cursing feminine anatomy, I placed a hand on the cool bathroom counter.

It was fine. It was totally, completely fine. I could always put the sweatpants over the skirt—but then Ethan would probably question why it looked like I was wearing a diaper.

Didn't want that.

I could also just suck it up and sleep in the skirt like I'd originally thought I'd have to. I could change into the sweatshirt he'd given me as an option and just deal with the skirt—and the way Ethan and I's legs would probably rub up against each other under the covers. We'd tangle together and—

Nope. I needed the skirt off.

There was absolutely no chance I was getting the zipper down on my own, however. I needed back-up.

"Hey," I called as I exited the bathroom, trying to act like I hadn't just been panicking. "Uh, would you mind helping me with—"

Ethan was in the midst of changing, too. Unlike me, he'd opted for the pants-first strategy. I'd never understood the hype around gray sweats—until now. They hugged his ass perfectly, and hung low enough on him where I could see the trail of dark hair and v of muscles that disappeared beneath the waistband.

That was the other issue—perk?—with the dressing strategy he'd taken.

Ethan was shirtless.

I knew he was strong. I'd seen him in enough shirts that hugged his muscles to figure that out. Then there were, of course, the occasional times when he'd held me in his arms, too.

Now, paused mid-way through putting on his shirt, his arms bent, biceps flexed naturally with the way they were positioned, I had absolutely no choice but to take note.

He was beautifully chiseled, not too brawny, but not too skinny, with abs that were just defined enough to make out, corded forearms that transitioned into perfectly swelled biceps, and a toned chest.

Those same arms had been wrapped around me on the couch. My head had rested on that chest. And his hands… I was already thinking too many indecent thoughts to dwell on those for long.

I'd been staring too long as it was.

"I, um—sorry. I—" Did words even exist anymore? I pointed at my skirt. "I have an issue."

"Shoot… I don't have any of that," Ethan said. "But there's a store down the street. I can run there and get you stuff if you need tampons or—"

"Oh, no, no, no! It's not that." Ethan Morimoto: a true angel on earth. "It's…" I turned and stuck out my hip a little. "My zipper is stuck."

"Oh."

I grinned and raised an inquisitive brow. "Can I get some help?"

"Right. Yeah. Of course. Let me just…"

He abandoned his shirt on the bed and made his way over to me. The proximity shouldn't have had any sort of effect on me; tonight alone we'd found ourselves in plenty of close-quarters situations. Yet I couldn't help the way my body tensed, then instantly relaxed as soon as I felt the brush of his fingers on the skin by the waistband of my skirt.

"I don't want to break it," he muttered as he tugged.

"It's okay."

I watched over my shoulder as he struggled, his face twisted in concentration. I should have known the moment I asked him for help that he wouldn't give up until he succeeded. That was the kind of guy Ethan was. Both because he didn't do any task half-assed, but also because he was helping me. Even in the short time I'd known him, I knew I could count on Ethan to follow through.

As if proving my thoughts correct, I heard the triumphant noise that escaped him, then felt my skirt loosen around my hips.

"Problem solved," he said, happy as a clam. Then, his tension radiated when I let my skirt drop to the floor, stepped out of it, and turned to face him.

The hem of his shirt fluttered around my upper thigh, just barely concealing anything below my waist. I commended myself, once again, for thinking ahead and wearing a pair of lace panties that matched my bra.

Ethan's eyes jumped around—my face, my chest, my legs, and back up again—like he didn't know how to give my entire body attention at once. I helped him by grabbing his hands and placing them gently on my hips. His attention immediately narrowed in to where we touched.

It didn't take long before he met my waiting stare. I took a small step forward, never breaking eye contact, until I was pressed against him. His sweatpants made it difficult to ignore how hard he already was.

My arms snaked around his neck, my fingers tangled in the hair at the back of his head. It didn't require much coaxing on my end to get him to lean down so my lips could reach his.

Ethan's hands roamed from my hips to my ass, squeezing enough to elicit a moan from me. The sound of it shattered whatever restraint he'd been trying to maintain. For what, I didn't know. But I was thankful as hell when he tugged me closer, my back arching in order to mold with him.

We were hungry. More so than we'd been in his office earlier that night. There, we'd just begun to explore what we could do with one another. Here, we were getting the chance to do it.

And, boy, did I need that chance.

Each place his hands—his lips—touched sent a new wave of heat through my body. If I'd struggled to form words earlier, there was no chance now. Only sounds escaped me, but he somehow knew how to interpret every single one.

The low moan when he sucked on the spot just below my jaw prompted him to keep going.

The hum when he grabbed the hem of the t-shirt I'd borrowed let him know it was okay to remove it.

The sharp inhale when his hand stopped exploring just above my panties told him to go lower… lower… lower…

"Shit," he moaned when his hand was finally where I wanted it. "You're so wet."

"I want you," I finally managed to say as I writhed on him, my body desperate to feel those same sensations from our night in his car. "I need you, Ethan."

I'd been right about him. There was something about Ethan where, when I made a request, he stopped at nothing until it was fulfilled.

We made it to the bed.

But we didn't get much sleep.

✕ ✕ ✕

SUNLIGHT FILTERED IN and forced me to open my eyes way before I wanted to. I could have sworn I'd just shut them. We couldn't have stopped more than ten minutes ago. Fifteen at max.

But when I lifted myself onto one of my elbows, the sheets falling just enough to expose my still-bare breasts, I found Ethan sleeping beside me.

I smiled at the way he was curled up, his face free of any worry creases, completely at ease. Given the night we'd had,

I couldn't say I felt much differently. I hadn't thought it was possible to have so many consecutive orgasms, yet here I was to tell the tale.

Ethan had been fantastic. More than fantastic, actually. I'd had my fair share of sex, but holy shit—I wanted to know all the secrets of how he'd gotten so good at pleasing a woman. I should have known what I was in for, given his performance in his car, but he'd exceeded all expectations.

I'd never had a man pay so much attention to me.

Realizing this wouldn't be like the last time, and Ethan wouldn't wake up when I moved, I laid back down. It was Saturday, and we couldn't have gotten more than four hours of sleep. Five, if we were lucky. There was still a whole night ahead of us.

I curled up beside him, acting as the big spoon, and that's when his arm found me. Ethan turned, trading positions, and hugged me to his bare chest.

His lips pressed a kiss to my shoulder blade. "Were you trying to escape?"

"Not yet," I assured him. "Only watching you sleep."

"How Edward Cullen of you."

"I don't know if I should be worried or impressed that you just made that reference."

I felt his chuckle more than I heard it, the vibration tickling my back, and goosebumps rose on my skin.

"You cold?" Ethan asked. He rubbed his hand up and

down my arm.

"I'm perfect." More than perfect. I couldn't remember a morning where I'd felt more content waking up somewhere that wasn't my own bed. Maybe at some fancy hotel or something? But definitely not in a guy's bed.

"Do you have anything going on today?" he asked.

"Not until our plans later." Ethan had gotten Brad to agree to handle the night shift so we could go scouting for a new act. Carla was on the schedule, so Ethan hadn't been too worried about leaving the restaurant in someone else's hands.

His hum was just as good as his chuckle. The kisses he littered my back, my shoulder, my jaw with even better than that.

"If you're not in a hurry, maybe we could make some breakfast?"

I made a noise like I was contemplating the offer, stretching my neck to give him better access to continue kissing me.

It was an excuse. A chance to buy time and figure out my next move. Hooking up in his office or in a car was one thing. What we'd done last night was another entirely. I'd known that when I'd made the decision to initiate it. But I'd done so thinking we were on the same page with this.

We were two people who were attracted to each other and conveniently spending lots of time alone. It made sense that we'd crossed the line we had. After the first kiss, it had only been a matter of time, honestly.

Staying for breakfast, though… something about that felt more intimate than the fact that we were currently cuddled up naked in Ethan's bed.

His lips found my earlobe, then he was whispering, "I make some mean scrambled eggs," in such a seductive tone, I couldn't help but laugh.

I turned in his hold, our legs tangled together so we could comfortably face one another. Ethan's eyes were tired, given the bags under them, but bright, shining with hope that I'd accept his invitation.

"You got a toaster?" I asked, my voice low, sexy. Two could play this game.

"Oh yeah. The four-slice kind."

"And bagels?"

"With cream cheese."

I bit my bottom lip as I groaned. "I'm gonna toast those bagels so hard."

That got Ethan to break character. "So that's a yes?" he asked through a laugh.

I stared at him—this amazing, goofy, nerdy man—a bit longer before I nodded.

What was one breakfast in the grand scheme of things?

# Chapter 18

♪ Poet | MALIA

*ETHAN*

WHEN I FIRST opened Mellow Cat Kitchen, I'd thought it would be cool to have some sort of competition. A Sinatra sing-off, dueling pianos—even though I wasn't sure where two pianos could fit—or even a search for Chicago's next great trumpeter. Stuff like that.

Never had I ever imagined a slam poetry-off—or whatever this was called; it was completely new territory for me—happening on my stage.

The two men at the mics—a bald one, probably a few years older than me and another younger guy who probably attended one of the city's universities—battled verbally, back and forth. In a way, it sounded like a rap without the production. They were keeping a rhythm entirely on their own. A small part of me found it kind of impressive. But the larger part was way too confused to focus too long on anything in particular they were trying to say.

I wasn't smart enough to comprehend speech that occurred only in philosophical-sounding metaphors.

Even if I didn't know what was going on, I couldn't deny it had brought in a halfway decent crowd. Nothing close to Holden, but still better than Leo. That had to count for something.

A girl dressed in patterns I was pretty sure shouldn't be paired together hummed her approval down the bar. I watched her sidelong as she lifted her fingers to snap.

I was learning that's what they did at these things. No clapping. Just snapping.

Another body slid up beside mine—one I'd been craving since the weekend before. When I'd made sure to learn every detail, every curve, every freckle as she'd writhed in pleasure on my bed.

"Sheesh," Heather muttered. She took up the same stance as me: leaned back against the rear bar countertop with my arms crossed over my chest. Technically, since she wasn't employed, she wasn't supposed to be back here, but there was no chance of enforcing rules once Heather decided she didn't care. I didn't really care either anymore. "The bald one is definitely winning this one."

"By a landslide," I agreed.

She tilted her head up to me, and when I glanced down, I found her grinning.

"You have no idea what's going on, do you?"

"I'm basing my opinion entirely on how much snapping happens."

She chuckled. "A fair strategy." After a pause, she added, "No more slam poetry?"

"Probably not."

Her grin widened and she nodded, electing not to respond as a fresh wave of snaps echoed around the restaurant. We'd been quick to learn that speaking over the performers was strictly forbidden. The whole place was silent for the duration of the battle, interrupted only by the soft cheers of affirmation and muted snapping.

Which made it that much worse when Jerry waltzed in.

"And here I thought I was late," he called out as soon as he saw me. "When's the show starting, E?"

The head of what I assumed was every hipster in Chicago turned, and Jerry became the recipient of the coldest glares I'd ever seen.

I quickly pushed off the bar and greeted him in his seat. Pattern Girl was clearly *not* happy about how close the stool he'd chosen was to her.

"The show *has* started," I hissed, and nodded toward the stage.

Jerry followed, and his brow furrowed as soon as he

figured out what was happening. "Isn't this Leo's night?"

"No, we bumped Leo to next week."

"What the hell is this then?"

I could have sworn I heard Pattern Girl mutter, "It's art, you asshat," but thankfully, Jerry didn't notice.

"It's something new we're trying."

"Like that kid last week?"

"He was part of it, yeah."

I didn't miss when Jerry broke eye contact, his attention straying somewhere over my shoulder. It wasn't hard to guess where. Heather hadn't moved, and I was sure she was waving and smiling, friendly as ever, behind me. As far as I knew, she was still determined to become Jerry's friend.

If the look on his face when we made eye contact again was any indication, I wasn't so sure he was willing to reciprocate.

"She's pretty," he said, his voice so low that even I could barely hear him. "But don't let her get in your head. This is *your* place."

"I *know* it's my place, Jerry," I replied. My voice had lost its customer service touch, but I couldn't help the twinge of anger that coated my words. "I'm trying to make sure it *stays* my place."

"Then *she* shouldn't step in so much."

He nodded towards Heather, and I knew she wouldn't miss it. Sure enough, when I glanced back over my shoulder she was watching with a furrowed brow, her jaw tense. There wasn't a doubt in my mind she was fighting the urge to step in and ask what was up.

I did before she had the chance to do so.

"Hey." I pivoted to face her. "Would you mind going up to my office to get the… thing?"

"The thing?"

"Yeah," I said and placed my hands on her shoulders. "The thing."

When she quirked a brow, silently asking me what the fuck I was talking about, I widened my eyes to let her know I, in fact, had no clue what the fuck I was talking about. I was talking nonsense. But I needed her to get out of there. Quick. Before the firecracker personality took over and spoken word night was taken over by fight night.

Thankfully, she seemed to take the hint.

"Oh, yeah—that thing," she said, snapping her fingers like she'd just remembered. "I'll be right back."

She disappeared through the kitchen door a second later— not without giving me another look. As soon as it smacked shut behind her, I spun to Jerry again.

"She's helping me, okay?" I said. "All the regulars are still on the schedule; they're just spaced out."

"That's not what your website says, bud."

The website? Shit.

I pressed my fist into my forehead, trying to ease the

tension building there. "I haven't had the chance to update that yet. Sorry." We'd posted about the new acts in the line-up on social media, but I'd completely forgotten about the events page on the Mellow Cat website. Of course Jerry wouldn't have known about the change in schedule. Nothing about him said, *I check Instagram frequently.*

Jerry leaned toward me, his face serious, like a father about to reprimand his son. "I don't doubt this is a hard place to run," he said, which, given how our conversation had been going so far, gave me some relief. "But don't lose sight of what you started. Mellow Cat has been a great addition to the neighborhood. It would be a shame to see it go to waste."

I wanted to argue that it wasn't going to waste. There had been more butts in chairs since Heather had stepped in to help with her reviews of our regular jazz acts and scouting out new entertainment than I'd seen in years. As a near-nightly regular, Jerry had to have noticed it too.

So I knew that's not what he meant. He was talking about the origins of Mellow Cat—how it had operated every day since I'd first opened its doors. Its *soul.*

I surveyed the room, taking in the crowd currently gathered. Many of their heads were bobbing. Some even had their eyes shut while they did it, taking in the sound of the spoken word more so than the performer. There were the snaps and foot-tapping to the rhythm the poet set.

These people were reacting the same way any jazz listener

would. It was just a different form of art.

This place hadn't lost its soul. It had just transitioned.

"That won't happen. I promise." Switching back into business mode, I asked, "Anything I can get you tonight? You've been here too long without a drink."

"Nah. I'll come back another night." My heart dropped to my stomach as Jerry scooted out of his stool. He tapped the bar top twice and gave me a closed-lip smile. "Women come and go. What you've got here could be for the long run if you do it right."

Yeah, easy for Jerry to say. He'd been divorced twice, and his current girlfriend clearly wasn't getting much of his time. I saw him more than she probably did. Of course, he'd see a career as a higher priority than a person.

But as I watched him walk back out the door—"Thank god," Pattern Girl muttered—I couldn't help but think of the person hiding behind the kitchen door. Like hell, Heather had actually gone up to my office to wait. I knew her better than that. She'd probably been watching through the tiny plastic window and would be back out here in three, two—

"What the hell was his problem?" she asked as she retook her place beside me. This time when she crossed her arms over her chest, it wasn't casual. She was pissed.

"He was mad about tonight's act," I explained. "I forgot to update the website's event page, and he thought it was something else."

Heather blew out an unimpressed *pft* of air and rolled her eyes. "Seriously? A hissy fit for that?"

I shrugged. "I don't know. Jerry's particular."

"Sounds like it."

Heather and I both looked towards the stage when a chorus of snapping filled the restaurant, along with a few surprising hoots and hollers at whatever had just been said on stage. The bald guy looked triumphant, but the kid he'd been verbally battling didn't appear too heart-broken over the loss. If people lost at these sorts of things.

Yeah, spoken word would be a very rare act at Mellow Cat Kitchen.

My attention was drawn back to Heather when she reached up and tugged at the collar of my Polo quarter zip sweater. The temptation to spin her around, press her against the bar, and kiss her overwhelmed me. She looked so damn beautiful tonight. She looked beautiful every night, really.

"I don't know if you noticed," she drawled as her hands ran down my chest, "but I never found that thing you needed."

"Oh?"

"Think you could come up to your office with me and we can look for it?"

Mischief shone in her eyes. My hands found their way to her hips, and my thumbs naturally brushed the strip of skin not covered by her jeans or crop top. Goosebumps formed immediately, and I fought the urge to smile at the effect I had on her.

If that was how she reacted to such a simple touch, I couldn't wait to remind her what else I could do.

"I think I have a little time for that," I replied, and she smirked as she tugged me upstairs.

# Chapter 19

♫ Disco Yes | Tom Misch



BEING AT A concert wasn't the weird part. It wasn't being at a concert without needing to write a review or scout a new act for Mellow Cat Kitchen either.

No, the weird part was realizing that when I'd accepted Ethan's invitation, I'd said yes to a date. A double date, to be specific.

When Ethan first asked me to join him at a MYTHIC concert, I hadn't thought much of it. The two of us? A concert? It was just another weekend, even though I did think electronic was a little outside of his usual choice of genre.

It wasn't until we were on the drive over here that he admitted the tickets had been part of a Christmas gift to

Eric—and his brother had chosen him as the lucky person who got to join.

"So it'll be the three of us?" I'd asked.

Ethan shook his head, eyes on the road. "Eric's bringing someone."

"A friend or something?"

"A little more than a friend, I think…"

It didn't take long for me to put two and two together after that.

Eric stood from his chair in the private balcony we occupied and cheered when the server returned with a tray of shots. He must have ordered them without us knowing, given everyone else's lack of enthusiasm. At least his date—I thought her name was Lauren, but Ethan said it didn't matter; Eric was a serial dater—put on a smile for him. That was, until she took the shot glass and saw what was in it. I couldn't hide my distaste very well either. Vodka and I hadn't been friends since college.

I turned to Ethan when he nudged my side and followed the downward motion of his eyes. He nonchalantly moved the plastic cup that had housed his last drink into the space between us. I grinned and nodded. What a genius.

"Here's to a great fucking night!" Eric announced. "VIP lifestyle, baby!"

How he and Ethan were related was beyond me.

The second his head went back, though, Ethan and I

simultaneously dumped ours into the cup.

"Oh god." I couldn't help snickering at the fake post-shot face Ethan managed, then realized I should have been doing the same. Didn't want Eric thinking I could handle any more.

I coughed, my face twisted in disgust. "Did you request the bottom shelf option or something?"

Ethan's cough sounded more like a laugh.

"Oh, okay, Miss Always VIP," Eric teased. For having only met him one other time, it was pretty ballsy. His confidence was sure to make for some entertainment later, though, once the alcohol hit. "Sorry we can't live up to your usual standards here."

"O-M-G!" Lauren's eyes went wide the same time mine did. I'd never actually heard anyone speak in text talk before. "Are you, like, secretly a famous person?"

I snorted. "No."

"Heather writes music reviews," Ethan explained. "So she meets a lot of people."

"Backstage access and stuff," I added with a shrug. "Nothing as fancy as Eric is obviously thinking."

Lauren squealed. "No way! Who have you met recently?"

"Um…" I tried to think back on the last few months. "There was Jonah Kidd—that rapper guy? Then I covered Lollapalooza last summer, so I met a lot of people there. And Ethan and I have been going to a lot of concerts lately. Stray Land, Jaxon Baker, Sixth Hero," I listed, including the main act of the show Holden opened for.

I was met with a blank stare from Lauren.

Sigh.

"I covered Taylor Swift a few months ago," I said flatly.

She lit up like house lights. From the corner of my eye, I watched Ethan take a sip of his drink, but it didn't quite hide his grin like I figured he wanted it to.

Thankfully, that conversation didn't go anywhere as the stage lights turned on and the general admission pit below us went wild.

The venue itself was only half-full so far. I knew, from previous experience here, people would be packed like sardines within a few hours, closer to when the headlining act went on. For the opener, this was still a decent crowd.

Instead of someone appearing behind the DJ table, however, a guy walked out to the front of the stage with a guitar.

"You're welcome, brother!" Eric called over the noise.

"You know this guy?" I asked.

"His name's Gavin Powell," Ethan explained.

"I think he's part of the reason why I got these tickets." Eric grinned. "A gift for yourself too?"

Ethan shrugged. "I said you could invite anyone."

"What kind of music does he play?" Lauren asked.

"He's a little funky."

"A little?" Eric challenged.

"Okay, he's all funk." Ethan pointed at his brother. "But you have to admit his stuff's good."

"The electronic fusion stuff, sure. But the rest is a little too old-school for me."

"What's wrong with old-school?" I asked.

"Shit, I forgot I was sitting in a balcony with two music nerds."

Ethan and I exchanged a smile. He wasn't wrong about that.

The building crescendo of the intro music cut out suddenly, and a single spotlight fell on the man on stage. The audience's cheers faded into a low murmur as we all waited to see what would happen. From our vantage point on the balcony, I was able to notice the loop pedal by his feet.

One dramatic pause later, he struck the first chord. I'd expected the backing production to come back, but instead one note followed the other until I realized he was playing an instrumental cover of "Fantasy" by Earth, Wind & Fire.

When the first chorus ended, the venue went quiet again. Then, the lights flared, the full stage production turned on, and Gavin went into his first full track, accompanied by the cheers of the crowd below us.

I watched as they danced, some with their hands in the air, vibing among the bright disco-era colors that perfectly matched Gavin's sound. Here was that electronic fusion Eric had mentioned, and while I'd been skeptical, this worked. It more than worked.

Lauren was on her feet in an instant, pulling Eric with her. He wiggled suggestive brows at Ethan and I as he took up a spot behind her and they began to sway to the music.

"I'm sorry about him," Ethan called over the music. Even though he was practically shouting, there was no chance anyone but me heard.

I shrugged. "If I got upset over every display of misogyny I witnessed, I'd be a very unhappy person. Besides,"—I nudged Ethan's side with mine—"he's the loud one, remember? This is to be expected."

I couldn't hear it over the music, but I knew a chuckle accompanied Ethan's smile from the crow's feet that appeared by his eyes. The lights flashed into our balcony, adding their colorful glow to the shine already created by his happiness.

My whiskey sour was in my hand in an instant, the straw between my lips, and I sucked in a long drink. Anything to get my attention away from Ethan in that moment. It was times like these when I lost control—where I let the more impulsive part of my brain win out over the rational one. The one that wanted me to climb into his lap and kiss him until we were breathless. That couldn't happen here. Especially not in front of his brother.

Sex with Ethan was… hell, it was some of the best sex of my life. Probably *the* best sex of my life. The man had only continued to impress me with his ability to get me off—and I happily returned the favor. I'd come to love those noises he made when my lips were wrapped around him, when I placed a trail of kisses down his body, when he was inside of me.

He hadn't said anything in regards to exclusivity yet—not that I was seeing anyone else. I doubted he was either. There was no way he'd be able to keep that from me, but I didn't think I'd care if he was. No labels meant no constraints. If I was in his bed one weekend and another girl was the next, so be it.

I wasn't exactly sure when he'd be able to find that other girl, though. With all this Mellow Cat revitalization going on, I'd inadvertently monopolized his time over the last month.

"So whatcha think?" he asked.

I set my drink down and shrugged. "He's not bad."

"Oh, c'mon." Ethan's hand found my knee and squeezed. "Admit it—someone might have better taste in music than you."

A huffed laugh escaped me. "Those are fighting words, Morimoto."

"I'm ready to battle to the death, Hansley," he retorted. "Just to hear you admit you might actually like some of the musicians I'm showing you."

"For the record," I said, holding up a finger, "my *job* introduced me to Stray Land."

"Yeah, but Stray Land introduced you to me, which I'd say

is *significantly* better than any singer.”

“I’m taking back what I said. You’re the loud one, Eric is once again the handsome one.”

Ethan put his hand over his heart, feigning hurt. “You wound me.”

I might have responded if my purse hadn’t started vibrating. Normally, I would have ignored it, but seeing as it was ten at night on a Saturday, there was a good chance it was Nia.

The name at the top of the screen was three letters, but it wasn’t my best friend.

*Mom.*

Shit.

“Um, can you excuse me?” I asked, more to be polite than because I wanted permission.

Of course, he didn’t object. He nodded, the joy that had just radiated on his face replaced by worry.

Before he could ask any questions, I dipped out of the balcony and brought my phone to my ear.

“Mom?” I asked by way of greeting. I hadn’t heard from her since the last money transfer had gone through. Not that I’d expected to have a loving mother-daughter conversation after that, but a *thank you* would have been nice.

“Hi, honey! I—wait, are you out right now?”

I plugged my other ear with my index finger. “I’m at a show.”

"Are you working? I'm so sorry, sweetie! But this should be quick!"

I glanced back over my shoulder. Eric and Lauren, as far as I could tell, hadn't even noticed I'd left. Ethan, on the other hand, wasn't even facing the concert anymore, his attention set wholly on me.

"What's up?" I asked and walked further away from the balcony entrance. Ethan's stare burned into my back.

"Your dad and I are in Denver right now and our regular friend raised his prices."

I shut my eyes and exhaled out my nose. "How much?"

"Only thirty dollars, but we only planned for the old price."

"Can't you just—I don't know. Ask him if you can pay him later? Or go to a store?"

"It's not as good in a store, and you know how these guys are, baby girl." No. I very much did *not* know how these guys were. "He needs it all upfront."

Fuck. Me.

I glanced back over my shoulder again. Ethan was talking with Eric and Lauren now, all three of them casting not-so-inconspicuous looks my way.

"Fine. But I can't until I'm done here."

"That's fine, baby! We can get it to him in the morning! You go have fun, and keep working hard!"

Yeah, *keep working hard,* not so I could build a successful career, but so I could fuel their lifestyle while they were between dead-end jobs.

"Will do," I said. "Bye."

"Love yo—"

I ended the call before she could finish.

× × ×

"EVERYTHING OKAY?" ETHAN asked as I took my seat in the balcony again.

My eyes lifted to Eric and Lauren. They were doing a mighty fine job of pretending they weren't listening, but their lack of smiles and tense dancing said otherwise.

"Yeah," I replied, my attention falling back on Ethan. I tried my best to offer him a smile. "All's good."

"Did I see that was your mom calling?" The same worry he'd worn before had returned. "Is your family alright?"

"Why wouldn't they be alright?"

My voice was harsher than I'd intended it to be, and Ethan reared back.

"You don't talk about your family a lot," he said, his voice as quiet as it could be with the set still going in the background. "I didn't know if someone was sick or something."

I shook my head. "No. She just… she had a question. No big deal, though."

It was impossible to miss the tension in his jaw. Ethan

wanted to ask more—I knew he did—but he was too polite to press. I'd probably receive some form of follow-up later, but for now, I appreciated the end of the conversation.

I was well and truly distracted now, though, and try as I might to turn on the positivity again, I struggled. The same pessimistic cloud that showed up every time Mom or Dad—usually Mom—contacted me wouldn't go away.

A hand appeared in my line of sight. I followed it all the way up until I found Ethan smiling at me. It wasn't the same as before. My bad mood had dampened his night too. But he was trying.

"What?" I asked.

"Let's dance."

"You remember karaoke?" When he nodded, I continued. "My dancing is about as good as my singing."

"Great, we're even then," he said.

He flipped his hand over again, palm up and expectant.

I smiled—as well as I could anyway—and accepted.

"First one to step on the other person's feet buys the next round," I said and allowed him to pull me out of my seat.

We maneuvered our way around the center table of the balcony until we were standing beside Eric and Lauren. I couldn't help but laugh when Ethan guided me through a slow spin then grabbed hold of my other hand. His hips swayed from side to side and our arms rotated like bike pedals. There was absolutely no fluidity to be found.

Oh my gosh, he was an absolutely *awful* dancer.

I loved it.

"Come here, you dork," I said through a laugh and used our clasped hands to tug him towards me.

I guided his hold onto my hips and began to sway with not very much more rhythm but a lot more elegance. My arms snaked around his neck, holding him close. With the tight quarters of the balcony there wasn't much more we could do, but it was probably for the better. I had a feeling our toes would be stepped on a lot if we tried to get more complicated. The spin was enough for us.

Ethan leaned in, his forehead against mine as he mouthed the words to the song. The groove was infectious, running through me in a way that made me forget all my worries. It helped that I had my dance partner who, try as he might, never could quite get the hang of the more complicated moves he tried.

We cheered him on, though—Eric, Lauren, and I. When he let down his walls, Ethan could put a smile on anyone's face.

Lauren and I doubled over in laughter when the brothers moved to the front of the balcony and started to perform something like a hybrid Macarena-Cha-Cha-Slide. It seemed rhythm didn't run in the Morimoto line at all. At least not when it came to dancing. For other activities…

I knew it wasn't the rising heat of the venue that colored

my cheeks, and when I peeked at Ethan to see if he'd noticed, he was watching me.

I realized I liked his lips too—especially as they were then, stretched in a wide, unguarded smile.

He extended his hand to me again, and this time, I took it without any hesitation, letting him serenade me in his off-tune way. Letting him put his hand on my lower back and pull me close. Even letting him kiss me, right there in front of his brother.

Butterflies formed in my stomach as soon as our lips met, and I knew it wasn't the result of lust.

It was another four-letter word that needed to remain caged.

# Chapter 20



*ETHAN*

IF THERE WAS one thing I'd learned from going out with my brother it was that no matter how confident I was feeling, shots were never the answer.

The pieces of paper in front of me were a blur. I didn't know if that was the result of my pounding headache or simply going cross-eyed from staring at them for so long. The information wasn't complicated. No—I'd put aside the spreadsheets for the time being, knowing I could go to those when I didn't feel like there was a herd of elephants stampeding on my brain.

I groaned and sat back in my chair. It was only the afternoon, so things were still relatively quiet downstairs. On occasion, a pot or pan clanked a little too loud, a server and cook shouted at each other, but overall, the noise was short-lived. Nothing like it would be tonight when Holden made his triumphant return.

There'd been no begging required for that one. Turns out, when a large enough crowd comes in, the artist sees it as beneficial for their image. There were a few details I'd worked out with Cal—basic rider requests, or so that's what Heather had told me they were when I'd asked if it was normal—but after that, Holden was officially on board. After this show, he'd come in one Saturday a month.

Even though it hadn't been my cup of tea, the requests for another spoken word night had come through on social media too. Apparently, people liked the change of scenery from the usual dives or bookstores that often hosted them.

In combination with our existing repeat acts, as well as the few that Heather had texted me contact information for—she was a wonderful solo scout when she was on assignment—I had weekends, and then some, filled through the summer.

It was the *and then some* that worried me, though.

My attention went back to the calendar and list of acts laid out on my desk. I was trying to cross this off the to-do list sooner rather than later. Jerry's mild hissy fit had stuck with me, unfortunately. I'd meant what I'd told him—this was my place and I'd run it the way I wanted to. That didn't mean I couldn't keep my website updated, though. Even if it was becoming harder and harder to maintain with all the new acts coming into the mix.

Now, I wasn't sure if the headache was hangover- or stress-induced.

Instead of reaching into my drawer to get some ibuprofen, I decided the better relief was checking if I was suffering alone.

How many shots did Eric convince us to take again? I texted Heather.

I didn't even have time to lock my phone before her reply came through.

I lost count at four ☺

That explained a lot.

Remind me to never listen to my brother again

I don't think Eric was the problem… ;)

What does that mean?

Instead of the teasing three dots, letting me know Heather was working on her response, her name lit up at the top of my phone.

"Do you seriously not remember?" she asked when I picked up her call. Humor touched her words, and I could imagine her face perfectly.

"Apparently not," I said. I leaned back in my chair and kicked my feet up on my desk. It was the closest I could get the desired horizontal position.

"Oh-ho-ho," she laughed. Muffled movements, like she was shifting positions, came from the other end of the line. "You, my friend, are a *blast* when your preferred drink for the night is tequila shots."

"What does that mean for the times that's *not* my preferred drink?"

"You're still a blast, but just in a way that involves less bad twerking."

"Oh *no*," I groaned. My hand went up to cover my eyes as I tried desperately to remember what Heather was talking about. "Please tell me you're fucking with me."

Heather's mischievous chuckle came from the other line, then two seconds later my phone vibrated. I pulled it away from my ear to see she'd sent me a text. Nope—worse. It was a video where I stood at the front of the balcony, my hands on the front wall. Multi-color lights from the electronic set happening in the background flashed, the kick-drum and deep bass combo almost drowning out Heather's—and it sounded like Lauren's—laughter.

Not even the shakiness of the video could hide how horribly I was dancing. I didn't even know if I could classify it as twerking. It was more like jumping with my ass out.

"Delete that," I said through a laugh. "*Immediately.*"

"Are you kidding? I'm texting you that video at *least* once a week from here on out."

"I'm never drinking tequila again."

"Famous last words, my friend."

The idea of any sort of alcohol made my stomach churn, but I didn't think that was the entire reason for the unease.

Heather and I texted every day. We usually saw each other three times a week—if not more. We were sleeping together. Last night… the dancing and stolen kisses had been the closest thing to PDA she'd allowed, but it had happened. Multiple times.

Yet, there that word was again.

*Friend.*

I wasn't stupid. I knew that was just how she spoke. But in the same breath, I'd thought with everything else going on between us, maybe she was finally starting to see me the same way I saw her.

"Does that mean you aren't suffering today?" I asked, trying to stay as nonchalant as possible.

"I'm not leaving my bed today if I don't have to."

"Lucky you."

"I take it you're out and about?"

"I'm at the restaurant." I sighed as I rested my elbow on my desk and put my cheek in my palm. "Had to work on a few things."

She was quiet for a little too long before she finally said, her voice hushed, sultry, "If you get bored you can come join me."

I would have been lying if I said the desire to leave the restaurant, hop in my car, and go over to her hadn't overwhelmed me at the invitation.

Still, that word lingered in the back of my head, taunting me.

"Maybe later," I said. "I need to get this done."

"Whatcha working on?" She didn't miss a beat. If she was disappointed in my semi-decline of her invitation, she wasn't showing it at all.

"I, um, just wanted to get the schedule nailed down so I could update the website."

"Lots of new acts to add in."

"Yeah, and it's a pain in the ass." I sighed and my lips trilled. "Who would have thought this would be a problem for me?"

"I did." I swore I caught a hint of irritation in her voice. "I knew this would be a success."

"Because it was your idea?" I teased.

"Kinda," she admitted, and I chuckled. "But I wouldn't have suggested it to anyone I didn't think could pull it off." Heather was quiet again, then, "You deserve all the success and more, Ethan. I'm really proud of you."

I'd been rendered speechless. No one—except maybe Dad and Kai; Eric, too, if I counted his well-intentioned backhanded compliments—had said anything like that to me before.

Apparently, I stayed quiet for too long because Heather continued. "So what's the issue with the schedule?"

"It won't fit."

"That's what she said."

"You're a child."

Heather snickered. "What won't fit?"

"Everyone who performs here," I clarified. "There's the regulars, most of whom you've seen by now. Then there's the new acts, but I'm struggling the most with the artists who don't come in as frequently."

"Why?"

"They depend on me, you know? They don't perform a whole lot, which makes it hard to establish relationships with the restaurants and bars that seek out live acts. Most of the places around here will go with their tried-and-true, but I like to give these people a place they can count on. Everyone has to start somewhere, and some people simply don't have the time to commit to performing full-time."

"That's really nice of you to think of all that."

"Yeah, but that means if I keep them on the schedule, I have to clear up other spots in some way."

"Could you open up weeknights?"

I shrugged, then remembered she couldn't see it. "A lot of them work. And if they don't, members of their band do. I tried the weeknight thing when I first opened, and it crashed and burned."

"Hmmm…" The same ruffling as before came from the other end of the line. She was getting in a thinking position. Even without seeing her, I could imagine the crease in her brow, the set determination in her eyes. "Sounds like you're in a pickle."

"That's putting it mildly."

"Have any back-up plan ideas?"

"Only one," I said, hesitant to even voice it aloud.

Now I'd opened the door. There was no way I'd get out of this without further explanation. Proving my point, Heather pressed, "*And?*"

"It will make you take back that compliment you just paid me."

"Why?"

"I might need to make some cuts."

"Oh." Clearly, she hadn't expected that. "Who are you thinking?"

"I have no idea."

I stared down at the list again. At the names I'd crossed off and re-written so many times in an attempt to make them all fit in the little squares of the calendar I'd printed out. Just when I'd thought I'd gotten it, I ran into a schedule conflict or double-booking. Not that the latter was awful, but all these people expected to be headliners. Telling them they'd been demoted wouldn't go over well.

Not that firing them would either. At least if they were fired, though, I wouldn't have to deal with the consequences in person.

"If you were to pick one person that you've seen," I asked, "who would it be?"

"To take off the schedule?"

"Yes."

Heather was quiet for a second. No matter how brutally honest she could be, I knew this was different. Maybe it had been a bit unfair of me to ask, now that I thought of it. The last thing I knew she wanted was for any musician to lose out on a chance to perform—to live out their dream.

So it was with some clear hesitance that she said, "I can sleep on my couch for free."

Deep down, I'd known that had been coming. Now that Chroma Groove Project had updated their setlist, there was only one regular act she held that opinion for. I hated to admit that was the direction I'd been leaning too.

I ran my hand down my face. "Got it. Thanks."

"No problem." Her sadness was evident, but still she went on, "The offer still stands. You know, if you aren't doing anything after you finish the schedule. Want some company, or whatever."

"I don't think I'd be a whole lot of fun today," I admitted, hoping she got my message without me needing to voice it explicitly. Foul mood aside, I'd hardly been able to walk up the stairs to the office without feeling like I could puke. Having sex was out of the question at the moment.

"That's okay," she said and sounded like she meant it. "We could just chill. Watch some TV. Maybe an anime?"

My lips curled in a slow grin. "Heather Hansley," I said. "Did you *like* watching anime?"

"Ope—sounds like Nia's calling for me. I have to go."

I chuckled. "I'll talk to you later."

The call ended, and I stared down at my phone.

The next time I picked it back up, the conversation wouldn't be nearly as fun.

✕ ✕ ✕

"YOU'RE *WHAT?*"

I grimaced, my eyes shut as I registered the anger I very much deserved to receive.

"I'm sorry, Leo, but our schedule is booked."

"I'm a standard slot," he argued. "Have been for the last year and a half. You're telling me after all that, I'm just done?"

How in the hell did people do this all the time? Downsizing the staff had been one thing. I'd called around to some other restaurants, made sure they were hiring and offered recommendations before I'd laid anyone off before.

This? This was different. Other clubs in the area already had their acts. Besides, Leo had made a name for himself in more than one way in this scene. Being labeled as difficult to work with wouldn't make it easy for him to find somewhere else to go.

I was kicking him out on the metaphorical streets.

"I'm sorry, Leo. I want to be saying this as little as you want to be hearing it. But the numbers show—"

"Fuck the numbers." I closed my eyes again. Deep breaths. "This is about talent. The people who know it will show up. They always do."

"Then wherever you end up, you'll have an audience," I said. "As a business owner, my numbers show that wasn't happening at Mellow Cat."

"Bullshit," Leo spat. "It's those new kids you're bringing in. You moved me around for one of them, didn't you? Now you're kicking me off the schedule for them too?"

I rubbed my temple. This was going about as well as I'd thought it would. "Leo, we can go around in circles about this until we're blue in the face. But at the end of the day, I don't believe you and Mellow Cat are a good fit."

Each word was a struggle, all of them an outright lie. Well, not all of them. After repeatedly going over the spreadsheets—hangover be damned—trying to find anything that might make me change my mind, there was nothing. If Heather's words hadn't solidified it, the revenue numbers from the nights Leo was on the schedule did.

But Leo fit. He was *exactly* what I'd wanted in an act when I'd first started Mellow Cat. Cool, old-school, knew how to craft an entertaining setlist.

Apparently, not everyone agreed with me.

*I can sleep on my couch for free.*

"You're gonna regret this," Leo said. "One of these days, those kids will flake on you and you'll come crawling back but oh-ho-ho—I'm not coming back. You're never gonna see me at your joint again."

"I understand," I replied, and I meant it. I wouldn't want to see me either.

With one more *fuck you* for good measure, the line went dead.

# Chapter 21

♫ Changes | David Bowie



"WOULD YOU LOOK who it is!"

Tonight's act was loud enough that when Eric came through the doors, he wasn't met with quite as much distaste. He did, however, earn mine and Heather's attention pretty immediately.

"The tequila shot champion of Chicago!" he greeted her. I watched unabashedly as she turned in her bar chair and they embraced. It was nice to see Heather smiling so broadly at someone so important to me. I supposed one crazy night out could make friends of even the most unlikely pairs.

"Brother," Eric continued, reaching across the bar to give me knuckles.

Kai and Dad trailed him, like always. As much as I enjoyed

watching Heather and Eric, seeing her greet Dad with the same, if not more, enthusiasm made me smile. He appeared equally as happy to see her.

"You never leave!" he teased her.

"Only on the weekends," she said, even though that was a little bit of a white lie. She'd been coming in on the weekdays too sometimes. When I'd asked why, she gave some noncommittal answer about craving her favorite cocktail. Seeing as she hadn't ordered a cocktail since her first visit to Mellow Cat, I'd been quick to internally call bullshit. Outwardly, I played along.

I knew it was really because she was concerned about me. Firing Leo had taken its toll, to say the least. Looking at that stage and knowing he'd never play on it again stung. I believed every word he'd said to me over the phone. Even if I changed my mind one day, Leo would never return to this restaurant. That, I was sure of.

"Are you still working on that editorial series?" Kai asked. He took up the seat a few down from Heather, leaving the seat directly beside her for Dad. Eric—who'd already made himself right at home and taken a beer from the fridge— stood beside me at the end of the bar.

"Yes and no," Heather replied. "I'm still doing the write-ups, but tonight I'm here for entertainment." She nodded toward the stage. "I covered this one a few weeks ago at a different show. Now I'm just here as a fan."

"Covered at a…" I saw the cogs working in my youngest brother's head. "Wait, is this woman *famous*?"

"Up-and-coming," Heather corrected with a shrug.

"And you got her to perform here?"

"No shit Heather did this," Eric said. "You think Ethan could score an act this fun?"

I rolled my eyes and when they settled, they landed on the woman on stage. In Eric's defense, this was way more his scene than any of the usual performers playing during his visits. A soft 808-beat embellished with a groovy guitar chord progression and some maracas came through the speakers at the front of the room while Evie Beats did her thing on the soundboard.

"She has the same name as a Pokémon," Heather had told me when she presented the option. "Isn't that fun?"

Her excitement over that, alone, had been enough for me to accept Evie as Mellow Cat's next new act, winning out over any apprehensions. Holden and poets were one thing. An electronic artist was another. In fact, given our last encounter with that particular genre of music, I'd been surprised Heather had even brought it up.

Now, though, as Evie continued to progress through her set, I found it hard not to bob my head along to the beat. It was rhythmic, smooth. Nothing at all like the blaring bass and shrill screeches from the MYTHIC concert.

It was clear the people in the audience felt the same way.

Even those engaged in private conversations were bobbing along or tapping their feet.

Once again, Heather had struck gold.

"What do you think?" I asked Kai, ignoring Eric's comment altogether.

"I like it," he said. "Reminds me of the music I listen to while I study."

"Dad?"

Kai nudged him to bring his attention away from the stage. Unlike the rest of us, there wasn't that hint of a smile curling his lips. No—Dad was analyzing.

"Where are the trumpets?" he asked. "The band?"

"Chroma Groove won't be playing until next week," I said, then cast each of my brothers a nervous glance. Kai shrugged and Eric took a convenient sip of his beer. "I updated my website. The whole list of acts is on there until July."

As soon as I said it, my gaze slid down the length of the bar. Jerry had only been back once since I'd put the full schedule out there, on a night Carla performed.

"I didn't check," was all dad said before he turned back to the stage, his brow furrowed and jaw tense.

I regarded him for a second before I addressed Kai. "Midterms go okay?"

"Straight A's except for one class."

"Hell yeah, man!" I said and reached across the bar to give him a high five.

"Still proving you're the smart one," Heather added.

"You're still on about that?" Eric asked with a smile.

"Oh yeah." She pointed her thumb at me. "Ethan's title has changed *at least* six times."

"Care to share what he's been awarded?"

Heather shook her head, and through gritted teeth said, "Not with your dad present."

Eric threw his head back and laughed, while Kai's mouth dropped open. I narrowed my eyes at her, smirking, only to be met with one in return. Heather lifted her glass and saluted me before she took a sip.

"She didn't even need the tequila shots to go there!" Eric said.

"Is that a reference to the concert I wasn't invited to?" Kai asked.

"Ethan got me the tickets, and I knew Lauren would want another female in the mix. Sorry for thinking rationally."

"Didn't you have midterms to study for anyway?" I asked and Kai shrugged. Guilt-tripper.

"How is Lauren, by the way?" Heather added. Mischief danced in her eyes. I'd warned her about Eric's dating habits, so I knew she already knew the answer.

And sure enough, my brother gave a nonchalant shrug and said, "Didn't work out."

Translated, that meant they'd slept together that night then had spoken for one or two days, max, after that before he called it off. But again, Dad was present. We couldn't go into too much detail. Much like every woman he met was in love with him, every woman we met was also in love with us. It ran in the Morimoto genes, apparently.

I hadn't introduced a girl to my family in years for just that reason. The second Dad got a whiff of any sort of romantic relationship, he assumed marriage was the only logical next step. Back in my early twenties, I'd thought he was nuts. But now, as I got closer and closer to thirty, he had reason to want to see his eldest son settle down, I supposed. Eric wasn't doing that anytime soon, and even Dad probably knew that. Kai was still in school, and therefore wasn't focusing on romance. I was his only reasonable hope for grandchildren at the moment.

Surprisingly, he'd said nothing about Heather yet. Maybe he actually thought this was strictly business. She was here to write her reviews, bring in some new acts from time to time, and nothing more.

My brothers weren't as naïve though. Now, their claims from the first night they'd met Heather were actually true, and Eric had seen more than a few indications we'd crossed from friends to something more—in my eyes, at least. Heather still remained extremely impassive to the whole… situationship we'd gotten ourselves into.

If it was anyone else I'd gotten tangled up with, I might have gotten myself out of it entirely by now. Unfortunately, however, I was wrapped around Heather's pretty little finger. And regardless of everything else going on, I wasn't sure I wanted to be unwrapped quite yet. A part of me feared the void that would overcome me if that ever happened. Even after only a few months, I couldn't remember a time where Heather didn't exist in my life.

"That's too bad," Heather replied, pouting. "She was super… bubbly."

"Nice save," I muttered.

"Okay, so we can all agree Lauren wasn't forever," Eric defended. "But she was good to have around for a night, wasn't she?"

"I think only you can really answer that one, buddy," Heather replied.

"What about you?" Eric shot back. "Everything go alright the rest of the night?"

Heather's brow scrunched. "What do you mean?"

"You seemed sad there for a little bit. Everything—*ow*."

Maybe I'd been a little heavy-elbowed, but it had succeeded in shutting Eric up, just like I'd intended.

I hadn't asked Heather anything more about what had happened that night between her and her mom, but given her reaction now, that was probably for the better. There hadn't been a good time to ask, really, even though I'd wanted to on more than a few occasions. But what right did I have, barging into her personal life like that? We'd been pretty open with each other so far, so her not telling me this said enough.

It was a bridge that I wasn't allowed to cross. Not yet.

Maybe not ever.

I dismissed that thought as soon as it came.

By the time I looked at her again, Heather had already composed herself, the picture of casual ease she always was.

"It was nothing," she said. "Just a call I wasn't expecting."

Thankfully, Dad saved us from whatever follow-up questions might have been asked when he turned around in his chair.

"The band won't come on after this?" he asked.

All four of us twenty-somethings exchanged a collective glance. Then, Heather picked up her drink, downed the rest of it, and looped her arm through Kai's.

"C'mon," she said. "Eric, let's show Kai all the moves we practiced at the concert."

"Go," I encouraged softly when my brother shot me a sideways glance.

Eric took another swig of his beer for good measure, then clapped a hand on my back before he joined Heather and Kai. She gave me a soft smile before she led them away.

I took the seat she'd vacated next to Dad.

"I can let you know when your favorite bands are coming, *chichi*," I said. "That way you won't make the drive over here to see people you don't like."

"I'm happy to support my son, no matter what he does,"

Dad replied. He grabbed my hands on the bar top. "And look—your brothers like it."

He was right. After only a few minutes, Eric, Kai, and Heather were already dancing. In classic Eric fashion, he was treating it like a rave with his fist pounding in the air while the sparse crowd around him took subtle steps back. Kai and Heather, on the other hand, were engaged in a dancing lesson where she was holding his wrists and guiding him in time with the music.

I didn't know what she'd been talking about being a bad dancer for. I'd thought she'd been great at the concert, and she was great now. Every time she doubted herself, she'd only proven how absolutely incredible she could be.

"But *you* don't like it," I said matter-of-factly.

Jerry could say what he wanted. Leo could cuss me out for all eternity. But the idea of Dad not being happy when he came to Mellow Cat was the breaking point.

But instead of confirming my fears, he said, "I don't understand is all. You worked so hard with your jazz. Why change it now?"

This was it—the perfect opening to admit to Dad how much I'd been struggling over the last year to keep this place afloat. He'd understand. Surely, he would. He'd just told me he'd support me no matter what, so why couldn't I just admit my failure. Even now with these changes, I still wasn't sure it would be enough to keep Mellow Cat's doors open. The variety of music was helping but…

I glanced at the empty barstool Jerry usually occupied. At the stage Leo used to play.

"It's something I wanted to try out," I said. "See if it resonates with people."

Dad nodded slowly. "It's resonating with your brothers," he said. Then he smirked. "It's also resonating with a pretty girl."

"Dad, don't start. Heather's not in love with you. Besides, she's, like, thirty years younger than—"

"Ach!" he spat and slapped the back of my hand. "I'm not talking about me. I'm talking about *you*."

"She's not in love with me."

Even as I said it, I had a hard time believing it. Something ran in the Morimoto genes, but it wasn't Dad's delusions. I was beginning to think it was hopeless romanticism. It was the reason why I fell so hard and fast. Why I'd sworn off relationships until I could get my shit together with Mellow Cat. I'd been searching for love my whole life—one like my parents' where even after one half of the partnership was gone, it never faded.

I'd thought I'd found love in my business, but if recent years were any indication, I'd been terribly wrong. That love had started fading as soon as my stress got too intense. It had only begun to be revitalized a few months ago when…

Holy shit.

I sat back in my stool and pulled my hands back to tuck them in my lap. Dad watched me like I was crazy, but my attention was focused elsewhere. On the dancefloor where my two brothers danced carefree with a girl whose personality was as fiery as her hair.

The girl I was in love with.

# Chapter 22

*HEATHER*

"NI, HAVE YOU seen my green sweater?" I called as I dug through our dryer. I really needed to be better about getting my shit out of there. Half of it wasn't even mine at this point.

"No!" my roommate called back. "Have you checked the dryer?"

I groaned into the bottomless abyss of a machine before I slammed the front-load door shut. Any normal person in Chicago would have been grateful for in-unit laundry. I was beginning to rue the day I'd ever decided to trust that clothes-eating machine.

Fuckity fuck.

I was going to be late. I was going to be *so* late on a night where I absolutely, under no circumstances could afford to be late.

Everything happened so fast that proper planning hadn't been an option—hence the whole missing portion of my outfit. One minute I was at a concert, talking with the headlining band after our pre-show interview. The next, they were asking if they could play at Mellow Cat Kitchen after I'd casually brought it up. For once, I'd had no intentions of scoring a new act for Ethan; he'd been more than preoccupied with the ones we'd already found. But even he knew he couldn't pass on this chance when I'd called him and explained the situation.

So tonight, Waking Fire was scheduled to perform at Mellow Cat Kitchen. A Billboard-charting band.

Between Ethan and I, we'd be a mental health researcher's dream with all the anxiety and what not.

I burst into the bathroom in my bra and a pair of light wash ripped wide-leg jeans. Nia didn't even flinch as she continued drawing on what would be a flawless winged liner.

"It's not in here," she mumbled.

"I think I've given up on the sweater."

She eyed me in the mirror's reflection. "Girl, you know I love a confident moment, but wearing only a bra isn't—"

"I'm going to find a shirt," I said. "First I needed to grab my—"

Shit. I didn't even remember what I'd come in here for.

I sat on the edge of the bathtub and put my head in my

hands.

"Breathe, babe," Nia soothed. She knew better than to actually pause her eyeliner artistry and do something sentimental like give me a hug. I wasn't a touchy-feely person when I was stressed. Anyone who came near me usually ended up in a worse mood after I verbally snapped at them in ways I later regretted. "Everything's gonna be fine. Ethan knows what he's doing."

"You still can't come?" I asked.

"No, my plans with my family still haven't been canceled," she replied. "If we finish dinner early, though, maybe we can stop by?"

"Sure." My response was about as noncommittal as her offer. They were going to some restaurant in the Loop. By the time that finished, the concert would be well on its way, and I couldn't promise there would be room for them to squeeze in. Ethan had hired actual bouncers to make sure no one got in once we hit capacity.

It was all-hands-on-deck, and I was pretty sure I was the only non-employee with guaranteed entry.

"Have you talked to Ethan at all today?"

"Here and there." I shrugged. "I think he's pretty busy prepping the restaurant. They closed at one today just to make sure they could flip the space in time." Nothing like a massive concert with two days' notice to prepare.

"Everything's going to be great." Nia finished her eyeliner

then met my eyes in the mirror's reflection, smiling. "You and Ethan are pros, and your friend from that other venue is going to be there too, right?" I nodded. "See? Nothing to worry about."

Except there was still everything to worry about. Finding the items from the band's rider. Making sure we had enough space for them to perform. Testing all the equipment. Making sure the stage lighting Ethan rented was set up in time. Doing a soundcheck for acoustics in the small space.

The list could have gone on and on and on in my head, but I left it at that and decided finding a shirt should be the main priority. I'd be no help if I continued to panic in my bathroom.

I switched gears and ended up going with a black corset bodysuit instead of the sweater. It matched the vibe of the band better, anyway. And once I stepped back and took a look at myself in my full-length mirror, I couldn't deny that I looked hot. Curl my hair a little, put on some red lipstick… outfit complete.

Damn, I couldn't wait until Ethan saw me in—

My confident smile faded into a straight line.

No. It didn't matter what Ethan thought of this outfit. I mean, had I picked the red lipstick because I knew it was his favorite? Yes—but that was because he was stressed, and I wanted to do something that would make him happy. And had I picked the bodysuit because I knew he'd love how my boobs looked in it? Also yes.

But that shouldn't have mattered. I shouldn't care what Ethan thought about me *in* my outfit. I should only focus on Ethan when it came to taking me *out* of my outfit. That's what this had become, I'd decided. A little friends-with-benefits situation.

Even if not hearing from him practically all day left me feeling a little down.

Or when I knew we had plans I always tried just a little harder to look nice.

Or if I equally shared his worry for tonight because I wanted nothing more than to see him find all the success in the world.

Totally normal friends-with-benefits thoughts.

Maybe the bodysuit was a bad idea. There was still time to change if I started—

"Holy shit, you look so hot."

Nia stood in my door, giving me a full-body once-over. Obviously, I didn't dress like this often, if the one person who probably knew the entire contents of my closet was impressed.

"Yeah?" I ran my hands down the curves of my sides. "Like in an, 'Aw, how cute you tried to dress up' way or an 'I'd totally fuck you' way?"

"The latter," she assured me. "But I'll let Beer Boy have those honors."

Okay, that was good. Maybe I'd thought too much about the outfit.

"You heading out?"

"I think so." With my outfit crisis averted, there wasn't any reason why I couldn't head over to Mellow Cat. "Just have to call a…"

With Nia at home and Ethan M.I.A. for most of the day, I hadn't been paying super close attention to my phone. So when I picked it up from its resting place atop my bed and saw the text from Mom, I was caught off-guard, to say the least.

CAN'T WAIT TO PARTY TONIGHT!!!!

I rolled my eyes. Definitely a wrong number situation. It wouldn't have been the first time she'd selected my name instead of Harry or Hailey or whoever else was in her normal crew.

"You good?"

I looked up from my phone to see Nia watching with a raised brow.

"Yeah," I said. "Yeah, all good." I waved my phone at her. "Just need to call a ride."

I closed out of my messages without bothering to ask Mom what she meant. It wasn't worth my time. There were plenty of other things I needed to worry about.

× × ×

I DIDN'T KNOW a whole lot about fire codes, but I was pretty sure Mellow Cat was at risk of breaking a few of them tonight.

It was absolute *madness*.

Nothing about the current scene was mellow. Lights from the rented stage equipment flashed, illuminating the restaurant in colors beyond the usual warm orange and yellow hues. All the tables had been put away—where, I had no idea—leaving plenty of room for the crowd that had shown up to stand. I felt like a teenager in one of those classic Y2K comedies—the ones that threw parties that turned into absolute ragers and they kept running around trying to protect their parents' favorite vase from breaking. My spot behind the bar allowed me to see most of the restaurant, where I watched over Ethan's décor vigilantly. If duty called, I'd risk the pit to save a lamp or two.

The crowd cheered, hands in the air, bodies pressed together as they shouted out the lyrics to the progressive metal song blaring through the speakers. Having grown up around this sort of music, I was used to the chaos—the sheer energy of the audience, the lingering smell of cigarettes on clothes, the bass drum beats that hit you straight in your heart.

As far as I knew, the amps weren't even at their usual volume. Noise ordinances and such. Still, every stroke of the electric guitar strings, every beat of the drums, every chord of the keyboard rang out loud and clear.

This right here. *This* was the setting that had made me fall in love with music. And for as loud and chaotic as it was, being around it had strangely calmed me down.

I couldn't say the same about anyone else who worked at Mellow Cat.

Liam, Brad, and the newly recruited Garrett rushed around behind the bar, trying to accommodate everyone who stood around it, asking for a drink. Even with his work at Sound Hall, I wasn't sure Liam had ever been hit this hard during a concert. Brad and Garrett—oh, Brad and Garrett. Those poor boys had definitely never seen a crowd like this. Each time I caught sight of their faces, their stress was evident. I was pretty sure there was even some sweat on Brad's forehead.

"Excuse me!" came a shout from the middle of the crowd. "*Excuse me!*"

"Hey, hey, hey!" I called out as I removed myself from my hiding spot and shoved past some burly middle-aged men. "Let her through! She's staff!"

I grabbed Sarah's arm and yanked her the rest of the way to safety when they stepped aside. She instantly fell under my arm, her breathing heavy. I wonder how long she'd been trying to make it past.

"You okay?" I asked.

She nodded, but her face betrayed her. "Have you seen

Ethan?" she asked. "Someone asked if we have earplugs for sale. Are we supposed to have earplugs for sale?"

"How about you go in the back for a second?" I suggested. "No earplugs, but you could use a break. Maybe some water?"

Sarah nodded again, her face still a little dazed, and followed my orders. I watched as the door flapped shut behind her, and not seconds later, it flew open again.

Ethan burst into the front of the restaurant, looking just as dazed as his hostess, but a lot less confused. He was definitely more frazzled—until he found me watching him. The shift from crazed to calm to… something else was almost instantaneous.

"Why hello," I greeted.

He gave me a once-over. Then again. "Holy shit."

Yup. The bodysuit had definitely been the right choice.

I chuckled as he seemed to forget whatever had been worrying him—probably everything—and his hands found my sides. They ran down the curves, where sheer black fabric disappeared into the waistband of my jeans. That's where his thumbs hooked, and I fought the urge to suggest we forget the concert and go have our own fun up in his office.

The effect his touch had on me was absolutely astonishing. But then again, I'd always loved his hands.

"Is this new?" he asked.

"Old, but rarely worn," I replied. "You like?"

His voice went low and sultry and he leaned in, his lips so close to mine as he said, "Yeah, I li—"

We both flinched, just as our lips brushed each other's, when a small sprinkle of something wet hit us.

"Hey," Liam called. "If you're done eye-fucking your girlfriend, we could use some help back here, boss."

He didn't stop moving the whole time he talked, which only further proved his point.

"I'll find you in a bit," Ethan whispered to me, loud enough so I could hear it over the music, before he kissed my forehead and rushed to help his employees.

I, on the other hand, was frozen in my spot.

*Girlfriend?*

No, no, no, no, no. I must not have heard him right because why would Liam be calling me Ethan's girlfriend? We hadn't put a single label on… whatever the hell we were.

No—we were friends with benefits. That was it. Nothing more. Nothing less. Just two people who'd found each other and didn't hate spending time together and talked all the time and gave each other mind-blowing orgasms.

But was that what Ethan was telling people? Probably not the orgasms part, but the rest of it? Why else would Liam have even suggested that if he hadn't heard it from somewhere else first? And there was nowhere else to hear it from except from Ethan.

God, this could *not* be happening. I wasn't ready to have

this discussion. Not tonight, when he was already so stressed from what was possibly the biggest turnout Mellow Cat Kitchen had ever seen. I couldn't fathom sitting him down and telling him that we were in no way, shape, or form in an actual, committed—

"Heather! Honey! Hi!"

I hadn't thought it was possible for my body to hold any more tension, but there it went, proving me wrong.

Whatever panic I'd possessed for the duration of the day was nothing compared to what overcame me when I slowly turned around, and to my horror, found Mom and Dad waving at me from down the bar.

# Chapter 23

♪ Ballroom Blitz | Sweet



MOM'S SMILE WAS exuberant, while Dad stood dutifully beside her, his attention still favoring Brad and the drink that was being prepared. Probably a beer, if their tastes hadn't changed much since the last time I'd seen them, and that had been… three years ago? Maybe four?

That meant I had approximately three minutes, max, to figure out how I wanted to handle this situation.

There was, of course, the easy way out. I could duck into the kitchen and hide in Ethan's office the rest of the night and no one would question me. Being falsely labeled a girlfriend had its perks, I supposed.

Or, there was the choice that I probably had to go with, given both Ethan and Liam kept casting me not-so-subtle glances each time Mom jumped in place and called my name, trying to get my attention.

*Shit.*

I was the perfect combination of my parents, with Mom's hazel eyes and heart-shaped face, Dad's nose and thick hair. Thankfully, I'd started coloring mine in high school, so there was no hint of the natural black anymore. If there had been, it might have been easier for the guys to realize these were my parents.

Ethan hadn't seen so much as a picture—not that there were any recent enough where he'd even recognize *me* in them. We weren't exactly a picture-taking family. That's what happened when you never saw one another.

Which led me to the question that had been screaming in the back of my mind: Why the fuck were they here?

I watched as Dad signed the receipt for his order then handed Mom a brown bottle of cheap beer. She took a swig then grabbed Dad's hand, pulling him through the crowd in my direction.

My heart pounded in my chest, and it no longer had anything to do with the bass drum. Speaking to them over the phone was one thing, but speaking in person…

I stole a glance at Ethan to see if he was still watching, and sure enough, he watched me as he shook whatever cocktail he was making, his biceps rippling with the motion under his black short-sleeve polo.

That could be another option. I could go to him. He would make sure I didn't have to deal with this if I didn't want to. But—no. I couldn't do that either. That was exactly what a girlfriend would do, and I was *not* that.

"Everything okay?" he mouthed. His eyes tracked Mom and Dad as they got closer and closer to where I stood.

I nodded. I was very much not okay, but fake it till you make it, right? I could get through this. My parents were easily distracted. A few minutes and they'd find someone they knew, probably, or want to dance or something that had nothing to do with me.

"My baby!" Mom shouted, breaking through the crowd. It didn't matter that I was behind the bar. She came right up and threw her arms around me in the biggest hug I'd probably ever received. Tentatively, I returned the gesture.

*Play it cool. Don't freak out. Play it cool.*

"Hey there, kiddo!" Dad added before he took her place.

"What are you two doing here?" I definitely sounded way more nervous than excited.

"We just got back from New Orleans last night, and do you know what we saw?"

They both said nothing more, leaving me no option but to play along and ask, "What?"

Dad pointed at the stage. "One of our favorite bands was coming to Chicago!"

"We were so upset when we missed the main show," Mom

said, pouting, her hand on my shoulder. "But then we saw this! A *free* concert!"

"Who can pass up a free show?" Dad added.

Certainly not them. Especially not after going to New Orleans. I was surprised I hadn't heard anything from them about needing money for one thing or another.

"And when we looked up the venue, you'd never believe whose name kept showing up!"

"Oh, I can make a few guesses," I muttered.

"Yours!" Mom said, no longer interested in the same games as before. "All sorts of articles with your name kept popping up, so we thought, let's go! What if our baby girl is at this concert too?"

So, that's how it was. Seeing me only worked when it was convenient for their lifestyle.

Mom wrapped me in her arms again, her cheek pressed against mine. I felt like I was trapped in a straight jacket. When I eyed the other end of the bar sidelong, Ethan and Liam were both watching the scene unfold, leaving the bar duties to Brad and Garrett.

"You did the main show too, we saw," Dad said. "You friends with the band or something?"

"Uh, no—not really."

"How early did you get here to get in?" Mom asked. "We ended up sneaking in through the back once the guy up front told us no more entry. Can you believe that? Who the fuck actually listens to capacity limits?"

"People who are getting paid to pay attention to that?" I suggested. From the corner of my eye, I caught Ethan clap a hand on Liam's shoulder then step around him.

He was coming this way.

No no no no no no—

"Uh," I stuttered. I hadn't paid attention to a lick of whatever Mom and Dad were babbling on about. "You guys shouldn't be behind the bar." They also shouldn't have been here in general, but I was going to let that slide for the sake of keeping the peace. "How about you go out there and enjoy the band and we can catch up later?"

"Will you be able to find us in this crowd?" To her credit, Mom actually looked concerned.

"We found each other here, right?" I said. Ethan was getting too close for comfort. "I'll find you again."

"C'mon, babe," Dad reached for Mom to pull her from behind the bar. "Our girl has to work."

"We're so proud of you, honey!" Mom called over her shoulder as Dad dragged her back into the crowd—just as Ethan finally made it to me.

His hand found my lower back and he ushered me just outside the confines of the bar. People immediately engulfed us, but there was something about being here, rather than in the direct line of sight of every person desperate for another drink, that was oddly intimate. Private. Just two more people in a crowd.

One we shared with my parents.

Ethan leaned down, his mouth right next to my ear as he asked, "You sure everything is okay?"

"Why wouldn't it be?"

"I don't know, you just seem like you've seen a ghost," he replied, then nodded in the direction Mom and Dad had disappeared. "Who were those people?"

I could lie. It would have been so easy, especially when it came to solidifying the line that had slowly been blurring between us. Those people could have been groupies I knew from the concert scene. An old colleague and their partner. Even a distant relative would have sufficed.

But the way he was staring down at me with genuine concern in his eyes made it impossible.

"Those, um, are my parents." It came out like a question—like not even I believed the words coming out of my mouth.

It was clear they'd surprised Ethan, too, given how high his eyebrows had lifted. "Your parents?" he repeated. "Does this have something to do with that call a few weeks ago?"

"No, they—uh—they surprised me."

Ethan's concern morphed into something softer. "That's really sweet."

Was it? "Yeah, sure."

I couldn't even pretend to sound convincing. Every thought that swirled in my head always came back to the same questions: Where were they? What were they doing? When would they leave?

They were lost in the crowd at this point, and with all the people surrounding Ethan and I, there was no chance I could see them, even if I tried. This hadn't been the correct night to wear flat shoes. My five-foot-four ass couldn't see anything over the mega-tall metalheads filling Mellow Cat tonight.

It wasn't that I wanted to interact with them again. If I could avoid that the rest of the night, I'd consider it a blessing. But I knew my parents—the trouble they were capable of causing. Next to when they needed money, their favorite time to call me was when they needed bailing out. Thankfully, my aunt had given Mom a mouthful for that once she found out and the habit had been broken.

Still, those were the kind of people my parents were. The last thing I needed was for them to wreak havoc on the night. And in order to do that, I needed to keep an eye on them the best I could.

"Hey."

I must have zoned out. Ethan's hand rubbed my back in soothing strokes, bringing me back to reality—or at least a reality that was easier to face.

"You know you don't have to work this event, right?" he asked. "You can go be with your parents if you want."

I shook my head. "No, I want to stay back here. It's better

if I keep an eye on them."

"What for?"

"They like to have a good time." That was putting it mildly.

Ethan chuckled. "How bad could they be?"

He didn't know the half of it.

✕ ✕ ✕

MY FINGERS DRUMMED on the bar top, subconsciously following the rhythm of the current song. My other hand supported my head as I leaned forward, my elbow on the counter, my gaze set intently on the crowd.

Ethan stopped by from time to time to make sure I was doing okay. Clearly, he was worried, but it wasn't like I was giving him any reason not to be. This was supposed to be an exciting—albeit stressful—night. After all our work scouting to bring in new acts to Mellow Cat Kitchen, we'd snagged one that had charted internationally. Of course, they'd never come back, but it would be a fun story to tell.

Instead, all that was ruined as I scanned the audience like a hawk, keeping an eye out for Mom's dried out bleached-blonde hair and Dad's spiky salt-and-pepper do.

A whiskey glass slid up under me. When I glanced down the bar, I saw Liam.

"Looked like you could use it," he said, then immediately got back to work with the next customer shouting their drink order.

I hoped he was getting great tips tonight. He more than deserved it. The whole staff did.

"Um, miss? Excuse me, miss—you can't—no, I don't think that's allowed!"

I hadn't so much as taken a sip, letting the burn of the liquor ease my tension for a few seconds, when Sarah's voice cut through the crowd. I tracked a bouncer as he moved from the front door through the sea of people. They'd become rather protective of her, I'd noticed, after the last mishap. Probably because she kept hovering near where the hostess stand would be and had gotten to chatting with them. Bouncers, in my experience, were always pretty terrific guys. Tough exteriors, but hearts of gold on the inside.

It was the tough exterior I was worried about when I realized what Sarah had caught.

Off to the side of the room, Mom stood on a chair, hands in the air. One of the decorative pillars of the restaurant had blocked her, but a simple shift in my position was all it had taken for her to come into full view.

"Play "Sacred Mutilation"!" she shouted at the stage, one hand cupped around her mouth, the other holding her drink in the air.

"Wrong band, lady!" someone in the crowd called back, earning a few chuckles from the people surrounding him.

"Oh, fuck off!"

The guy who'd called her out groaned in disgust when beer showered down on him.

Oh my god.

I downed the rest of my drink in one swift gulp, knowing I'd need the liquid courage for whatever situation I was about to dive head-first into. I didn't even bother seeing if Ethan had noticed what was happening. There was no way he hadn't, but then again with all the chaos at the bar, he might have become too preoccupied.

What was one more woman shouting when there were a sea of people doing the same thing around him?

"Bitch!" the beer-showered guy shouted as he turned on Mom. She didn't seem the least bit worried. In fact, she wasn't even paying attention to the guy anymore as she cheered, both hands in the air.

I pushed my way through the audience, not caring in the slightest as I elbowed past some people who couldn't—or were pretending not to—hear me calling out, "Excuse me! Let me through! I'm event staff! Excuse me!"

"Hey!" He hit the base of the chair, hard enough where I could hear it over the music. "What the fuck was that for?"

I pushed harder when the guy grabbed onto Mom's leg. Oh, hell no. Damaged relationship or not, I didn't put up with assholes touching women so aggressively.

Thankfully, Dad was there to step in where I couldn't. "Watch it, man! That's my wife!"

My attention frantically darted to the bouncer when Dad shoved the guy. He was on them now, guiding a wide-eyed Sarah behind the pillar before he stepped between the two men. I was caught between a woman with too-strong perfume and a Dave Grohl doppelgänger who refused to move.

If the fiery pits of hell opened up right below me, I would have accepted my fate with open arms. Maybe being smote by lightning? Anything would be better than this.

"Break it up, guys. Break it up," the bouncer instructed. He stood between Dad and the guy, one hand on either of their chests trying to keep them separated. Someone in the guy's group held onto his arm too, holding his friend back.

"They started it," he accused, pointing at Mom. "She's the one pouring her drink on me!"

The bouncer turned his attention upward only to find the accused completely oblivious to what was happening on the ground below her. She danced, happy as ever, on her chair.

"Excuse me!" I shouted and elbowed Dave Grohl Jr. in the ribs and shoved past. I'd lost all ability to care about anything other than de-escalating the situation at hand.

"Let's keep everything civil here, alright?" the bouncer said. "Sir, if you'll come with me—"

"No, I'm not leaving without my wife!"

I broke into the little circle that had formed around the chair just as Dad climbed up on top of it to stand with Mom.

I watched with wide-eyed horror as they nearly toppled over sideways, only to find their balance, arms wrapped around one another, and immediately begin singing the song. Well, kind of. Most of the words were mumbled or wrong, but the notes were correct.

"Can you two *please* get down from there?" I pleaded.

"You know them or something?" the bouncer asked.

"They're my parents," I informed him, then hit the back of Dad's leg. "Earth to Dawn and Tim! Time to get the fuck down! *Now!*"

It was a mistake. I should have just let the bouncer continue to handle it because the second Mom and Dad realized it was me calling for them, their excitement increased ten-fold.

"Heather! Baby!" Mom shouted.

"Great show, isn't it, kiddo?" Dad added.

"Yeah, fabulous. Now can you get down? You're causing a scene."

"These people can mind their own fucking business!" Mom said, much to the dislike of the guy she'd showered with beer and the bouncer.

"No, they absolutely cannot. Not when you're acting like a fool." I extended my hand, offering it to either one of them to take. At this point, I didn't care who. All I wanted was for this to be over.

"But, sweetie, we're having a good time! *Wooooo—*"

Turns out they didn't need my hand. My parents got down on their own, at the expense of one of Ethan's dining chairs.

A few people standing nearby shrieked as the sound of splitting wood pierced the air, followed by the loud *boom* of my parents toppling to the ground. Mom lost hold of her beer bottle and it shattered, splattering me and a few others with what had remained of her drink.

Then, the whole room went silent.

My heart dropped to my stomach when I realized the band had stopped playing, and all eyes in the entire restaurant were on us.

My mouth hung agape and my chest rose and fell with heavy breaths as, somehow, through the gathered crowd, I managed to lock eyes with Ethan. He was stone-faced, assessing, behind the bar, but his eyes held the same softness they always did when they were on me.

I looked away, unable to handle his sympathy right now.

Dad groaned as he rolled over on the floor, right into the puddle of Mom's spilled drink. She hadn't moved aside from turning onto her back and putting her hand on her head.

"That's it," the bouncer said, his voice loud and clear for everyone in Mellow Cat to hear. "You two are out."

He grabbed Dad by the collar of his shirt and yanked him up, but I stepped in before he could do the same to Mom.

"I've got them," I said.

"I mean it. I don't care who they are. I don't want them

in—"

"I know. I know. They aren't going to stay," I assured him, and his stern face softened some. "I just—please let me get them out of here myself."

He regarded me for a second before he sighed. "Fine." He shoved Dad in my direction and we both bent down to get Mom off the floor and back on her feet. "But if I see them back in here again, I'm kicking them right back out, and you'll be with them."

"Hey!" Ethan called from behind the bar. "She's done nothing—"

"Ethan, please," I interrupted. One of my arms was looped through Dad's, the other around Mom's shoulders. There was no way I wasn't keeping them in some sort of hold right now, even if they were still dazed from their fall. "Don't worry."

I knew that was asking a lot, especially when I saw his face twisted in a way that told me he wanted to say more. But he was doing his best to respect my wishes.

In the end, he gave me a curt nod. I tried my best to give him an appreciative smile in return before I dragged my parents out the front door.

# Chapter 24

*HEATHER*

"WHAT THE HELL was that?" I seethed.

I shoved Mom and Dad into the alley beside Mellow Cat. The street outside the restaurant had still been packed with eager Waking Fire fans, trying to catch glimpses of the band through the windows at the front of the restaurant. None of them had been too rowdy, but maybe that was because they, too, had seen the incident with my parents unfold. They'd backed away from the windows the second I stormed through the front door, Mom and Dad in tow. Any passerby might have thought I was dragging them to their execution the way we were regarded.

Might as well have been.

"Oh, calm down," Mom said. Her hand was still on her

head. It was also the first time in a long time where she hadn't immediately addressed me with some sort of nickname.

Maybe even she knew there was no point in trying to butter me up now. They were very much in the doghouse.

"Who brings such weak chairs to a metal concert?" Dad added and Mom nodded along.

I, however, was staring at them like they'd each just sprouted a second head.

"Weak? Dad! This is a restaurant!" I shouted. "Where the hell did you even find that chair anyway?"

"Hiding behind a curtain with a bunch of other fancy shit." He shrugged. "If they didn't want us to use it, they should have locked it away."

"That's not how that works. Regardless of where you found it, it was put away, so you don't get to—*ugh*!"

I threw my fists down at my side. Even from where I stood, I could smell the alcohol on their breath. There was no telling what else they were on—if they'd chosen to partake this evening, that was. Trying to reason with them now would be like trying to reason with a toddler.

Mom groaned. She slid down the wall of the alley until she was sitting on the ground, her knees pulled up to her chest.

"That bouncer was *such* a buzzkill," she complained. "So we broke *one* chair. Big deal."

"It *is* a big deal, Mom," I ground out. "This is a small business. It's not meant for big concerts like this. Do you know how much the damage is going to cost Ethan?"

The chair was all I'd seen, but my heart sank at the possibility of other assets that might have become the victim of my parents. It seemed they'd been the only ones at the concert who hadn't gotten the memo that yes—it was a metal concert. But there had been no moshing. No rushing the stage. Certainly no dancing on furniture or spilling drinks on other people. Everyone else had been completely rational and well-behaved.

"Who's Ethan?" Dad asked. "Friend of yours?"

Mom gasped, perking up. "Do you have a boyfriend, baby girl?"

"Don't worry about who Ethan is," I said, ignoring her question. I still hadn't quite gotten over Liam's use of the g-word earlier, but the matter at hand had been a useful distraction. "The point is you two were ridiculous and now you've gotten yourselves kicked out."

I didn't bother bringing up how they shouldn't have even been there in the first place. That was a whole different issue—one that would require me suggesting to Ethan that he get a better security system.

"That?" Dad stared at me incredulously, his thumb pointed back over his shoulder toward the entry to the alley. "Ha! That was nothing."

"Hey, hey, hey," Mom said through a giggle as she swatted Dad's leg. "Do you remember that one time LuLu took all those shots then got called on stage?"

I never heard the punchline of the story. Mom and Dad both broke out into a fit of laughter, only adding little interjections of "And then they," and "And she was," before doubling over again.

I gaped at them, completely dumbfounded, before I found the ability to say, "I can't believe this. You two are ridiculous."

"Oh, honey, it's just another night of fun," Mom said, waving my comment off.

"We'll get that Evan guy a new chair if that's what you're so worried about," Dad added.

"Ethan. His name is Ethan," I corrected. "And this isn't about a *chair*, Dad. It's about how you two acted in there!" I extended my arm, pointing down the alley. "This was a huge night for him—a huge night for *me*! I interviewed that band a few nights ago. What if all this gets back to my boss?" There was no way *someone* wasn't recording in there. The search for "Waking Fire Chicago" would populate with my review, followed by a clip of Mom and Dad collapsing to the floor.

"We know, baby girl! We're so proud of you for your job!" Mom babbled. Then, she lit up, like an actual lightbulb had turned on in her head. "Speaking of, you have a nice apartment, don't you? Think we could crash the night?"

The thought of bringing these two home terrified me. There was no way in hell I was subjecting Nia to them either.

To think, she was out having a perfectly enjoyable dinner with her perfectly normal family, while I was in an alley trying to reprimand my own parents.

"You haven't heard a single word I've said tonight, have you?" I asked, my voice soft. I'd lost my fight. Now, I was simply operating on fumes as I tried, one last time, to get my point across.

"What?" Dad asked as he turned quickly to face me. He stumbled and almost tripped over Mom, and had it not been for the side wall of the building where he caught his balance, he might have still landed on the ground.

Unbelievable. Absolutely unbelievable.

My hand shook as I pulled my phone out of my back pocket and sent Ethan a text. Can you make a call for me?

Mom and Dad had fallen into a fresh fit of laughter when he responded mere seconds later, like he'd been waiting for some sort of update from me. Whatever you need

I gave him the instructions before I put my phone away and simply watched my parents. There was nothing more I could say. They were a lost cause, and the only thing left to do was stand there and make sure they didn't injure themselves.

How had I ever lived in their household, even if it was only intermittently between stays with my aunt? God, I didn't want to have to call her after this. I knew she wouldn't be mad, but how the hell did I explain my decision?

I leaned back against the opposite wall and my face fell into my waiting palms.

"Oh, honey, are you crying?"

I hadn't been, but as soon as I lifted my head, gravity won and tears spilled down my cheeks.

"Oh, honey!" Mom tried to push herself off the ground, but hardly made it a few inches before she slumped back down. I wanted so badly to believe it was the result of her hitting her head when she'd fallen off the chair, but I knew it was a combination of things working against her.

Dad tried next. "C'mere, kiddo," he said, reaching out to me—or trying to. With his aim, there was a chance he was seeing a few of me.

"No." I swatted his hand away and backed flush against the wall of the alley. "You don't get to pick and choose when you get to be actual parents."

"What're you talking about? We're always here for you, sweetie."

"Are you fucking kidding me?" I pushed off the wall, and when I stepped forward, Dad had the good idea to step back. "You two have *never* been there for me. I take care of you more than you've *ever* taken care of me!"

Mom let out a *pft* of air and rolled her eyes. "Name one time."

Oh, the challenge was *more* than accepted.

I held up my hand to begin counting as I listed, "You were

never around when I was a kid. You missed not only my high school graduation, but also my college graduation. I left a voicemail letting you know I got my first job offer and didn't hear back from you for *two weeks*. You didn't bother helping me move to Chicago. I haven't seen you in *years*—should I keep going?"

"That's not fair," Dad accused. "You know we're busy people."

"So busy you can't pay attention to your only kid?" I shot right back. "But, oh wait—never mind! I do hear from you guys every now and then when you need me to fork over some cash. Nothing like making a bank account out of your own offspring instead of actually working. Have *either* of you ever had a job longer than two months? Seriously."

Mom actually pouted. "Now you're just being mean."

"What do you expect me to say? Huh?" I was shouting again, my voice reverberating off the walls of the alley. Each word fought out against the tightness in my throat as more and more tears streamed from my eyes. "Do you want me to act like what we do is *normal*? Like we're a happy family? Because we are so fucking far from that it's insane!"

Flashing blue and red lights filled the alley, illuminating the surprisingly somber faces of my parents. Maybe something I'd said had finally stuck, but I was far beyond caring if it had. I was far beyond caring in general.

"I'm done," I breathed, hardly believing the words were

finally coming out of my mouth. They'd been there for years, but this was the final straw. "I am absolutely, one-hundred-percent done with your bullshit."

"What does that mean?"

"It means you're cut off." I brought my hand up to count again. "No more playing nice. No more money. No more sympathy." The slam of car doors echoed down the alley. "And no more bailing you out."

"Excuse me," one of the two approaching police officers said. "We received a call about disorderly conduct. Was that one of you?"

I'd never seen Mom get to her feet faster, and Dad managed to stop swaying as soon as he realized what was happening.

"That was me," I said. I sniffled and wiped at my nose with the back of my hand. Anything other than turning to face the betrayed looks my parents wore. "Well, it was my friend who made the call for me. Ethan Morimoto?"

The officer who'd spoken first nodded to me, then to his partner.

"Heather," Mom said as one of the officers took her and the other took Dad. "Heather, honey—what is this?"

"I told you." I watched as my parents twitched frantically, their heads turning from the officers to me to one another. It didn't do any good. "I'm done."

✕ ✕ ✕

OFFICER SCHULTZ KEPT me busy with questioning for another thirty minutes. Mom and Dad watched me from the back of the squad car, but I did my best to avoid looking at them—especially when I was questioned why I felt it was necessary to call the police on my parents.

It wasn't unheard of, but all the details were needed, regardless.

Which was why I'd even included trespassing in the report I delivered. That was only after Officer Schultz told me they'd be let out after they were booked. Consider it my last kindness to them: guaranteeing they had a place to sleep for the night—even if it was a jail.

"Thank you," Officer Schultz said, flipping his notepad shut and stuffing his pen back in his front uniform pocket. "You'll likely be called in as a witness for the court hearing, but would you like us to provide you with any other updates in the meantime?"

I turned my head just enough to finally look at my parents in the back of the squad car. Thankfully, this was one of the times they were talking frantically amongst themselves instead of watching me.

My jaw tensed, and I sniffled as I shook my head in response.

He gave me a tight smile and a curt nod of

acknowledgement before he went to join his partner in the car. I didn't watch as the flashing lights turned off and they drove away with Mom and Dad in tow.

The night suddenly felt so quiet. Waking Fire still played inside Mellow Cat Kitchen, and a few members of the crowd had snuck outside to smoke cigarettes—or more likely try to figure out why the cops had showed up. I felt their stares, but I refused to meet them.

I was a fucking mess.

I didn't regret what I'd chosen to do, but still—it didn't make me feel any less numb.

My arms wrapped around my torso, both to shield against the springtime chill and to provide some level of comfort. It was stupid to think it would help either of my problems, but I didn't know what else to do.

The front door of the restaurant creaked open then was shut gently behind whoever had joined the smokers and I outside.

"Heather?"

My name was a caress from Ethan's lips, gentle in a way that told me he didn't want to overstep any boundaries, but also didn't want to stay away completely.

As conflicted as I'd been only a few hours before—less than that, perhaps—I realized now, being away from him was the absolute last thing I wanted at that moment.

I met his eyes just long enough to communicate a silent

message before I walked back into the alley. The soft shuffle of his shoes followed behind me.

Only when I believed we were far enough into the darkness, the only illumination coming from a light by the back door of Mellow Cat, did I stop. Ethan did too.

We stared at each other, and I took in the tension in his body, like he wanted to come to me, but knew better than to do so unwarranted—especially given the night I'd had. I was probably a sight to behold too, with puffy, red eyes that hurt the longer I tried to keep them open and make-up likely running down my face with my tears.

So, I made the choice for us both.

It took me three eager strides to get close enough to Ethan where I could grab his face in my hands and bring his lips to mine. Given the night's events, there was nothing soft about this. I kissed him with a pure hunger that he returned, his arms snaking around my middle to pull me closer as I opened for him.

I sucked his lower lip into my mouth, eliciting a groan from him that made me melt, and his hands found their way to my ass then to my thighs. I hopped up into his hold as my lips found his jaw, his neck, his earlobe. Fuck—I couldn't get enough of him.

My legs tightened around his waist when my back hit the wall of the alley. Even through my jeans I could feel how hard he was for me, and heat pooled in my core.

"Let's leave," I panted, breathless as he took his turn to explore the skin on my neck, my collarbone, my breasts. "Please."

Any other night I might have said *fuck it*. I would have had sex right there in the alley. But I'd just sent my parents away to jail. I wasn't about to join for public indecency charges.

Not to mention I wanted to be as far away as possible from Mellow Cat Kitchen at the moment. I didn't want the crowd. I didn't want the unwanted stares when the daughter of the crazy people reentered the space. I just wanted Ethan.

His head lifted, and for a moment he looked conflicted. The business owner was battling with whoever he became when he was with me. Even through this back wall, the rumbling bass of the current song and the cheers of the crowd could be heard.

My Ethan won, though.

He put his hand on my cheek and stroked it with his thumb. "I'll go get my stuff."

# Chapter 25

*HEATHER*

WE WERE IN his car within ten minutes. Liam had been left in charge of Mellow Cat, seeing as he had the most experience out of the staff with music venues. I got a text from him, expressing his concern and saying he hoped everything was okay, but I didn't answer. There hadn't been time before we arrived at Ethan's apartment, got upstairs, shut the door, and immediately began to tear each other's clothes off.

They laid scattered around the space, a testament to our desire, as we laid quietly in his bed, our skin slick with sweat, trying to catch our breaths.

I stared up at the ceiling, trying to make sense of all that had just happened. Not just with my parents, but with Ethan.

It had been different. The hunger from our alley make-out

session had still been there, but the way he touched me had been the perfect blend of heated but sensual. Like he'd wanted to fuck me like he always did, but something was preventing him from doing it. Something softer, more tender, than just lust.

His hand found mine under the covers and he brought it to his lips, kissing each of my knuckles before he turned and wrapped himself around me. I stiffened as his face burrowed into the crook between my head and shoulder, and he began to kiss the skin there too.

My heartbeat quickened, and it had nothing to do with desire anymore.

"No," I said. He apparently didn't understand I wasn't kidding—he would have stopped immediately if he had—so I shoved him gently with my free hand. "Ethan—fuck. No, I can't do this."

I rolled away, out from under the covers, not caring that I was naked as I began to search for my underwear. I could have sworn he'd taken it off me when we were already on the bed.

Ethan propped himself on his elbows, his eyes tracking me like search lights as I moved around his apartment.

"Do you need me to drive you home?"

The question made me instantly feel like an asshole. We'd come all the way here. I'd been so sure he'd be the answer to my worries the way he always had been all these months.

Now, I was realizing, it had been a mistake. A massive, *massive* mistake.

"No, I just need to go." I swiped my panties off the ground and pulled them on. At least I was a little less exposed now.

"Why the hurry?"

"Because I need to get away from whatever"—I gestured between us—"that was."

Ethan quirked a brow. "Fucking?" he asked.

I huffed a laugh. "I've been fucked a lot of times, Ethan. *That* was not fucking."

"Then what was it?"

I shrugged as I snagged my bodysuit off the floor, not wanting to use the phrase, but he did it for me.

"Love-making?"

I turned on him, an accusatory finger pointed. "Don't," I warned. "Don't call it that."

"Why? Because then you have to admit that's what it was?"

"No," I said, more as a dismissal than as an answer to his question. I shook my head and turned away from him to step into my clothing. "No, I'm not talking about this."

"Why not?"

"I put my parents in the back of a fucking cop car tonight, Ethan! Excuse me for not wanting to talk about my feelings right now."

"You brought it up!"

"No, I got out of bed to *avoid* bringing it up."

"So… what? Are we just going to dance around this even more now?"

"What do you mean 'even more'?"

Ethan shook his head at me as he pulled his briefs on then approached. Aside from when we were hooking up, this was the most heated emotion I'd ever seen from him.

"I *mean*," he said, "that we'll keep ignoring whatever it is that's going on with us."

I busied myself with my re-dressing, unable to meet his eyes, as I mumbled, "Nothing is happening between us."

Ethan stayed quiet long enough that I was forced to look at him. What I found was a man—a beautiful, wonderful man—who looked like he'd just had the air punched out of him.

"Are you serious?" he finally asked on a breath.

I slipped my arms into the straps of my bodysuit and shrugged. "Yeah."

"You mean to tell me you haven't felt *anything* in these last few months?"

If I told him no, I would have been lying, and I couldn't do that. Not when it was so clear my words had already hurt him. So I decided to take the omission of truth route. "We weren't supposed to have the chance to feel anything. We should have gone down the same route I go down with everyone else I meet at a concert."

"And what's that?"

"We text for a few days, pretend to be friends, then never speak again."

"Pretend to…? Do you realize what that sounds like?"

"What? Like *you* always thought this would turn into what it did?" I accused.

"Maybe I didn't at first, but I hoped it would be something after we kept talking—yeah," Ethan admitted, and my traitorous heart actually skipped. "Did you really not want that too?"

It wasn't that I didn't want it. It was that— "It can't happen, Ethan. Whatever you thought, it's not—it's impossible."

"It's not impossible," he argued. "I'm proof that it's not impossible." He pointed at his bed. "What we just did was proof that it's not impossible."

"I said I'm not doing this."

I pushed past him, headed for the front of his apartment in a desperate attempt to find my jeans. They'd been the first thing to go, so they had to be somewhere by the door— which was what I'd be walking out of the moment I was dressed. No energy remained in my body for this conversation. Even if I'd known it was coming sooner or later, tonight was not the night it needed to happen.

He was right—I'd opened the door for it. But I'd hoped so badly he'd let me have this one moment after such a shit night and leave in peace. My head was far from clear, and I knew I wouldn't say everything I wanted to. Or if I did, it would come out wrong. Hell, it already was.

That was only further proof I needed to hurry up and finish getting dressed before—

"Holy shit," he muttered. "This is about your parents, isn't it?" Ethan huffed a laugh, and when I glanced back at him over my shoulder, he wore the expression of someone who couldn't believe he hadn't come to his conclusion sooner. "You're so afraid of being hurt like you were by them that you won't even *try* to let anyone else in."

"That's not true," I said as I finally managed to find my jeans. How they'd made it into the kitchen, I had no idea. "I have friends."

"Who? Nia?" Ethan shrugged. "Liam? I might have even said me, but now I'm not so sure."

"Of course, you're my friend, Ethan." The fact that he was even questioning that pained me. "You think I'd do half the shit I've done in the last few months for someone who *wasn't* my friend?"

"To be honest, Heather, what you've done in the last few months is something I would expect from someone who's *more* than a friend."

He was right again. There were very few people in my life that I'd go through the lengths I'd gone through for Ethan. Even fewer now, given the choices I'd made earlier that evening.

I stepped into my jeans in silence, the sound of the denim sliding against the creaking wood floor the only sounds in the whole apartment.

"I'm going," I announced when I finished buttoning my pants.

"Heather, wait."

Ethan's hand wrapped around my wrist just as I reached for his door. I was still half-turned and ready to escape when I met an expression that I was sure mirrored my own: defeated and near tears. At least for one of us, it would only be the first time that night.

"What do you want, Ethan?" I whispered.

He inhaled, then exhaled deeply. "Tell me I wasn't imagining things," he said. "That I wasn't the only one who thought... who fell."

Oh my god. He'd...

I guess I'd known it for a while now, or at the very least I could have guessed that's where he was headed. But to hear him say it out loud was different than my own silly assumptions I could brush off. Pretend I was imagining things—the same way I'd been doing for my own feelings.

"I'm not going to lie to you, Ethan. That would be unfair. But it's also unfair that you've put me in this position that I've already told you I don't want to discuss."

I'd thought he'd been pained by my earlier words. Nothing—not one thing—would have prepared me for the way he looked at me now.

"So what now?" he murmured.

I forced my attention elsewhere, unable to meet his eyes. Really, I could have left. If I so much as moved my arm, even a little, he would have dropped his hold, and I could have gone home.

Instead, I was frozen in my spot, not quite ready to do that. I knew the answer to his question as well as he did: once I was out that door, the chances of us talking again were unlikely. What I'd thought would happen between us after only a few days was finally going to happen nearly four months later.

And the only thing that could make it worse, was the purple plush I found sitting on the ground by his TV stand.

Gengar stared back at me, its red eyes and menacing grin a damning reminder of the first night I'd come here. Of falling asleep on Ethan's chest. Of the scent of the shirt he'd let me borrow. Of the heat that had overwhelmed me the first time we'd slept together.

If I walked out that door, I'd never experience those things again.

But enduring the pain now would be a hell of a lot easier than enduring it later, after we allowed whatever this was to grow even more.

I forced myself to meet Ethan's hopeful stare one last time.

"I'm sorry," I said.

Then I tugged my arm free and walked out his door without looking back.

# Chapter 26

♪ you were good to me | Jeremy Zucker, Chelsea Cutler



I'D BEEN HEARTBROKEN before. In high school, the guy I'd sworn I'd been in love with, ended things right before he went to college, claiming he couldn't handle distance. Then, a few years later when I was in college myself, the bartender I'd started seeing ended up dating three other people—at the same time.

Oh yeah. I'd definitely been heartbroken.

But the pain had never existed after *I'd* been the one to end things.

So when I woke up the next morning feeling like I'd been hit by a bus—or five—I had no idea what to do.

It wasn't just heartbreak over Ethan, I supposed. The emotional rollercoaster that had been the night as a whole was taking its toll.

The soft buzz of my phone vibrating came from my bedside table, and for a moment, I felt the smallest glimmer of hope. Had Ethan forgiven me? Had he seen my point of view? Was this our chance to carry on as friends?

But instead of his name above the text message, it was Nia's.

let me know when you're up! i wanna hear all about last night!!

I'm up, I texted back and almost immediately it was followed by the sound of her bedroom door opening, the creak of the old apartment floor as she checked if I was in the living room, then a knock on my door.

"Come in," I groaned. My voice was barely there.

Nia followed instructions, a bright smile lighting her face, as she cracked the door open slowly. Once her head peeked in, she asked, "How was the concert?" just like she did every time I had a show.

The normalcy of it, combined with Nia's unsuspecting cheer, almost comforted me. Almost.

"Fine."

"Holy shit—your voice," she said through a laugh, and stepped further into the room. "It was that metal band you saw a few nights ago?" When I nodded, she added, "Were you just absolutely head-banging and screaming?"

"Something like that." More like yelling and wanting to bang my head against the wall, but those were minor semantics.

"Sorry I didn't come say hi when you got home. I figured you were with Ethan. Let me guess." Nia pointed her thumb to the right. "He's hiding in the closet."

I shook my head, and immediately felt the sting of a fresh wave of tears. That's when Nia seemed to really get a good look at me, and her smile fell.

"Oh no…" She came the rest of the way into the room and sat down on the edge of my bed. I propped myself up on my elbows and instantly regretted it. Sorrow could hit harder than a hangover sometimes. "Did something go wrong at the concert?"

I couldn't help the huffed laugh that escaped me. "I think it's easier to ask what went right."

And then I told her everything—about the absolute chaos in the restaurant, about Mom and Dad showing up unannounced, about the broken chair and being kicked out, about the cops and the most amazing sex I'd ever had in all my life, until I finally got to the choice I'd made.

By the time I was done, the tears had spilled over.

"Damn," Nia said on an exhale. She reached onto my nightstand and grabbed a tissue from the box that was there. "That's… a lot."

"I feel like shit," I replied, taking her offering and wiping at my eyes then my nose.

Nia nodded slowly, the joy she'd worn when she entered

the room completely gone. I didn't blame her. I'd just dropped a million bombs in the span of five minutes. If she'd had any sort of immediate response, I would have been shocked.

So, after a few moments of information digestion, she managed, "And Ethan just let you go?"

"Obviously," I said, a little harsher than I'd intended. Nia didn't flinch, though. She knew me well enough to understand I meant no harm. "I slept here."

"Wow."

"What?" I pressed.

She only shrugged. "I don't know. It just seems out of character for him, I guess?"

"Not at all," I disagreed. "He isn't really the combative type."

"No, I guess not." She sighed, almost like she wanted to say more on that topic, but moved onto the next. "Do you have to do anything for your parents?"

"The officer said he would call me if he had any updates, but I made it clear I wanted nothing to do with them." I did still have to call my aunt, though. I'd get to that when I felt like I had just a little more energy. I'd sure as hell need it.

"I had no idea you were doing all that for them."

"How would you? I didn't advertise it."

"No, but I'm your best friend, Heather. I should have been paying more attention."

"No one knows, Ni. Or no one knew, I guess, now that I'm officially cutting them off."

"That's fucking ridiculous." Any sadness that had just accompanied her previous statement had been entirely replaced by anger. "What parents do that to their kid?"

"Mine," I said, rolling my eyes.

"Fucking ridiculous," she repeated.

I made an *oh-well* face then groaned as I laid back down, my energy quota officially hit. Time to recharge—if I even managed to muster up enough energy to make it out of bed. Something told me it would be a doom scroll on social media in between take-out orders kind of day, and I wasn't sure I was mad about it.

Nia's hand found my leg over my duvet. "You want me to get you anything, babe?" she whispered.

"Do you have a time machine?"

She chuckled. "Sorry, no. But I do have some leftover coffee in the pot? I can heat it up and add your favorite flavored creamer?"

A strangled laugh escaped me, and I nodded. "That sounds amazing."

"The sweet cream or hazelnut?"

"Sweet cream, please."

"Okay." She offered me a small smile, but didn't get off the bed. I knew what she was doing. Nia Thomas was the one person in my life who I'd fully let in. It was why we were best friends—why she was sitting there offering to serve me coffee.

She was the one person who knew me when I was broken. It didn't happen often, but right now… yeah, it was one of those times.

She got up and patted my leg before she left the room, door creaking closed, but not shut, behind her. The small crack it was left open allowed me to hear her begin to prepare the coffee. And if I wasn't mistaken, I thought I heard her getting the toaster out.

If she brought me a bagel, too, I'd break down again—if there were even any tears left in me.

My ceiling fan spun in dizzying circles as I stared up at it, the position bringing me back to the night before. I imagined a lot of simple things would now haunt me. But why did it matter? I'd been the one to make the decision. Ethan had given me the chance to stay, and I'd rejected him.

Now I was left with a puffy post-cry face and the realization that only bagels and coffee could bring me any sort of happiness. The idea of going outside was sickening, especially in my neighborhood. The chances of running into happy couples and normal families was too high. And call me a shitty person, but I had a crazy feeling it was the former that would bring me more pain.

*That* was how much Ethan had gotten to me—that the thought of losing him was harder for me to grasp than the fact that I would likely never speak to my own parents again.

It scared the shit out of me and simultaneously proved I'd made the right choice. Why put myself through the pain of loss twice when I could knock it out in one night?

Because that's what would happen. I would eventually lose Ethan the same way I'd lost everyone else. He'd fail me, one way or another—or I'd fail him. This little business plan we had going would come to an end. We'd fall out of the honeymoon phase. We'd find someone more exciting to fuck—not that I could even imagine kissing another man right now, let alone sleeping with one. But one day. One day that would happen to us. We were just too different. Fire and ice. Oil and water. Completely incompatible in the long run.

Or at least that's what I kept telling myself as I tried to shake the mental montage of the last few months that wouldn't stop playing.

Nia's reappearance in my room—ugh, thank god she brought the bagel—was the only thing that released me from my agony.

"We only had plain cream cheese," she said as she set the plate on my lap. The coffee cup went on my nightstand atop a book I hadn't picked up in months. "Figured you wouldn't want to wait for me to go get some more garden veggie."

"You're correct, and you're also an angel for bringing food at all." I ripped off a bite of circular, carb-y goodness and for a moment all my worries faded. It only lasted until I swallowed, though.

Nia chuckled, then we fell into a moment of silence before she asked, "I assume you're gonna take it easy today?"

I nodded. "Ideally I won't leave this bed." It had been a long time since I'd had a lazy Sunday, so I didn't feel terrible about wasting the day away.

"Normally, I'd feel guilty about having a shift tonight—since, you know, we should be drowning your sorrows with vodka tonics—but now I don't feel as bad."

"Go save lives," I said. "I'll be perfectly fine here, wallowing by myself."

"Okay, now I'm officially unsure if I should go save those lives or help you with yours."

"The sick kids need you more than I do. I'm just being dramatic, per usual."

"You sure?"

"Oh my god, you can't seriously be considering not helping children in favor of me." I placed the plate with my bagel to the side and propped myself up on my elbows again. "Ni, I'll be fine. You're not calling off work to—what? Probably watch chick flicks and eat Chinese food?"

Though I would admit, this was the first time either of us would be going through… well, it wasn't a breakup, per se, but it was close enough to an event that would prompt us to get rip-roaring drunk, blast girl-power and emo rock tunes, and find new men or women to distract us.

"Fine, you've got me there," she conceded. "But maybe we can do something later this week if you don't have any assignments."

"Just one on Tuesday." A rising pop-star, so the genre would be completely bearable, even if the setting wasn't.

God, concerts were going to be ruined for life. It was possibly a fate worse than death for someone like me.

"Great, because I was going to ask about Thursday."

"What's Thursday?"

"My aunt and uncle who are in town?" I nodded in reply to the clarifying question. "They want to go see my cousin's show and asked if I could join."

"Show?" I asked. "What does your cousin do?"

"He's the musician. You know—the one who was in band in high school?"

I nodded, vaguely remembering her mentioning some cousin who played some instrument. It didn't help that Nia and I hadn't known each other until college, so anything high-school-related was uncharted territory, even if it wasn't *her* high school experience.

"Would you want to come?" she continued. "I'm sure we could snag you a seat. Plus, it'll be good to get you out for something that isn't work."

Her hand found my leg again, and she met me with a soft but warm smile.

Honestly, if I wasn't being paid, I didn't think I would even go to the concert on Tuesday. Being around music sounded terrible. There were too many genres that had been breached—too many memories associated with them now. But I knew this was Nia's attempt at being there for me during a hard time, and it wasn't like she knew I needed a long, hard break from live shows. In her eyes, she was probably asking me to do the one thing she knew I loved most.

So, fighting against the tightness to make sure my smile came across as genuine, I said, "Yeah, sounds great. I'd love to join."

Maybe it's what I needed—to make new memories that would erase the old. Start fresh.

Something told me it would take a lot more than one show to ever be able to erase Ethan, though.

# Chapter 27

*ETHAN*

NEVER AGAIN. NO amount of popularity or buzz or peer pressure would ever again convince me to host a metal concert at Mellow Cat Kitchen.

Liam had done a great job with the closing, but still—there had been plenty left for me to handle in the morning. As much as I'd wanted nothing more than to lay in bed all day and indulge in self-pity, I'd somehow gotten my ass out of bed and gone to the restaurant.

And thank god I had.

The smell of cigarette smoke lingered in the air. The floor was as sticky as a dive bar that hadn't been mopped in a decade. There were stains on most of the velvet seats of the bar chairs. At least one person had tracked mud in. And then, of course, there were still shards of wood from the broken chair.

The larger pieces of that, thankfully, had been cleared away, but what remained was enough to leave my chest aching with memories from the night before.

All these months. All we'd shared. Somehow, I'd never learned the biggest part of Heather's life. The part that had made her who she is. And in the end, it was exactly what had torn us apart.

That had to be it. I was sure of it. Why else would she have kept that aspect of her life hidden from me when she'd been open about so many other things, only to run the moment it was brought up?

The thing was, as painful as watching her walk out my apartment door had been, I didn't blame her. I remembered those months following my mom's death—how I'd absolutely shut down for everyone except Eric and Kai. It took a long time to find the strength to get back out there and create relationships—with friends and otherwise—knowing that any of them could end the same way.

Heather, even though her parents were still alive, had essentially lost them forever. She was a strong woman. I'd known that from the minute I'd spilled my beer on her. The way she'd reacted last night had been that of someone whose life had been altered forever.

That's why I'd fought as much as I thought was

appropriate before, ultimately… I let her go.

She needed to heal on her own time, and if she thought that was better done without me there with her, then that's what I would allow. Even if I hated waking up alone in my bed, hated how silent my phone had been all morning, hated being here, knowing Holden would show up later tonight—knowing how he'd come to play at Mellow Cat in the first place—I'd allowed it. That's what you did when you loved someone, I supposed.

I only hoped that when her healing was finished, she didn't forget me. Because I sure as hell knew I'd *never* forget Heather Hansley as long as I lived.

She was already haunting my thoughts as I went around the currently closed Mellow Cat Kitchen, cleaning up what the rest of my staff hadn't managed to get to the night before. I knew one thing for sure: I'd rather be cleaning the main floor than doing any sort of work in my office. I'd probably never be able to look at that space the same way again.

Or at the very least, I'd have to wait a week or two before I felt confident enough with my emotions to remain in there for extended periods of time.

Liam and Brad would have to get used to me camping out at the bar to do paperwork for a little bit.

I sighed as I leaned my broom and long-handled dust bin against the polished wood of my new, hopefully temporary desk the same time there was a knock on the front door.

Eric waved at me from the other side, then tugged as if I needed a reminder it was locked. Closing for the first half of the day had been the greatest decision I'd ever made.

"Damn, would you look at this place?" my brother said when I unlocked the door and held it open for him to enter. I quickly locked it again behind him—not that I expected a huge flood of people waiting to come in. "Was last night wild?"

Oh, he didn't know the half of it. "Yeah, it was nuts."

"Sorry, I couldn't make it," he said as we settled into our normal spots at the bar. Well, almost normal. With Dad and Kai not here, Eric took one of the barstools while I settled in the back. Apparently, he'd deemed it too early to steal a bottle of whatever IPA I had in stock at the moment. "I wanted to, but some guy brought his car in and told me he needed it first thing this morning for a road trip."

I raised a brow. "Kinda last minute, isn't that?"

Eric only shrugged. "Can't help when your car decides to stall on you. Besides, with the cost of rentals these days, I didn't blame him for choosing to spend the money on a repair. Even gave me a little extra for the quick work, which was nice."

"Maybe now you can upgrade your dates to a real restaurant and not just fast food," I joked.

"Ha-ha," Eric said, rolling his eyes. Truth be told, my brother was damn good at his job as an auto mechanic. For as much of a smart-ass as he could be, he offered great customer service. "But seriously—how was it last night? The guys at the shop listen to Waking Fire all the time. They're pretty good."

"It was good," I replied, feeling like an idiot for repeating essentially what he'd just said.

Eric must have thought the same thing, given the face he was making, but surprisingly didn't say anything. "I can't believe Heather got them to play here. You're going to be so busy now."

"Doubt it. The audience wasn't exactly my normal clientele."

"No, but with all these new acts the two of you are bringing it, maybe some people will come back."

I nodded slowly, my eyes on the bar top. I couldn't bring myself to correct him that "the two of us" weren't doing *anything* together anymore, let alone finding new acts. Honestly, I hadn't thought about what that would mean until now. How long would I be able to keep up with these new performers? It was Heather who'd known all the connections. Heather who'd gotten this revival plan going in the first place. It was only a matter of time before things went back to how they'd been before.

Visions of spreadsheets with too much red on them flashed in my mind.

"Got anyone I would be interested in on the docket?" Eric

followed up when I neglected to respond. "That Evie girl was sick. Is she coming back?"

"I think more this summer."

A sparkle lit my brother's eyes, and he leaned back in his barstool. "Heather was totally onto something with that one. You've gotta tell her that—"

"Can we not talk about Heather?"

It was the absolute wrong thing to say, but I couldn't take it anymore. She'd already been consuming my thoughts all morning. Now, hearing my brother go on and on about her like everything was totally normal, I couldn't take it. I didn't need the added reminders that everything was, in fact, very far from normal.

Eric's face fell immediately.

"Shit…" he muttered. "Are you…? You guys hitting a rough patch?"

It was hard to hit a rough patch with someone you weren't officially in a relationship with. "Yeah. Something like that."

"What's that mean?"

"I don't think she wants to talk to me right now."

Eric's jaw actually dropped, and he stared at me with incredulous eyes, like what I'd just told him was the most absurd thing he'd ever heard from anyone, let alone me.

Eventually, he shook himself out of it. "Wait, wait, wait. You mean to tell me Heather—Heather Hansley, who the last time I saw her couldn't stay away from you—suddenly decided no more?"

I nodded. That pretty much hit the nail on the head without going into too much detail. As much as I loved my brother, divulging the details of her relationship with her parents wasn't my place. Hell, even *I* hardly knew the details. I'd intended to talk with her about it after the police left, but then she'd kissed me, and the next thing I knew, I was putting Liam in charge and we were going back to my apartment.

After that, speaking had been the last thing on our minds— until, of course, we'd gotten in the closest thing to an argument as we'd ever had.

"I have a hard time believing you did anything wrong," Eric said, his voice rising at the end so it sounded more like a question. Out of the three of us brothers, I'd say I fell in the middle of most likely to fuck up a relationship. Eric wasn't naïve enough to think he fell anywhere but the top of the list. Not to say I hadn't been the culprit of failed relationships before, it was just less likely.

"No," I said. "At least, I don't think I did? It was a rough night for her. Bad timing. I think… I think she just needs to be alone. That's what it sounded like, anyway."

"Don't tell me you just accepted that."

My brow furrowed. "Why wouldn't I?"

Eric's entire head rolled with his eyes when he groaned. "Seriously, E? Do you know *nothing*?"

"I definitely know *some* things." But where he was going

with this was not one of them.

Eric leaned forward on the bar, crossing his arms and resting his weight on them.

"Listen," he began. "I like Heather—seriously. She's a great time, and if you hadn't made it so obvious that you were in love with her right off the bat, she's someone I would have tried to shoot my shot with."

"I'm not in—"

Eric wasn't buying it because he held up his hand to stop me before I could fully voice the lie.

"I like Heather," he repeated. "But whatever she told you last night that made you believe she's not into you? It's bullshit."

I couldn't stop my eyes from widening at the bold statement. "What?"

"You heard me," Eric fired back. "And the fact that you didn't realize that is bullshit. And seeing you here, alone in this place you've worked so hard to build up is—"

"Let me guess. Bullshit?"

"I was going to say depressing, but sure." Eric shook his head. "Dude, I can't believe you didn't see it."

"See what?"

"That she's in love with you too."

As much as I wanted my brother's words to shock me, they didn't. Even though Heather had never told me, I knew what he said was true. She didn't *need* to tell me. I saw it in the way she softened for me. How she let her guard down. How she laughed without abandon and wore smiles that lit up the room. How she could be utterly exhausted and still show up to help me or notice I was stressed and say or do just what I needed.

Then, the moment her parents showed up, that wall I'd slowly been taking down, brick by brick, went right back up again.

This wasn't because of me. This was because of them.

I'd never despised two people I'd never met so much in all my life. To dim that light that was so brilliantly Heather was unforgivable.

It didn't matter if I'd never been told the whole story. I knew enough to decide that much.

"Yeah, she might be," I agreed. "And you're right—I do love her." It wasn't worth hiding anymore, but it did feel strange having Eric be the first person I admitted it to. "But because I love her, I know what she needs, and it's not me. Not right now."

"Dude, what are you—"

It was my turn to hold up my hand to him. "She's not someone who's going to accept coddling," I said. "That's all I would be able to offer her. She needs to be with her friends or busy doing her thing. And if it's meant to be…" I sighed. "I guess we'll see how it pans out."

"I know I'm just your pesky little brother," Eric said,

prompting a much-needed laugh from me, "but I can honestly say I haven't seen you this happy with anyone in a long time."

"That's because I don't let you see me with anyone," I retorted. "You know what happens when we bring girls home."

"Yeah, Dad thinks we're getting married to them," he agreed with a nod. "And if we don't, then it's obviously because they're in love with him and they don't know how to tell us."

"Exactly."

"So why'd you let us meet Heather?"

"She introduced herself to you."

Eric shrugged. "Sure. But you're pretty good at dodging things. You didn't exactly play it off like you were only business partners, or whatever you wanted us to believe."

He wasn't wrong.

"I'm just saying," Eric continued. "I don't think it would be the worst thing in the world for you to be a little selfish for once. Go after what you want. Stop worrying about what makes other people happy."

"There's a difference between going for what I want and completely disregarding someone's wishes."

"Well, yeah, don't piss her off," Eric agreed. "But also just… I don't know. Make sure she knows *you* aren't pissed off. Let her figure her shit out. Do what she's gotta do. But let her know you're there for her. That if she wants to come back, you'll be there waiting."

Wow. For all his usual trouble with women, it was amazing to hear that Eric actually had some sound relationship advice. Sometimes it was easier said than done, I supposed.

Which was exactly why I knew it wouldn't be as simple as picking up my phone and sending a text. An act I'd been doing for months now was something that frightened me. Now, I could be left on read. I could be ignored. I could be forgotten. That wasn't something I'd feared until now.

Still, I told my brother, "Yeah, I'll send her something later. First, I have to finish dealing with this," I finished through a sigh.

I didn't know if Eric bought it or not, but thankfully, he didn't press any further. It was probably weird for him, having another one of his brothers be the one with relationship issues for a change. Not that Eric had ever been in a relationship before. I guess his problems were more women-related than commitment-related. Or maybe a combination of both.

He nodded toward the broom I'd been using when he first arrived. "You got another one of those?"

"In the back." He hopped off his chair and I held out my arm before he had the chance to sneak into the kitchen. "What are you doing?"

"Helping you, dumbass," he said, shoving my arm down.

"Someone's gotta help you while Heather's out of the picture."

I appreciated how he still spoke like Heather and I had a chance. It gave me hope that we might. But I appreciated his offer to help even more, now that my attention was once again focused on the state of my restaurant.

"There's a mop in the storage closet by the stairs to my office. That might be best for what's left."

Eric smiled. "You've got it, bro."

# Chapter 28

*HEATHER*

I KNEW NIA'S invitation had come with good intentions, so that's why I tried my best to keep a smile on my face as I walked into the old-school jazz club with her and her family. It was clear she might not have known the venue for her cousin's concert either and turned over her shoulder, meeting me with concerned eyes.

"I'm good," I said with a forced smile. "Really."

I was not, in fact, good, but the lie did its job. Nia turned around, responding to something her aunt had just said, as my face fell again.

It had been proven. Concerts were forever tainted. Well, jazz concerts at least. I'd been proud of how well I'd done at the show I'd covered on Tuesday. That setting had been easier, though, and work had been enough to distract me. Here, there was nothing stopping my mind from going straight to Ethan.

This place wasn't nearly as neat as his, but that probably had something to do with the fact this one boasted a "Chicago staple since 1942" sign on the wall. It was one of the lucky spots that stuck to its roots and continued to survive.

That was enough to earn a grin from me, albeit a small one.

"Here we go," Nia's aunt, Rosalyn, announced.

She stopped at a small round table in the front and center of the room. A tiny "reserved" sign sat atop it. I wouldn't have expected her to be anywhere else for her son's performance.

The only problem was there were six of us and only four chairs available.

"NiNi, why don't you and Heather take that table?" Nia's mom, Jasmine, suggested. She leaned in closer to us with a grin. "I figured you girls would want to enjoy yourselves. My sister gets a little wild at these shows."

"Of course I do!" Rosalyn said, turning on us with mock offense. She wrapped her arm around Jasmine's shoulders. "I've got to cheer on my baby!"

When she began cheering at the empty stage, a genuine smile found its way onto my lips. While she was distracted, however, Jasmine widened her eyes at Nia and me.

"Got it. Taking the other table," Nia said.

"Thanks, Mrs. Thomas," I added.

Somehow, with the help of her brother-in-law, Jasmine managed to get her sister to sit down at their table. Turns out, ours had the same little reserved sign the "adult table" did.

"Mom must have thought ahead," Nia commented as we took our seats.

"I might have more fun watching your aunt than the actual show," I said.

"Aunt Rosa is a hoot, that's for sure." She smiled fondly at where the rest of her family was seated before her attention returned to me. "You sure you're good, babe?"

"Why wouldn't I be?"

"Oh, I don't know." She gestured to the space around us. "This whole place?"

"It was my choice to end things, Ni," I reminded her. "Besides, I can't hide from an entire genre of music forever. I'm in a really bad city to try and do that, anyway."

"I guess."

I reached out and put a hand on her knee. "I'm fine," I repeated. At this point, I wasn't sure if I was trying to convince Nia or myself of the sentiment. "Now, did you invite me here to pout and be sad or did you invite me to have a good time?"

She smiled. "Definitely the latter."

"Good," I said, pulling my hand back. "Because I could

have done the former on my couch for…"

I trailed off, clearing my throat to distract from the thought I didn't finish. That same forced smile from before returned.

"Is it too aggressive to order shots?"

× × ×

THE PLACE WAS absolutely packed by the time the emcee for the evening got on stage to announce Nia's cousin's band: Kick Brass. The trio strutted onto stage, instruments in hand, to a roaring chorus of applause, none of which was louder than Rosalyn one table over.

Nia and I both clapped, eyes set on the excited mother as her son and his group took the stage. It was easy to pick Anthony out, given he waved directly to his parents' table then to us. Nia cupped her hands around her mouth and let out an enthusiastic cheer in response.

Only when the young men took their places did I notice a fourth person had come on stage and taken up his spot behind a soundboard. I watched him with the most curiosity. The two trumpeters and singer were expected. This fourth person, however…

The lights dimmed and spotlights shone on Anthony and his fellow trumpeter as they lifted their instruments to their lips. Silence befell the audience as a melodic harmony filled the room, powerful, commanding our attention.

They stopped what could have only been a minute later, the instruments falling to their sides, as the lights went out and the room went completely black.

Then, I realized why the soundboard guy was there.

Colorful stage lights illuminated the jazz club as his production started, slow at first until it built to an R&B rhythm that I couldn't help but bob my head to. The crowd's enthusiasm grew with it until people were standing in their seats, clapping or with their arms above their heads moving in time with the beat.

Anthony and his cohort raised their trumpets again and played in time with the backtrack, adding an element that made the whole ensemble come alive.

It was absolutely electric. Not at all what I'd been expecting when I'd first set foot in the jazz club. And I couldn't help from thinking—

"These guys would be perfect for—"

I stopped myself when I realized what I was doing, but it was too late. Nia had heard me, despite my pleas to higher beings that the trumpets might have drowned out my words.

"Perfect for what?"

"Never mind."

Her excitement visibly faded as she leveled me with a look. "Perfect for that little project you and Beer Boy were working on?"

"Seriously, Nia. Forget I said anything," I tried. "We're not talking about that, remember?"

"Just because we aren't talking about it, doesn't mean you won't be thinking about it *constantly* now," she argued. "Kinda defeats the purpose of this whole outing."

I didn't bother saying anything back because she was right. And it wasn't just tonight that was making me think about Ethan. All week, he'd been at the forefront of my thoughts—especially after he'd sent me a text a few days ago.

Don't feel pressured but I'm here if you need to talk.

I'd run out of his apartment with little to no explanation as to why I wanted to end things, and he still had the heart to text me that.

Yet another reason why I didn't deserve someone like Ethan Morimoto.

I hadn't responded. Much like on Saturday night, I still didn't know how to properly articulate the it's-not-you-it's-me reasoning behind my decision without sounding like a total cliché. He deserved more than that.

Apparently, I was taking too long to respond now too because Nia's hand found its way atop mine on the table. The moment I lifted my eyes to her, she appeared blurry. Shit—I definitely thought I'd cried all the tears out by now. Obviously not.

"Ugh," I groaned, lifting my free hand to try and wipe them away before they fell. "I'm sorry."

"What for? You're allowed to be upset."

"No," I said, shaking my head. "I'm not. Or I shouldn't be." I huffed a laugh. "I'm being stupid."

"Okay, I'm going to need you to stop that talk right now," Nia said in her serious voice. "You're not being stupid. Well, actually you are a little bit, but not when it comes to your emotions."

I sniffled. "Huh?"

"You're being a *little* stupid," she repeated, holding up her thumb and index finger centimeters apart to visualize what she meant. "Being upset? Totally understandable. But…" Nia sighed. "I'm not going any further until I ask this. How honest do you want me to be with you?"

If there was one thing that had drawn me to Nia Thomas when I first met her at a bar in college, it was her take-no-shit attitude. It matched perfectly with my own, which, in the end, gave us both the perfect person to call the other one out when they were very clearly making a mistake. Our honesty had helped us avoid red flag after red flag, but this time, I knew what she was about to say wasn't that.

Nia was about to drop an atomic truth bomb on me if I gave her permission to continue. Those were the only times we ever asked if honesty was okay, because sometimes, hearing the truth was the hardest when it came from friends.

Even though I was afraid, I nodded.

Nia's hand grasped mine. "I'm your best friend. We're ride or dies—you know that, right?" I nodded my response and she continued. "So as your best friend, I've seen you at your highs and lows. I've never—not once—seen you at a high like when you were spending time with Ethan. I mean, you were fucking *glowing*, babe."

I couldn't stop the strangled laugh that escaped me. Only Nia could manage to make me laugh when I was crying.

"Which leads me to ask why you're torturing yourself by not talking to him," she concluded, her voice softer, eyebrow raised in a way that let me know she was genuinely confused.

All I could do was shrug. "I don't... I don't know," I admitted. It would have been a miracle if she could even hear me over the on-going medley. "It felt like the right thing to do, I guess?"

"Does it still feel that way?"

Now it was my turn to level a look at her. My head tilted to the side, and I pointed to my clearly not-glowing face. Unless she counted the tears.

"I'm going to take that as a no," Nia whispered, just loud enough for me to make out over the music.

I sat back, pulling my hand away, and shook my head, unable to meet her eyes. Instead, I lifted them to the ceiling that was colored by the stage's flashes of lights.

"It was supposed to be easy, you know?" I said through a half-sob when I finally faced her again. "I'd just called the police on my parents, so ending things with some guy? Piece of cake."

"But was he really just *some guy*?" Nia tilted her head at me. "I've seen you with *some guys*, Heather. Ethan was not one of those scumbags."

No, Ethan was definitely not like any other guy I'd ever dated. That was part of the reason he'd been so special. He was exactly the opposite of every person I'd ever tried to love.

He was… perfect. Sweet and kind. Gentle. Funny. Quirky. He didn't push me to do anything I didn't want to do, and knew exactly when I was joking or being serious. Even better, he played along with the jokes and opened up in a way I was pretty sure only his brothers and dad had seen before. The idea that another woman might get the chance to see that side of him now…

Nia was right. If Ethan were just some guy, I wouldn't want to run out of this show and go straight to Mellow Cat Kitchen to mark my territory like some crazy-possessive girlfriend.

I didn't want anyone else to make him laugh.

I didn't want anyone else singing bad karaoke duets with him.

I didn't want anyone else having sexy rendezvous in his office.

I didn't want anyone else hugging Gengar while watching anime with him.

Those moments were mine. Ours. No one else could have

them.

"I could be totally wrong here," Nia continued, probably prompted by my thoughtful silence, "but do you think the shit that went down with your parents might have influenced you a little?"

"I know it did," I said. "I know I fucked up, Ni. I… I didn't know what to do. I just wanted him so much it scared me. Like—" I swallowed the fresh lump in my throat and met her waiting stare. "I know you were out to dinner, but I also know you would have dropped *everything* if I called you that night. It was one text. You would've been at Mellow Cat in a heartbeat and would've taken me home and gotten us Taco Bell and turned on some trash reality show to distract me."

"Nothing like a cat fight to extinguish the pain."

"Exactly," I said through a strangled laugh. Then I shook my head. "But I didn't. I didn't even *think* to call you because I knew Ethan was right there and… and he was all I wanted."

At first, I'd thought I'd just needed the distraction of sex— of the heat and pleasure I knew he could give me. Looking back now, though, I hadn't wanted his body at all. I'd wanted Ethan. As a whole. As much as Nia would have been an amazing shoulder to lean on, she wasn't him.

"I know I should be offended by that," my best friend said, "but I'm not—only because I know you love me." She lowered her chin and stared at me from under her lashes. "I think what you need to do now is admit that I might not be the only one anymore, though."

When I blinked that time, the tears finally won. They spilled down my cheeks until they met my smile—although it probably looked more like a grimace.

"You're not," I said.

"You love him?"

I nodded. "I do."

"Are you scared?"

"Shitless."

We both laughed at that, some of the tension of the conversation breaking. The more Nia prompted me, though, the more at ease I felt.

I love Ethan Morimoto.

I *love* him.

"I don't think it would be any fun if you weren't scared of it, you know? Love is *supposed* to be a little scary," Nia said. "But he's not your parents, babe. He's like me—another person who's going to be there for you no matter what."

"I know," I said, then wiped at my nose with a cocktail napkin. "I know—really. But now…" I lifted my eyes to her again. "I really fucked up, didn't I?"

"'Really' seems a little strong," Nia replied. "Moderately fucked up seems more accurate."

I groaned and tilted my head up to the ceiling again. There wasn't a single person I could blame this on but myself. The first real chance I have at falling in love and of course I go ahead and mess it up.

This wasn't something I could admit over text, even if Ethan had opened the door for me to talk with him. And asking him to meet up… that seemed way too casual. I'd said awful things to him when I'd left. Even if he was okay with talking, that didn't, by any means, guarantee he'd be willing to go back to the way things were—or go beyond that.

Because that's what I wanted. I wanted—needed—it all with Ethan.

"That doesn't mean it can't be fixed, though."

That time, when I brought my attention down again, I found my friend wearing that same mischievous grin that originally made me decide I needed to have her in my life. Nia had an idea.

"Talk to me," I said.

"It's nothing you haven't already suggested."

I tracked Nia's nod towards the stage. Of course—I'd just continue with our plan and bring Kick Brass to Mellow Cat. It would be easy enough to convince them to do it, seeing as one of the members was related to my best friend.

But that felt like the easy way out. The obvious answer. What would be different between me bringing Ethan different acts before and bringing them now?

I needed something more. Something bigger. Something that said, "I'm all in no matter what." A true testament that would let Ethan know I understood him and loved every part of him.

And then, as Anthony's trumpet blared through the venue, I couldn't help but realize exactly what that was.

# Chapter 29

*ETHAN*

SOMETHING FELT... OFF.

In reality, everything was operating at Mellow Cat as it should on a Saturday night. Holden was setting up. There was a steady crowd forming—as was expected from his performances now; no longer were they standing room only, but they were still far from sparsely attended—and the bar and kitchen were engaged in a steady flow of activity.

Still, I couldn't shake the feeling that something wasn't right. I just couldn't put my finger on it.

"Boss man," Liam greeted as he clapped a hand on my shoulder. "You look tense."

I straightened my posture and averted my attention from the hawk-eyed stare-down I'd been giving the room. "Not tense at all."

Liam smirked. "You're an awful liar." He squeezed my shoulder once then dropped his hand. "Lighten up, man. It's gonna be a good, easy night."

I huffed a laugh and rolled my eyes. Yeah, anything would be easier than the last Saturday we'd both been here together. I was still trying not to think about it—and the fact that Heather had never responded to my text even though almost two weeks had passed.

Maybe Eric hadn't been right. Maybe she was truly done with me. Moved on. Going about bigger and better things. Honestly, helping me was a major setback in her career. *That's* what she needed to focus on. Not some restaurant that was slowly creeping back to its old ways, the hype of the new acts and novelty of a new venue wearing off a bit.

I couldn't deny that with Heather out of the picture, trying to find new people to entertain the diners was difficult. I'd had half a mind to call Leo and beg him to come back, but knew better. That call would only leave me disappointed, and I'd had enough of that for a while.

"Holden looks like he's almost ready to go," Liam continued.

I hummed then looked down at my watch. Not long until show time. A couple minutes, maybe. Though I hadn't heard much of a soundcheck happening yet. It wasn't out of the question for him to be running a little behind, but it was definitely rare.

There wasn't much time to dwell on it before the front door opened, and I saw three familiar faces enter the restaurant.

"Okay, are you sick?" I asked Eric as he sidled up beside me and nudged me with his elbow. Liam asked what he wanted, but I waved him off to help someone else. My brother knew where to find the drinks. "You've been showing up here way too much for someone who hates jazz."

"Can't a little brother visit his big brother at work from time to time?" he argued. When I leveled him with a stare, he shrugged. "Dad likes this Holden kid, too."

"He's very catchy," Dad confirmed as he and Kai slid into their normal bar chairs.

I chuckled at that. Dad had been very engaged with my new lineup the last few weeks. He'd skipped the Waking Fire concert—probably for the better—but Kai and Eric did a good job of accompanying him down here pretty frequently. I'd thought it was because he wanted to offer as many reassurances as possible that the changes to the lineup of acts didn't bother him, but maybe he did actually enjoy a few.

"You happy to be done with classes for a bit?" I asked Kai.

He nodded. "I'll be able to help around here a bit more now. If you need it, that is."

"Thanks, but I think I'm—"

"Hello, hello, hello. How's everyone doing tonight?"

A chorus of cheers and clapping followed Holden's greeting. I couldn't help but smile as Dad joined them, rather enthusiastically. Eric nudged me in the side again to make sure I saw, and Kai had his face in his hand to hide his laughter.

Our little fanboy.

But my attention was drawn away again when, from the corner of my eye, I saw the front door open. This time, Sarah stopped the newcomers: two middle-aged Black women and… Nia?

Heather's friend smiled sheepishly at me in the small gap through which we could see each other. It was clear she was trying to remain inconspicuous, and with good reason. I didn't know a whole lot on the topic, but I was pretty sure showing up to the restaurant owned by your best friend's… whatever we were, was against girl code.

I offered a polite nod of acknowledgement when her and the two women she was with passed by, and she returned it with a shy wave.

"Who's that?" Eric muttered beside me.

"Heather's roommate."

I expected him to say something about that—maybe a follow-up to check if I'd had the balls to reach out to her. I was more than ready to report that yes, I had actually done as he'd advised, but my brother was silent. Oddly silent. And it had nothing to do with the fact that he was taking a drink.

If anything, that was an excuse not to speak.

If things hadn't felt off earlier, they certainly did now.

"What's up with you?" I asked. "Seriously."

"Don't know what you're talking about." He gave a shrug that definitely contradicted that statement. It had guilt written all over it.

"Eric…" I chided. "What do you know that I don't?"

"Nothing, nothing," he assured me a little too quickly. His beer clanked on the counter when he set it down, then his arm was around my shoulders. "Just sit back and enjoy the performance, alright?"

I glanced at Kai and Dad sidelong, but they appeared clueless as to whatever Eric was up to. For some reason, that made it worse.

My suspicions were temporarily forgotten, however, when Holden said, "Let's get this show started, shall we?" into the mic, and I couldn't help but focus on him, on the stage, on the door where a new influx of patrons streamed in—

"What the hell?"

Eric didn't stop me as I made my way from behind the bar to go assist a frantic-looking Sarah at the host stand. So much for a calm, quiet night. This was more along the lines of what I'd seen for the Waking Fire concert, except the people gathered fit a vastly different aesthetic.

"If everyone could please calm down," I tried, calling over the noise. "We have a show in progress, but we can get you seated as soon as we can."

"Wait, that's not Kick Brass," someone said.

"I thought you said Kick Bass was going to be here?" another added.

Something was in the water. I was sure of it.

"Tonight, we have Holden Young on stage," I said and placed a hand on Sarah's shoulder to calm her down. It sounded like a lot of these people were in the wrong spot. "We post our schedule online, so if you ever want to double-check—"

"There they are!"

My brow furrowed at the claim before I turned around. There was no way Holden wasn't on that stage. I'd seen him set up—listened as he greeted the crowd and started playing his guitar.

But sure enough, he wasn't alone anymore. Two other young men had joined him on stage, both with trumpets in hand. One of the women at the table where Nia sat threw her hands up in the air and called out, "That's my baby! Show 'em what you've got, Tony!"

Normally, I might have panicked. I'd never had to handle stage crashers. Why would they have tried to do something like that here when there were hundreds of bigger venues in Chicago they could go to? But these guys… they walked on stage like they knew they belonged there, settling themselves on either side of Holden as his rhythmic sound turned into something more fitting of the venue.

Jazzier.

I held Sarah back with my arm as the people at the door gave up waiting, and quite frankly I didn't care where they went. These weren't rowdy concert-goers. They were slow-moving, their steps and hips following the rhythm as they made their way into the restaurant. I'd need to call an immediate staff meeting once everything settled, but until then, I didn't sense trouble.

No—the energy in the room was joyful. Smiles graced the lips of every patron, and even the younger crowd that had shown up to enjoy a couple apps and drinks while they took pictures seemed more engaged than I'd ever seen them.

"Everybody on their feet!" Holden said into the microphone. "C'mon!"

Just as he finished his command, it happened. A backtrack picked up, started by another young man I didn't recognize behind the musicians up front. More cheers filled the room as the diners followed orders, some even leaving their tables to join the group that had just come in on the small dancefloor.

And to top it all off, a third trumpeter found his way onto the stage.

I was sure I was going crazy the moment I saw Leo up on that stage, clapping hands with the fellow musicians. Given the broad smile he wore, no one would have guessed we'd ever gotten in a squabble over him performing at Mellow Cat. That seemed to have been forgotten as he lifted his instrument to his lips and his first note filled the room.

The other trumpeters joined in, the three of them and Holden playing off the backtrack in a way only true musicians could. There was no way they'd been able to rehearse beforehand. I couldn't fathom any possible way these three acts had found their way together.

Unless…

"What do you know about this?" I asked, back at the bar and pointing an accusatory finger at my brother.

He held up his hands in defense. "My lips are sealed."

"What about either…of…you…"

My arm lowered and my words came out on nothing more than a breath when I turned on Kai and Dad and saw who stood with them. I don't know how I hadn't noticed her to begin with, but I supposed my curiosity made me blind.

Heather gave me the same shy smile her friend had. "Guilty," she whispered.

I stared at her. My brain was broken. Words didn't exist. Her appearance here explained a lot, but it also created about a hundred other questions that were now swirling in my head.

"And on that note," Eric said, downing the rest of his drink before he moved from behind the bar. "We'll leave you two to chat."

He grabbed Dad and Kai's collars and tugged them out of

their stools.

That little shit. He'd known this whole time what had been coming.

"Don't be mad at him, okay?" Heather said when they were gone, mixed into the crowd up front. "I asked him to keep it a secret."

"Where did you…?" I tried. "How did you…?"

My chaotic pointing at the front door and stage area was enough for her to figure out what I was trying to ask.

"Liam let me in the back. I was waiting out there for, like, twenty minutes."

Did *everyone* in this place know she was coming except for me?

"I didn't mean to bombard you," Heather continued, taking a step closer to me. "But I didn't know another way to do this. I thought if I texted you, you might not answer."

"I told you I was here to talk if you wanted to," I reminded her.

The reference to my text that had gone unanswered was enough to make some of her guilt show.

"I'm sorry," she said. "I… I'm getting used to this whole letting-people-in thing."

I hated the way her head drooped and she wouldn't meet my eyes.

It was clear she wasn't expecting my thumb and index finger to find their way to her chin, lifting it enough so I could look at her as I asked, "How's it working out so far?"

"Not great," she admitted softly. "But hopefully it will get better soon."

I nodded my chin towards the front of the restaurant where Holden and Leo had stepped back to allow the two young trumpeters to do a song with a new singer I didn't recognize—and Clara Calloway. "What is all this?"

"My apology," Heather said. "It took a bit to get everyone to agree,"—my eyes naturally found Leo when she said that— "but everyone was more than eager to get involved when I explained what I was doing."

"What's that?"

"Same thing I've always been doing. Finding the perfect act for your restaurant. Except this time, I worked with what I had."

"Who are the trumpet guys and producer?"

"Okay, so I brought in a *few* newbies."

I chuckled as my eyes finally left Heather's to watch what was happening on the stage. Each act—young or old; classical or modern; musician or singer—worked perfectly together bringing a sound to Mellow Cat that was exactly what I'd hoped to find. The audience reacted the same way. Age didn't matter. Preferred genre didn't matter. They were all getting bits and pieces of what they wanted.

It was the perfect blend.

"Before," Heather said, drawing my attention back to her,

"I was always looking at them as separate things—the original sound you curated and the revival sounds—because… well, because I think I was afraid to admit they might work together."

Something told me she wasn't just talking about the music, but still, I asked, "And what gave you this idea?"

Heather shrugged. "I think I always knew they would, but it was hard to come to terms with it. It was easier to keep them separate because that way no one got hurt."

Now, I *knew* she wasn't just talking about the music.

"Heather." My hand drifted from her chin, up to cup her face. "I never would have hurt you."

"How can you say that?" she asked, her voice growing weaker. Beneath my hold her chin trembled. "How would you have known?"

"I guess I didn't—not at first," I admitted. "I knew I liked you, though. Enough that being your friend would have satisfied me." My thumb stroked the soft skin of her cheek. "Until it didn't."

My other hand went up so I could hold her face. I didn't want there to be any chance that she could shy away from me now. Every word I spoke, I needed Heather to hear it. I needed her to know how sincerely I meant all the things I'd been dying to voice for the last two weeks.

She was right. A text conversation wouldn't have been enough. We needed this. Here. Now. Where all our emotions were on the line, and I could let her know her fear wasn't necessary. It never would be.

"I was scared too," I said. "I don't think I've ever really given myself the chance to fall in love with anyone since Mom died. I was still young then, but I knew what loss felt like. I didn't want to feel it again, and keeping myself from situations where that might happen..." I shrugged one shoulder. "It was easier."

Her eyes softened in a way that told me she understood completely. We were both two people that had been broken by our parents. In different ways, of course, but there was damage left behind that neither of us would ever fully be able to shake.

"How did you do it?" she asked.

"How did *you* do it?" I fired back then nodded in the direction of the performance again. "I don't think this would be happening if you hadn't had some sort of epiphany."

"It was easy," she said, much to my surprise. "Once you weren't a regular part of my life anymore..." Heather shook her head. "I needed you back, Beer Boy. Anime, jazz, and all."

There she was. The firecracker of a woman I'd fallen in love with.

I laughed before I brought my lips down to her forehead for a chaste kiss.

"I'm glad to hear you missed me too," I said when I pulled

back.

"So much."

Then, her arms were around my torso, her body pressed tight against mine. I adjusted to cradle her head to my chest, and realized just how much I'd actually missed this feeling. It had only been two weeks, yet it felt like a lifetime since I'd been able to hold Heather like this. Hell, for a second there, I'd thought I never would be able to again.

"So I take it this means you've changed your mind," I asked. She lifted her head just enough to meet my waiting stare. "You aren't done with me?"

Heather's lips pursed with a tight grin, and she shook her head. "No," she said. "You're okay with taking me back?"

"Are you kidding me?" I asked, the incredulous tone in my voice making her laugh. God, I loved that sound. I loved that smile. "You're the Simon to my Garfunkel."

"The Sonny to your Cher," she added, smile growing.

"The Hall to my Oates."

"The Peaches to your Herb."

"Okay, show-off." I kissed her head again. "I get it—you know more duos than me."

"Sounds like I have a lot to teach you."

"I look forward to it." When I pulled back, Heather's confusion was evident. "But first, how about a dance?"

She took my waiting hand with a smirk. "You sure that's safe? These are paying customers. Might look bad if the owner or his girlfriend steps on their toes."

I quirked a brow as soon as she finished speaking. "Is that what you are now? My girlfriend?"

"Well, *I* was planning on introducing you as my boyfriend, so…"

I'd never heard her say something so incredible. It was enough for me to use my hold on her hand to tug her closer and bring my lips down to hers. There was no point hiding now. No more cars or alleys or alone in my apartment. Even if another spotlight shone on us, it wouldn't matter.

I was hers, and she was mine. And it didn't seem to scare her one bit.

"Let's go break some toes," Heather said through a smile when I pulled away.

And I happily followed her onto the dancefloor.

# Epilogue



*HEATHER*

2 YEARS LATER

AS A MUSIC columnist and now the entertainment manager at one of Chicago's hottest jazz clubs, Mellow Cat Kitchen— according to various Chicago activity guides, news outlets, and social media, not just my own personal opinion—it was nice to be at a concert for something other than work for a change.

The personal invite from the headliner was a nice touch.

When Jaxon Baker's team had reached out to me, I'd almost thought it was a scam, but then I got the DM on Instagram too. Definitely not a fluke. Apparently, Ethan and I had made a lasting impression during the last tour. Now, we were part of the private crew with VIP accommodations at the slightly upgraded venue. Jaxon had gotten bigger after the release of his new album, but the same casual, tequila-shot-loving guy from last time remained among the growing stardom.

So far, we'd only taken two tequila shots, but I couldn't tell if the spinning was from the alcohol or if Ethan, whose arms were wrapped around my torso, my back to his chest, was really swaying so aggressively.

Something told me it was the latter. I'd gotten better with shots over the last two years, given Eric made us take them pretty much every time we went out with him, but dancing? That was something that would never improve for either of us.

Jaxon strummed his guitar one last time and the crowd standing around us erupted into cheers as the note faded out. That hadn't changed in the last few years, either. Ethan and I still stood in the back, enjoying the music and each other more than the proximity to the artist on stage. It didn't take long to realize maybe that's why I'd been so hell-bent on being up close when I was younger. I just hadn't found the right person to enjoy the show with yet.

Now, I couldn't imagine going to a concert without Ethan beside me. Whether it was a new act we were scouting for Mellow Cat—even as entertainment manager, I never signed anyone onto the schedule without his approval—just for fun, or him accompanying me for work, he was always there.

I wouldn't have it any other way.

"How we doing out there, Chicago?" Jaxon called from the stage.

In response, we all cheered. Ethan lifted his chin off my head to shout while I hit my hands on the back of his in a half-hearted attempt at clapping.

"Think we could get Jaxon to come to Mellow Cat?" I asked with my head tilted up so Ethan could hear me. I was half-joking. After Waking Fire, neither one of us was too keen on major acts coming to the restaurant. But Jaxon might be acceptable.

"Think Jerry will approve?" he countered.

To that, I had no rebuttal. Jaxon wouldn't be Jerry's favorite, but he might tolerate him. He was usually our tie-breaker when Ethan and I couldn't agree. Given our history, it was pretty amazing how many times he actually sided with my choices. I was getting better at finding the happy medium of jazz and modern sound, that was for sure.

And, lowkey, Jerry loved me. He didn't have to admit it. The conversations we shared over drinks said enough.

I was just happy he was back to being a regular at Mellow Cat again. Next to Leo, the night of his return was one of the top happiest moments for Ethan—I was sure of it.

"I'm gonna slow things down a bit now," Jaxon said, and the lights dimmed from warm hues to cool tones. "If any of y'all were here on the last tour, you'll remember this. I'm bringing it back for y'all tonight, Chicago!"

As expected, the crowd went nuts. Nothing like special treatment to get people going.

Then, the music started and while the audience got even louder, I couldn't help but sit there and smile.

"It's our song," Ethan said, his lips at my ear.

That it was, and it was obvious, just like the last time, that the big Jaxon Baker fans knew what this song was too.

The spotlight kiss.

It was incredible to think that was what had really started everything between Ethan and I. Now here we were, two years in and falling deeper and deeper in love every day.

Still, even though kissing him wouldn't be an issue this time around, I didn't know that I wanted the spotlight to fall on us again. There was no way Jaxon would do that, anyway. Two tours in a row? The odds were slim. Besides, another couple deserved their romantic moment.

I smiled as Jaxon's singing faded out and we got to the point where the instrumental took over. This was it. The energy was palpable as the couples in the crowd wondered whether they'd be the lucky ones.

One by one, the chosen appeared on the screen. A middle-aged man and wife. A young gay couple. Two teenagers who I was surprised were even allowed at the show. A pair that was a little too sloppy.

"They need to get a room," I said, my head half-turned so

I could still watch the screen—only to find we were now on it.

The spotlight hit us next, and the sudden brightness made me squint. Ethan's arms unwrapped from around me, probably so he could shield his eyes too. With the intensity of it shining right in my face, I could hardly even see Jaxon on stage anymore.

"Oh my god, again?" I asked, completely aware that the headliner couldn't hear me at this distance from the stage.

"It's your turn, Miss Heather," he said into the microphone anyway.

I shook my head. Yup, he was the exact same as he was two years ago.

"Okay," I said through a sigh and turned to Ethan. "Here goes round—"

But Ethan wasn't there. At least, not at the height I expected to find him. Instead, he was down on one knee, staring up at me with a smile that was half nervous, half absolutely radiant. In his hand was a small black box.

"Holy shit." They were the only two words I could think of, especially as the crowd realized what was happening and began to cheer.

Jaxon hushed them through the microphone and the music softened. I knew there were at least four hundred people on the floor with us, but with the spotlight, it felt like only Ethan and I in the room.

"Heather Hansley," he said. "I knew you were special from the moment I spilled beer on you."

A strangled laugh came out of me, and my hand flew up to my mouth to smother it.

"I know we've had our challenges, but there's no one else I would have rather spent the last two years of my life with. Now, I'm hoping I'll get to spend forever with you."

The crowd went absolutely wild when he flipped the box open, revealing the oval diamond set on a gold band.

"Will you marry me?" Ethan shouted over the roar.

I was speechless. No matter how badly I wanted to vocalize yes—there was nothing I wanted more, all I could do was nod.

It was enough for Ethan, and he rose from the ground. The crowd went silent once more, watching with great interest as he removed the ring from the box and slipped it onto my waiting finger.

"Holy shit," I repeated once it was there.

Then I threw my arms around his neck and kissed him.

The house lights flashed, the music flared, the crowd—and Jaxon—went absolutely wild. Yet in that moment, it was only Ethan, me, and the promise of our future together.

He rested his forehead against mine when we finally broke the kiss.

"I love you," he whispered. Even over the noise, I heard it perfectly.

"I love you too," I replied, then kissed him again just as Jaxon started singing the final chorus.

I'd always loved concerts. They'd always been my safe space. But here, in Ethan's arms? I couldn't help but think I'd found a new place where I belonged.

# Acknowledgements

I almost shelved this book. When I first started writing it in the spring of 2023, I didn't think I had it in me to finish it. It took almost a whole year for me to pick it back up again, and I'm so glad that I did.

So, I want to start by thanking everyone who was so encouraging and helped me regain my self-confidence and love of writing. This book would very much not exist without you.

Thank you to my parents and little brother who continue to be so supportive of this journey. I love you guys so much, and couldn't do this without you!

I want to give an additional thank you to my brother for helping me figure out all the criminal justice-related questions I had.

Thank you, Falen, for being my beta/sensitivity reader for this project. I'm honored to have been your first beta read ever!

Thank you to my editor, Jessica, whose kindness helped get this story polished and published much quicker than I thought it would be.

And an extra "thank you" to Jessica as well for coming in clutch and helping me format the eBook version of this story.

Thank you to my friends and family who continue to show

support for all my projects.

Thank you to my colleagues at my full-time job for cheering me on while I work this "part-time job" of mine.

Thank you to the online writing and bookish communities for your endless support. You all continue to give me the courage I need to put my stories out in the world, and I cannot thank you enough for that!

Thank you to all the people I have met while alone at concerts for welcoming me into your groups or becoming my buddy if you were also attending solo. You're all the reason this story exists.

Thank you to any artist I have seen live (and there's a lot of them), especially the ones that inspired the experiences in this story. That includes Magdalena Bay, Russell Dickerson, Galantis, and Public Library Commute, but all my concert experiences have had an impact on this story.

And thank you, dearest reader, for picking up this novel and giving it a chance. I appreciate you endlessly for helping me achieve my dream!

# About the Author

MCKENZIE BURNS is a multi-genre author from Chicago with a passion for writing stories that involve different cultures, witty banter, and women who don't take 'no' for an answer. Her spare time is spent drinking copious amounts of coffee and searching for obscure music.

## Encore

Haven't gotten enough of Heather and Ethan?
Listen to the songs that inspired their story! Scan this code in
your Spotify app to access the official *Love on Tour* playlist.

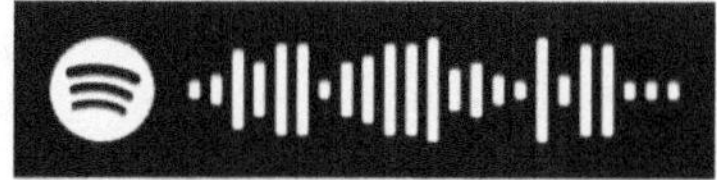